"You tou**
coldest, **
her life.

The man growled and launched himself at Liam, aiming Quinn's Nikon at Liam's face... He dropped her camera, and Liam picked it up, tossing it to her. One hard hit to the man's jaw and he crumpled to the ground, out cold.

"Let's go," Liam said.

She was all for that.

He grabbed her hand, and they ran through the woods.

At the car, she tried to catch her breath. "Not fair. You're not even breathing hard," she said.

He grinned. "I could give you mouth-to-mouth."

Did nothing faze this man? "We almost got killed and all you can think about is kissing me?" He'd been magnificent and seeing him in his element had been hot. She could have done without having a gun pointed at her, though.

"I think about kissing you all the time, and trust me, you didn't come close to getting killed. I wouldn't have allowed that to happen on my watch. Now, let's get out of here before they come looking for us."

Dear Reader,

Thank you for choosing *Dangerous Affair*. Three boys were kidnapped when they were in high school. They bonded, and after their rescue, they became fast friends, brothers. As adults, they started The Phoenix Three, their mission to rescue children in trouble.

In *Dangerous Affair*, the last thing Liam O'Rourke expects is to find *her*. You know, *the one*. Quinn Sullivan, a photojournalist, doesn't want to be *the one* for any man, but she does like the chemistry between her and Liam.

The journey Liam and Quinn travel to find their happily-ever-after was such a fun story to write. If you haven't read the first book in The Phoenix Three series, *Dangerous Secret*, go do that now. I think you'll really like Grayson and Harlow's story.

I love hearing from readers, and here are some ways we can connect. I'd love to have you join my Facebook reader group, Sandra's Rowdies. We laugh a lot and play games, and my Rowdies are the first to see cover reveals and teasers. Then there are my giveaways. You can join here: Facebook.com/groups/owens.

Sign up for my newsletter here: app.mailerlite.com/webforms/landing/e7q6o9.

Lastly, follow me on BookBub here: BookBub.com/authors/sandra-owens.

Happy reading!

Sandra

DANGEROUS AFFAIR

SANDRA OWENS

ROMANTIC SUSPENSE

If you purchased this book without a cover you should be aware that this book is stolen property. It was reported as "unsold and destroyed" to the publisher, and neither the author nor the publisher has received any payment for this "stripped book."

ISBN-13: 978-1-335-47156-7

Dangerous Affair

Copyright © 2025 by Sandra Owens

All rights reserved. No part of this book may be used or reproduced in any manner whatsoever without written permission.

Without limiting the author's and publisher's exclusive rights, any unauthorized use of this publication to train generative artificial intelligence (AI) technologies is expressly prohibited.

This is a work of fiction. Names, characters, places and incidents are either the product of the author's imagination or are used fictitiously. Any resemblance to actual persons, living or dead, businesses, companies, events or locales is entirely coincidental.

For questions and comments about the quality of this book, please contact us at CustomerService@Harlequin.com.

TM and ® are trademarks of Harlequin Enterprises ULC.

 Harlequin Enterprises ULC
22 Adelaide St. West, 41st Floor
Toronto, Ontario M5H 4E3, Canada
www.Harlequin.com

Printed in Lithuania

Sandra Owens lives in the beautiful Blue Ridge Mountains of North Carolina. Her family and friends have ceased being surprised by what she might get up to next. She's jumped out of a plane, flown in an aerobatic plane while the pilot performed death-defying stunts, and ridden a Harley motorcycle for years. She regrets nothing. Sandra is a Romance Writers of America Honor Roll member and a 2013 Golden Heart® Finalist. Her books have won many awards and she is an Amazon bestselling author.

Books by Sandra Owens

Harlequin Romantic Suspense

The Phoenix Three

Dangerous Secret
Dangerous Affair

Visit the Author Profile page
at Harlequin.com for more titles.

This book is dedicated to all the book lovers in the world.
Y'all rock!

Prologue

"I have to go to work." Liam O'Rourke gave his new girlfriend a quick kiss as they stood on the school grounds after the final bell. He was going to be late, and his father wasn't going to be happy. When Patrick O'Rourke wasn't happy, no one was. Late to work at his father's Kansas City pub meant he was going to be put on dishwasher duty as punishment, the job he hated the most.

"You always have to work," Christina whined. "Can't you come with us just once?"

"I can't." She wasn't going to stay his girlfriend for long if he never got to spend time with her outside of school.

She and their group of friends were meeting up at Charlie's, their favorite after-school hangout. While he was buried up to his elbows in suds, they would be eating cheese fries, drinking milkshakes, and having a great time. Sometimes, he hated his father.

His senior year in high school should be all about having fun with his friends, having a girlfriend he could spend time with, and being a carefree kid. Instead, he was in training to learn all about the family business from the ground up so that someday he'd be qualified to take over Danny Boy's Irish Pubs International. Someday being in the far distant future because his father would have to be on his deathbed before he gave up control of his empire.

Liam left Christina and his friends and ran the one mile to work. It burned that he wasn't allowed the time to just be young. It also burned that as rich as his father was, he'd refused to give Liam a car so that he didn't have to run everywhere just to be on time when at his father's beck and call. A lot of the senior kids had cars, and Patrick O'Rourke could afford to buy Liam a fleet of them, but no…he couldn't even have one measly used car.

Resentment bubbled up in his chest as he raced for the pub. No matter what he might want to do with his life, the choice wasn't his to make. His resentment wasn't that, as the only child, he was being groomed to take over the business one day. He was good with that. He just wanted to be like his friends who were allowed to have fun the way teenagers were supposed to.

Two blocks from the pub, he glanced at his watch as he ran. He was only going to be five minutes late, but as far as his father was concerned, five minutes might as well be an hour. His backpack bounced against his spine as he picked up speed.

He was crossing the street at the last intersection before reaching the pub when a white van screeched to a halt in front of him, and unable to stop in time, he ran into the side of it. His head bounced against the van and, dazed, he stumbled back.

"Hey, watch where you're going," he yelled as white stars floated in front of his eyes. He rubbed his forehead, and already, a lump was forming. Great, he was going to have a big fat egg right between his eyes.

The side door of the van slid open, and before he could comprehend what was happening, he was yanked inside.

He was pushed face down on the floor, and a knit cap was pulled over his head and halfway down his face, covering his eyes. He'd been stunned, unable to comprehend what was happening, but when he realized someone was binding his hands behind his back with a plastic tie, the first wave of panic hit. He struggled to get his arms and hands away before they could be bound, making him helpless.

Something small, round, and cold was pressed into his cheek. "That's a gun, Mr. O'Rourke," a man with a gravelly smoker's voice said. "Unless you want to die right here, you'll stop fighting us."

Us? How many were there? Had anyone seen them abduct him? Was someone calling the police right now to report a kidnapping? He hadn't noticed anyone around, but he hadn't really been paying attention to his surroundings as he ran. His father was going to be so pissed when Liam didn't show up for work.

The van hit a bump in the road, and the rough metal of the floor scraped his chin and the tip of his nose. That hurt. Through the fear pounding in his chest, he tried to focus on the van's direction, but he didn't have a clue. He needed to calm the hell down and think.

Wait... They'd called him O'Rourke. They knew his name? This wasn't a random kidnapping. He'd been targeted. Was that a good thing or a bad thing? Danny Boy's Irish Pubs International was worldwide, consisting of over five hundred pubs. His father was a millionaire many times over, and that wasn't a secret. Was this a kidnapping for ransom? If so, that was good, right? They'd need him alive to collect any money.

"What are you going to do with me?"

Someone kicked his thigh. "Shut up."

"Ow." The plastic tie was too tight, making the tips of

his fingers tingle, but he didn't want to get kicked again, so he kept quiet.

He lost track of time as the engine droned on, and even though he was frightened out of his mind, he dozed off. He didn't know how long they traveled, but it had to be two or three days, and he mostly slept the miles away.

He never had a chance to escape because they never let him leave the van. The knit cap was kept over his eyes, and he was good with that. If he never saw his captors' faces, they'd have no reason to kill him.

The plastic ties had only been removed long enough for him to go to the bathroom in a bucket and to let him eat the hamburgers they'd gotten for him at fast-food drive-throughs as they traveled.

"If you try to yell or call for help, we'll shoot the worker," one of the men said the first time they got food.

Since that was something he couldn't live with on his conscience, he kept quiet.

Where were they taking him? Sometimes he heard the low murmur of voices from the front of the van, but he could never make out what they were saying. He thought there were only two men, but there could be three. If he tried to talk, he got kicked, so he stopped asking questions. On what was the second or third day, the van stopped, and he was roughly dragged out. Standing for the first time after so many hours of lying face down on the floor, his legs buckled when he tried to stand on them.

Rough hands grabbed his arms on both sides, and he stumbled along between two men as they dragged him into what he thought was a house because a door slammed behind them. After walking for a minute, he was pushed down onto a hard floor. It felt like wood under his face. The ties were cut off his wrists, and then he heard receding footsteps and a door closing. Afraid to move, he lay there for...he didn't know how long. He'd lost all sense of time.

He was hungry, his body was sore all over, and he was scared out of his mind. He'd give anything to be at his dad's pub washing dishes. If he ever got out of this, he'd never complain again.

His family would know by now that he was missing and would be searching for him. Would they even know where to look? He had no idea which direction they'd traveled, but he did know he was far from Kansas City. He tried not to cry, but tears welled up and spilled down his cheeks. He wanted to go home.

Suck it up, O'Rourke. Crying wasn't going to get him out of this, and he needed to figure out a way to escape. At least they'd untied his hands. It felt like he was alone, and he tentatively pushed the knit cap up, uncovering his eyes. When a kick to his body didn't come, he sat up.

The room was dark, and he crawled until he found a wall. On still shaky legs, he stood, leaned against the wall, and waited until his legs agreed to do their job of keeping him on his feet. Once he was steady, he circled the room, trailing his hands at the height that light switches were usually located.

He came to the door and tried the knob, unsurprised to find it locked. Switches were usually near the door, so he searched to the side of it. "Yes," he exclaimed when he found it, and a light came on. It was nothing more than a single light bulb hanging by a cord from the ceiling, but he could see.

There was nothing to see.

Other than a bucket in the corner, the room was empty. No bed, no chair, no blanket or pillow. Nothing, nothing,

nothing. The windows had thick boards nailed over them. How was he supposed to escape?

Fear and helplessness washed over him, and he slid down the wall. He cried, and he hated himself for being weak. He wanted to go home.

"Oomph!"

Liam startled awake when the silence of the room was broken. He'd left the light on, and he blinked to clear his eyes, doubting what he was seeing. A boy his age was sprawled on the floor, and another boy, also his age, was standing, glaring at the closed door.

"Am I dreaming?" He had no idea what day it was, how long he'd been asleep, or if he was even awake now. Maybe he was hallucinating.

The standing boy tore his attention from the door to Liam. "Who are you?"

"Liam." He pinched himself as he got to his feet. Okay, that hurt, so not dreaming. "Did they kidnap you, too?"

"Yeah, me and Cooper. I'm Grayson. Do you know who they are and what they plan?"

"I don't know. Where are we?"

"South Florida. It's spring break here."

"No shit? Florida?" He'd always wanted to go to spring break in Florida, but willingly. Not as a kidnap victim.

"Yeah," Grayson said. "You didn't know that?"

"They took me in Kansas City, where I'm from. I've been blindfolded and in the back of a van for two or three days."

Grayson frowned. "This all seems really odd. Why take you from Kansas and me from Florida. What's the connection?"

"Yeah, weird."

"They knew my name," Grayson said.

"They did mine, too. What do you think that means?"

Grayson shrugged. "Who knows, but I'm hoping it means that they kidnapped us for ransom. Is your father rich?"

"Very. Yours?"

"Same."

He studied the other boy. His clothes didn't seem to be as expensive as Liam's and Grayson's. Maybe he was from a rich family, too, and was just slumming? Cooper caught him staring, and Liam jerked his gaze away.

"He wasn't targeted," Grayson said. "He was with me when they took me, and they grabbed him, too. They didn't know who he was." He tapped Cooper's foot with his own. "Sorry for that."

"Not your fault." Cooper rolled over and sat up.

"Is your family rich?" Liam asked.

Cooper laughed as if that was the funniest thing in the world. "We don't even know what money looks like."

He and Grayson glanced at each other, and even though they'd just met, they both understood the message passed between them. If this was to get ransom from their rich families, what did that mean for Cooper if his family couldn't pay?

That was the moment Liam was more worried about someone other than himself. Somehow, he was going to get out of this and take his new friends with him.

Chapter 1

"I got one for you," Cooper Devlin said.

Grayson Montana groaned. "Not another dad joke. I beg you."

"You might as well try to stop the tide," Liam said to his friend as they sat on the deck of Grayson's beach house. Cooper had an entire book of dad jokes in his head.

"What do you call a fake noodle?" Cooper grinned when no answer was forthcoming. "An impasta."

"Don't encourage him," Grayson said when Liam chuckled, but there was amusement in his eyes.

"Sorry, that laugh slipped out. Won't happen again."

Cooper clutched his chest. "Bro, you wound me. You love my dad jokes. Admit it."

What he loved were these two men. Getting kidnapped sucked, but he wouldn't change a thing. An act of violence had brought these men he considered his brothers into his life. Didn't matter they weren't of his blood, they were his family.

The three of them had started The Phoenix Three because of being kidnapped when they were teens. They'd bonded during their time in captivity and had become the best of friends. After graduating high school, each of them had enlisted in the military to learn the skills necessary to plan and complete missions.

The Phoenix Three's purpose was to save children who'd been kidnapped like they had been, to find runaway children and get them help before the streets ate them up, even to save children from the very people who were supposed to love and protect them. Really, just to save children whenever and wherever they could. It was a mission they each had dedicated their lives to and fervently believed in.

They'd dreamed up the idea of doing this work when they'd been young and idealistic...and very naive. But they'd made it happen, and Liam felt a sense of completion and satisfaction that he never would have achieved working for his father.

When he'd told his father he was enlisting in the Marines, they'd had a fierce argument, his father refusing to understand why Liam needed to do that. What his father didn't understand was that the kidnapping had changed Liam.

If there had been another son to groom for the business, maybe his father wouldn't have disowned him. He'd never know. How things had gone down between them was a hurt Liam kept buried and tried not to think about.

Tyler, the son of Grayson's fiancée, raced out the door with the energy only a five-year-old possessed. "I'm here! Let's go surfing."

Liam chuckled. The kid already had on his wet suit. Grayson had said Tyler took to surfing as if he'd been born on a surfboard.

"Do you have any homework you need to do first?" Grayson asked.

"Mama said I could do it after we surf."

"All right then. Let me put on my wet suit." Grayson eyed the ocean. "The waves are good today."

Five minutes later, man and boy were walking across the sand, Tyler's surfboard half the size of Grayson's. Of the three of them, Grayson had the best role model for a father, no doubt why he'd fallen into the role as a father to Tyler so easily.

"Grayson told me that Harlow's ex has been writing her, demanding she bring Tyler to see him," Cooper said.

"That bastard might as well wish for the moon to fall in his lap."

Cooper grunted his agreement.

Tyler's no-good father was in prison for murder. He didn't give two figs for his son. He was just trying to manipulate Harlow. Harlow had hired The Phoenix Three to help her get her son back. They had, and Grayson and Harlow had fallen in love.

It was a warm summer day, but there was a nice sea breeze and big fluffy white clouds floated by, blocking the sun about the time it started to feel too hot. Liam hadn't slept much the past few days, and his eyes slid closed.

"They're coming in."

He blinked awake and focused his gaze on Cooper. "What?"

"They've been surfing for an hour, and now they're coming in. Enjoy your nap?"

Actually, he had. He shifted his gaze to the ocean. Grayson rode the small wave next to the boy he planned to adopt. The two of them grinned at each other as they hit shallow water and hopped off their boards. Grayson held up his hand and they high-fived.

His friend lived on the beach, had found a wonderful woman, and had fallen in love with her and her son. His life was about perfect. Liam was happy for Grayson, and although he tried not to be envious, he was. He hadn't let himself be serious about a woman while he was in the military. As a Special Ops Marine Raider, he'd lived a dangerous life and was gone more than he was home. That wasn't conducive to having a relationship. Now that he was out of the military, he was ready to settle down and find his own happiness.

The dating scene—going out to clubs, one-night stands, and meeting women who were just out to have fun—wasn't his thing. Also, and surprisingly, he wanted kids, something he'd started thinking about after seeing how much Grayson enjoyed being around Tyler.

"Are they finally coming in?" Harlow said, joining them on the deck. She carried a bucket of beers on ice that she set on the table.

"Looks like." Liam grabbed a bottle and twisted off the cap. "I think they're going to turn into fish as much time as they spend in the ocean."

"But such cute fishies," Harlow said. She smiled fondly at the man and boy as they walked across the sand, carrying their boards.

Liam grinned. "Well, the little one, anyway."

"Yeah, the word *cute* just doesn't cut it with the big one," Cooper said.

"Hush, both of you. My boys are the cutest things ever." Harlow moved the beer bucket to the other side of the table, away from them. "No more beer for either of you until you take it back."

"Do I need to kill them for you, love?" Grayson said as he joined them on the deck.

Tyler raced up the stairs behind him. "Please don't kill them, Dad. I like Liam and Cooper."

"Hey, I was just kidding, okay?" He put his hand on top of Tyler's head. "Why don't you go change out of your wet suit?" After he ran inside, Grayson gave Harlow an embarrassed smile. "I need to remember that kids take things literally."

"Like when he asked what the brown things in his soup were and you told him monkey toes?" Harlow said. "He'll never eat cream of mushroom soup again."

A snort escaped from Liam. Although she was going for stern, he picked up on the amusement in her voice.

Grayson grimaced. "Uh...sorry?"

"Bro," Cooper said. "You gotta work on your jokes."

"Wait. Back up a minute." Liam pointed his bottle at Grayson. "Tyler calls you Dad?" That was big.

"Yeah. Started that a few days ago. Said he needs to practice getting used to it for when his mommy marries me. Kid owns my heart, man." He and Harlow shared an intimate smile.

That. That right there was what he wanted. A family of his own. A woman who looked at him like that. He just needed to find her.

Chapter 2

Quinn Sullivan hurriedly packed her suitcase. She wanted to be gone before Jasper returned. What she thought of as a temporary fling while they were both in California covering the wildfires differed from Jasper's growing possessiveness. When they'd first hooked up, he was fun, but now, if she even said hello to another man, he would get jealous and mentally abusive. That was shit she didn't put up with.

This morning he'd hurled insults at her after she'd told him she planned to leave soon. According to him, she was a cold bitch and only cared about herself.

"You'll leave with me, and I'm not ready yet," he'd said. He'd sneered at her then. "What's the big deal? There's no place important you need to be. You just take pictures of kids, no big deal."

Jasper hadn't been the first man to tell her that her work wasn't important, and that her priority should be him. He had no idea how much of a trigger hearing him say that was. She'd told him she was leaving, and he didn't want to hear her, so she wasn't waiting around to have another fight with him.

He was a photojournalist embedded with a team of hotshots, and she was covering the devastation left in the wake of the fires, especially the children who'd lost their homes. Also a photojournalist, children were her forte.

She'd documented the horrors of war on children, the gaunt faces of hungry children in Africa, the fragile bodies of abused children living on the streets of cities around the world. Wherever children were suffering, she went. Her hope was that her photos would make a difference in the lives of those lost souls. That people seeing them would feel compelled to reach out a helping hand however they could.

When Jasper had asked her to stay with him in the house he was renting, she'd first refused. She was a nomad and didn't do relationships. He'd convinced her that he didn't either, and when it was time to leave—a few weeks at the most—they'd go their separate ways. The icing on the cake, though, was the money she'd be saving on a hotel room. She should have listened to that little voice telling her staying with him was a mistake.

She carried her suitcase into the second bedroom. Jasper never went in there, so if he did come back before she could leave, he wouldn't see it. Her cameras and accessories were her life and needed to be packed carefully to prevent damage while traveling. Some of her accessories were on the dining room table along with Jasper's. She was almost finished packing everything up when she heard Jasper's car arrive. Panicked, she grabbed her thumb drives and stuffed them in her camera bag.

Her rental car was parked out front, so he would know she was here. She ran to the spare bedroom, put the bag in with her suitcase, then left the room, closing the door behind her. The last thing she wanted to do was talk to him right then, and the only thing she could think to do was take a shower. He never bothered her when she was in the bathroom.

She'd just locked herself in when she heard him come into the house. He was talking, and at first, she thought he'd brought someone home with him, but after a minute of listening, she realized he was on the phone. The bathroom door was thin plywood, and Jasper had a loud voice. She could hear his conversation.

"I told him I'd give him the photos for a million dollars," Jasper said.

Huh?

"Well, he's not happy, but what can he do? If he doesn't pay, I'll release the photos to the news outlets. See how he likes that. He sure as hell doesn't want the world to know kids are getting sick because of him."

Who wasn't happy, and why were children getting sick? She put her ear to the door to hear better.

"Yeah, it was pure luck that I stumbled on their dumping ground when I was in Hope Corner."

Dumping ground for what, and where was Hope Corner? He'd told her that he'd been in West Virginia before coming to California. Was that where it was?

"Million-dollar payday, dude."

Who was he talking to?

"No, just hang tight. I'll let you know when the meet is. I'll make sure it's in a public place where you can watch my back. Later, man."

Quinn took a second to panic that Jasper would be suspicious she'd heard the conversation. *Do something*, she screamed at herself. The shower! She hurried and turned it on. She had no intention of disrobing and getting in. If Jasper did suspect she heard him, she wasn't about to be naked if he forced his way into the bathroom.

"Quinn?" He knocked on the door.

"Oh, hey. You're back already? I'm in the shower. Be out in a few minutes." Or never.

"Walked out without my wallet. Why don't you put on something pretty tonight, and we'll go out to dinner."

"I'd love that." Not.

She left the shower running as she put her ear back to the door. After a good ten minutes of silence, she turned off the shower and ventured out. The relief that he wasn't tricking her and waiting for her to emerge was so great that she almost fell to her knees. But no time for that.

It was time to boogie.

Quinn was hot, hungry, and tired. She'd been in Hope Corner for three days and had nothing to show for her efforts. She had found a lake and was working her way around it, looking for any sign of illegal dumping. She had also found a textile plant, a big one, but it wasn't on the lake. It was about a half mile from Black Bear Lake, and the plant would have barrels of dye and other chemicals, so it seemed possible it was the place Jasper was talking about.

She'd briefly stopped home to do some research after leaving California. Hope Corner was in the Appalachian Mountains in West Virginia. After deciding this had to be where Jasper was talking about, she'd made a reservation in a motel in the small town.

The people here were tight-lipped, and her inquiries about children getting sick were met with silence until this afternoon. A man who she wouldn't want to meet up with in a dark alley told her it was none of her business when she'd asked her questions and that she wasn't welcome in Hope Corner. She was getting a little scared to be here, but if Jasper was right, children were getting sick. What if they started dying? She couldn't turn her back on that.

The little that she'd learned while here was that the largest employer was the mill, Hanson Textiles, Inc. About 80 percent of the people in Hope Corner worked there. What she needed to do was go home and regroup. Take the time to research the mill, and if they were involved, how? Who owned it? What chemicals did they use and what illnesses would those chemicals cause? Then she'd call her friend Brett, a professor of environmental studies. Get his input on where to go with this.

First, she needed food, a shower, a glass of wine, and a good night's sleep. Oh, and she had to call her father. It was Wednesday. The deal she'd made with him when she'd told him at nineteen that she was going to be a photojournalist was that she'd call him every Wednesday and Sunday evening when she was traveling. Because she'd be traipsing the world, he needed to know she was safe. She hadn't missed one promised call.

Too tired and sweaty to eat at a restaurant, she went through a fast-food drive-through. Back at the motel, she grabbed her purse, her camera case, and the bag of food to take with her into the room. Food first, then a shower. After she ate and was clean and in her comfy clothes, she'd call her father, then pour a glass of wine from the bottle in her room to enjoy while she went through today's shots on her camera.

The motel still used actual keys to open the door. She should have thought to get it out while she was still in the car. With her camera bag strap over one shoulder and food in one hand, she fished around in her purse for the key with the other.

"There you are." She slid the key into the lock, and as she opened the door, something hit her from behind, pushing her into the room. "Umph." She tripped, and she dropped everything she was holding so she could put her hands down and catch herself to keep her face from hitting the floor.

Before she face-planted, an arm slid around her stomach and pulled her back against a body. "Hello, Quinn."

She stilled. "Jasper?" What the devil was he doing here? After leaving him in California, she'd hoped to never see him again.

"I came for you," he said, his breath hot on her neck.

"Let go of me." When she tried to step away from him, he tightened his hold.

"I don't think so. You left without a word. I have to wonder why."

She tried to elbow him in the stomach, and he only laughed. It never occurred to her that he'd follow her. Even more alarming, how did he know she'd be in Hope Corner? She pulled away from him again, and surprising her, he let go. She stumbled a few steps, her foot landing on the bag with the hamburger and fries she'd dropped, smashing them.

"Damn it. That was my dinner." She turned to face him and gasped at seeing him pointing a gun at her. "What the hell, Jasper? Put that thing away."

"This is how it's going to be. You're coming with me."

"I'm not going anywhere with you." He laughed, and the sound of it sent shivers snaking down her spine.

"You have a choice, darling. You come with me, or I shoot you." He picked up her camera bag. "All your equipment in here?"

"That I brought with me, yes. Why?"

"Let's go."

What was going on? This couldn't be because she'd left California without telling him. That wasn't a reason to threaten her with a gun. It had to be because, somehow, he'd found out she'd overheard his conversation. She glanced around the cheap motel room and decided it wasn't a place she was willing to die in. If she went with him, she could find a way to escape.

"I need my suitcase."

"No, you don't."

She looked into eyes that were flat and dead. Eyes that said he might just shoot her if she didn't do as he said. Her purse was at her feet, and she scooped it up. Her phone was in it, and somehow, she'd escape and call the police.

"You don't have to do this. We can talk here."

"Shut up." He pushed her toward the door. "You try anything when we walk out, and I'll shoot you and anyone you try to talk to."

When she left California early because he was raising all kinds of red flags, she'd instinctively known that he was a man who could be physically abusive. The kind of man who'd claim it was for her own good. What she hadn't anticipated was that he would hunt her down and threaten her with a gun.

As they walked out the door, he pressed the barrel of the gun against her hip. To anyone seeing them, it would just look like a couple checking out of their motel room. The one good thing was that she hadn't called her father yet, and when she missed her scheduled call, he would know something was wrong. Her father would move heaven and earth to find her.

"Remember what I said I'd do if you tried anything." He let go of her to open the back door of his car. After setting her camera bag on the back seat, he opened the driver's-side door. "Get in and slide over."

She glanced inside. "There's a console. Can't I just get in on the passenger side?"

"And have you try to run when I'm coming to this side to get in? Don't think so."

It was awkward, but she managed to climb over the console.

"Put your seat belt on," he said as he buckled his. "Can't have the cops stopping us because you're not belted."

Her mind was racing with a million thoughts, but there was one thing that was certain. She had to get away from him as soon as possible. As they drove through the dark, deserted mountain roads, she tried to come up with a plan. She could feel Jasper's eyes on her as he watched her every move. She had to be careful.

They drove for about an hour, and finally, they arrived at a secluded cabin in the woods. Jasper parked the car and got out. She opened her door and stepped out, her gaze stopping on the cabin. It was old and run-down, with weeds growing up around it.

He waved his gun toward the cabin. "Inside."

Should she make a run for it now? She glanced around. It was dark and the cabin was surrounded by forest. There were probably bears and mountain lions in those woods. And she didn't know where they were, so she had no idea which way to run. She'd be better off escaping when it was daylight.

She followed Jasper into the cabin. It was just as run-down on the inside as it was on the outside. It was clear that no one had lived in it for quite some time. It was small, with a living room, bedroom, and kitchen area combined. Next to the bed was a closed door, which she assumed was the bathroom.

The power must not be on because there were oil lamps

scattered around. They were burning so that meant he'd already been in the cabin. "Who lives here?"

"No one." He motioned to the worn-out couch. "Sit."

A spider crawled up the wall behind the couch, and she shuddered. God only knew what all might be living in that couch. And she didn't even want to try to guess what the stains on the cushions were. "I think I'll stand."

"Suit yourself." He set his gun on the kitchen counter, went to the small table, and started removing the contents of her camera bag. When he got to the two thumb drives she'd brought with her, he stared at them and frowned.

"Leave my stuff alone." He knew better than anyone not to mess with a photographer's cameras.

He dropped the thumb drives as he faced her. "Where is it?"

"Where's what?" The rage in his eyes was scaring her. She eyed the gun. It was about halfway between them. Could she get to it before he did?

Thanks to her father, she knew how to shoot. It was one of the things he'd insisted she learn when he'd accepted that she was going to go after her dream and that meant she'd sometimes find herself in dangerous countries. She owned a gun, which unfortunately was in her gun safe at home. It hadn't occurred to her that she'd need it here. A mistake she wouldn't make again. From now on, wherever she went, her gun would go with her.

"Don't play games, Quinn. Where's my thumb drive?"

"Why would you think I'd have anything of yours?" Had she accidentally taken what he was looking for when she'd hurriedly packed up her camera bag? In her haste, she had scooped up several thumb drives that were on the table. During her brief stop at home, she'd sorted out her cameras and accessories and had only brought with her what she would need for a day or two of snooping. If she had his thumb drive, it was at home. Not something she was about to tell him.

"Because you're the only one who could have taken it." He glared at her. "If it's not here, I'll start shooting you in places that won't kill you but will hurt like hell until you tell me where it is."

"And here I thought you liked me." She didn't know where her bravado was coming from because she believed him. When he returned his attention to her camera bag, she took a deep breath. "I'm thirsty." The gun was her aim, not a glass of water. Just a few steps, and she would be closer to it than him.

As if he had eyes in the back of his head, he spun, going for the gun, too. Their hands reached it at the same time, and they wrestled for it. What she didn't see coming was his fist. It was hard to see anything when her world turned black.

Chapter 3

Liam answered the ringing phone. "The Phoenix Three. Liam O'Rourke speaking. How may I help you?"

"I need you to find my daughter," a man said, his voice urgent and tinged with fear.

"To whom am I speaking?"

"Robert Sullivan. My girl is missing. I was told that if anyone could find her, it was you people. I don't care what it costs, just find her for me."

"How old is she, and how long has she been missing, Mr. Sullivan?"

"Since at least yesterday, but the last time I talked to her was Sunday, so it could be since then. Something's wrong. She never misses our scheduled phone calls every Wednesday and Sunday."

Not a small child then. "And she's how old?"

"Twenty-eight. Quinn's a photojournalist. A damn good one, and she travels all over the world."

Liam frowned. "So, she's missing in a foreign country?" That was going to make it harder...if he accepted the case. The Phoenix Three's emphasis was on saving children, which Quinn Sullivan was not.

"I didn't say that. She's supposed to be in West Virginia."

More than likely, he would be wasting time on finding

a woman who simply got busy and forgot to call her father. "Mr. Sullivan, I think you should give her a few more days to contact you, and if she doesn't, call the police. Our company focuses on finding missing children."

"She is a child, my damn child!"

Liam pulled the phone away from his ear. The man could shout. "Sir, I'm sorry, but—"

"Your father said you could find her."

Liam almost gasped. "My father?" That was not something he ever expected to hear. His father hadn't spoken to him in over ten years, not since the day Liam had told his dad that he had a higher purpose in life and was enlisting in the Marines. That was the day his father had disowned him. Said Liam was turning his back on family, on his inheritance.

"Yes, he gave me your name and number. Said if anyone could find her, it would be you. I don't care what it costs."

That his father even knew his phone number was shocking. "Has anyone been hassling her that you know of? An ex who might want to hurt her? Anything like that?"

"No, no one would want to hurt my Quinn, and she doesn't have a boyfriend."

That you know of. "Mr. Sullivan, send me everything you have on where your daughter is supposed to be, along with a photo of her and any other information you think will be helpful. Also, include her cell phone number. I'll find her for you." He gave the man his email address, then disconnected.

His father! Liam couldn't wrap his mind around that. The old man had disowned him, said he'd never utter Liam's name again. Yet, after ten years, he had, and apparently with praise. How was he supposed to feel about that? It had taken years of not hearing from his father, but he'd finally accepted that his old man meant it when he said he no longer had a son.

Liam pulled open the bottom drawer of his desk. He stared at the folder for a moment before picking it up and setting it on his desktop. He hesitated before opening the folder and spreading out the contents.

His gaze roamed over the photos of his father and mother, the place that used to be his home. For the first time in what felt like forever, he let himself miss being a part of his family. He secretly talked to his mother once a month, but that only made him feel guilty because it meant that she had to lie to her husband. He picked up the photo of his father. What did it mean that he'd given Liam's name to Robert Sullivan? *Probably didn't mean a thing.* Liam closed the folder and slid it back into the drawer. He was dead to his father, and he wasn't going to wish for a change that would never happen.

A few minutes later, his computer dinged, signaling an incoming email. Mr. Sullivan hadn't wasted any time sending the information on his daughter. Included was a message saying that a deposit of ten thousand dollars would go in the mail tomorrow. Liam had been so gobsmacked by the mention of his father that he hadn't thought to discuss payment. He printed out the attachments then settled back to learn about the missing woman.

The first item he looked at was her photo, and it was the green eyes with laughter shining in them that caught his attention. She looked like a woman who would be fun to know. The most striking thing about her was her curly hair the color of copper. His gaze moved to her face. A phrase he'd heard somewhere came to mind. Peaches and cream perfectly described her complexion. Her smile was infectious, and he almost smiled back at the photo.

"Get a grip, O'Rourke," he muttered. She was a case, not a woman he needed to be lusting over. Even if there was something about her that had him wanting to meet her.

He set the photo aside and read her father's email. Quinn Sullivan wasn't just a photojournalist. She was an award-winning one. Her specialty was the children of the world. Her photos of children caught in the middle of war zones were heartbreaking.

There was a long list of links in the email, and by the time he reached the last one, he was impressed with not only her heart-wrenching photos posted online and in magazines and newspapers, but with the attention she brought to children who needed the world to save them. He had much in common with her.

Her father was adamant that his daughter wouldn't willingly miss their scheduled calls, and after reading about her and seeing through her lens the love she had for children, Liam believed that Quinn hadn't voluntarily gone radio silent. She wasn't a woman who'd worry her father like that.

According to her father, she was supposed to be in West Virginia, in a small Appalachian mountain town he'd never heard of. He did a search on Hope Corner and decided to drive, since there wasn't a flight out of Myrtle Beach until the following day. He could get there faster by driving, and that would give him the added benefit of being able to carry his weapons without having to declare them to the airline.

He called Grayson, got his voicemail, and left a message for his teammate to call him. Grayson was in town, searching for a fourteen-year-old boy who'd gotten in a fight with his father and had run away. Cooper was in Texas, tracking down a mother who'd kidnapped her two-year-old daughter. He was on the woman's trail and should wrap the case up in a day or two, so Liam didn't call Cooper.

Next, he went to their weapons room, and after putting his palm against the reader to unlock the door, he went in. The three of them had a wide assortment of weapons, some they'd collected over their years in the military and some they'd bought after starting The Phoenix Three.

Not sure what he was walking into, he decided on two handguns and a long gun, along with plenty of ammo. He added a KA-BAR—his knife of choice—to his weapons, along with a handful of smoke grenades and night-vision goggles. Hopefully, he wouldn't need any of the items he was packing up, but it was always better to prepare for the worst.

On his way to his condo to pack, he stopped and topped off his gas tank. He was packing his duffel bag when Grayson returned his call.

"Hey, man," Liam said on answering. "Any luck finding the kid?"

"I got a tip that he's couch surfing among his friends. I'm sitting on a house that he's supposed to be sleeping at tonight."

"No doubt you're bored. Hope you can get the kid home to his family tonight."

"Tell me about it. What's up?"

"Got a job, and I'm heading out to West Virginia."

"Now?"

"Yup. Woman who her father swears is very reliable is missing."

"Thought we agreed we were only going to take on cases involving children."

Liam had expected that response. "I have to take this one. My father told the woman's father to call me, that I could find his daughter."

"That's unexpected."

"Understatement." Grayson and Cooper were aware that Liam's father had disowned him. "Not sure what the deal is, but I'll keep in touch. I'm leaving now, and I'm driving. I need you to track the cell phone number I'm going to send you and text me the coordinates."

"I'll do that, and, Liam, be safe."

"Back atcha."

He made coffee, filled a travel mug, then grabbed a box of power bars. In the car, he started the ignition. "All right, Miss Sullivan, let's find out what kind of trouble you've landed in."

Liam arrived in Elkins, West Virginia, at five in the morning. It was the closest good-sized town before Hope Corner. He found a decent-looking hotel, checked in, and in his room, he stripped down to his boxer briefs. A few hours' sleep, and he'd be ready to go.

Three hours later, he was up and in the shower. Twenty minutes later, he was dressed and ready to leave. He slipped his wallet and phone in the back pockets of his jeans, his duffel bag over his shoulder, and with his car keys and travel mug in hand, he went to the lobby. After dropping off his room key and getting a receipt, he went to the breakfast area.

"That's what I'm talking about," he said when he saw that the hotel served sausage, cheese, and egg biscuits at their free continental breakfast. After filling his travel mug with coffee, he stacked two of the sandwiches on a napkin, added an apple, and he was good to go.

He'd already programmed the Hope Corner motel where Quinn was supposed to be into his car's GPS, and he brought up the directions. According to the GPS, he had a two-hour drive before reaching the Sunset Motel.

The drive along the country road was beautiful, and he enjoyed the scenery as he ate his breakfast. Since Quinn hadn't been in contact with her father, Liam didn't expect to find her at the motel. His hope was that someone there might have seen something. Maybe she'd asked the desk clerk directions to somewhere or talked about places she wanted to go.

The Sunset Motel was appealing. The grounds were well-kept, bright flowers lined the entrance to the parking lot, and the yellow paint was cheery. He parked in front of the office and went in.

Mr. Sullivan had said that he'd called the motel several times when Quinn missed her scheduled check-in, and she hadn't answered the phone in her room. He'd left messages for her to call him, but she hadn't.

Liam expected to be told they couldn't give out her room number or any information on her, and he could respect that, especially if he just walked in, a stranger, and started asking questions. He'd considered his options before leaving Myrtle Beach, and he'd decided the best approach when asking anyone about her would be a brother looking for his sister. He'd created a fake license with his name as Liam Sullivan, and he'd photoshopped a picture of him with her to put in his wallet.

An older woman was at the counter, and he hoped she'd be willing to help after hearing his sob story. He smiled as he walked up to the counter.

"Good morning," she said. "Are you needing a room?"

"I'm not sure. I'm Liam Sullivan. My sister's supposed to be staying here. Quinn Sullivan. Can you tell me if she's still booked in a room? If she is, I'll want a room, too."

The woman narrowed her eyes. "How do I know you're

her brother? You could be one of those sex predators they talk about on the TV."

"It's smart of you to be suspicious, ma'am. It makes me feel better that my sister is staying in a place where you're looking out for her."

"Well, I got daughters, and I'd want someone to watch out for them if some stranger came looking for them. Your sister...if she really is your sister...is a pretty girl like them. Some men don't have good intentions, you know."

"I do know." He took out his wallet. "This is my driver's license with my name on it. As you can see, Quinn and I have the same last name. And this is a picture of my sister and I together, taken two years ago at our father's house." He'd given the photo a Christmas theme with him and Quinn supposedly standing in front of a decorated tree.

She took the picture and brought it close to her eyes. "I see the resemblance."

It had always fascinated him how you could lead someone to believe what you wanted them to with a few details, whether they were true or not. "You see, Miss..."

"Just call me Betta. Everyone does."

"Betta, my father and I are worried. Quinn was supposed to call him Wednesday night, and she didn't. She's not answering her cell phone, and he's called here several times, but she's not answering the room phone either. He's left messages, and—"

"Oh, I've taken those messages. They're right here." She turned and pulled several pink message sheets from a cubbyhole. "Your sister hasn't stopped by so I could give them to her."

"When was the last time you saw her?"

"Hmm. Not sure. Maybe two days ago. Her car's still here. Haven't seen it move for a few days now. It's the nice blue one parked in front of her room. She's booked for a week, so I just assumed I hadn't noticed her coming and going."

"Something's not right. I feel it in my bones. Will you let me see inside her room? Please, Betta. My father and I are so worried."

Betta's eyes widened. "You think she's dead in there?"

"No!" He sure hoped not. "But I think I need to see inside her room."

"I'll have to go with you."

"That's fine."

She picked up a key on a large ring and dangled it in front of him. "The master key."

"Do you have maid service?" he asked as they walked toward the room. If there was anything unusual—such as a dead body—in Quinn's room, housekeeping would have reported it.

"Yes, but Miss Sullivan asked that no one enter her room unless she was in it. She said she had some expensive cameras and stuff that she didn't want bothered. We've cleaned her room twice since she checked in, and she was there both times."

They stopped at the door to Quinn's room, and Betta inserted the key. He put his hand on her shoulder. "Let me go in first." He didn't know why, but he didn't expect to find Quinn Sullivan's body. There was the possibility that he was wrong, though, and if so, he didn't want Betta to see.

"Oh, Lord, please don't let her be dead," Betta said.

He stepped into the room. There was no body. *Thank you, Jesus.* "You can come in." He walked farther into the room.

"There's her suitcase," Betta said. "She must be around."

A small white bag on the floor caught his attention, and

he picked it up. The smell of rotten meat hit his nose as soon as he opened it.

Betta scrunched her nose. "Good Lord, what stinks?"

"I'm guessing this was going to be her lunch or dinner. It stinks because it's a day or two old." And smashed. Someone had stepped on it. His gaze shifted around the room. There wasn't any sign of a struggle, and her suitcase was still open on the suitcase rack. He glanced inside but didn't touch anything.

Quinn Sullivan was gone but had left her things behind. Because of the smashed meal and that her car was parked out front, his gut said someone had come to her room, and that she hadn't left willingly.

"How long is the room paid for?" he asked.

"Sunday. Do you think something happened to her?"

Yeah, he did. Today was Friday, so only a few more days on the room. It needed to stay untouched. If the worst had happened to Quinn, the police would need to send a crime scene tech to the room, where hopefully whoever took her had left fingerprints behind.

"Betta, I'm going to pay for another week on the room. I need you to keep it locked up and everyone out."

"You think something happened in here?"

"I hope not, but maybe." He lifted his chin toward the door. "Let's talk outside and not contaminate the room any more than we already have." As he followed her out, he grabbed the Do Not Disturb hanger and put it on the outside of the door.

"Should I call the police?"

"Not yet." He didn't want the police to hinder his search for Quinn. "I'm an investigator, so I know how to find people. Why our father sent me here. Did my sister have her camera bag with her, do you know?"

"She had a large purple backpack every time I saw her, so that could have been a camera bag. Like I told you, she said she had some expensive camera equipment, and nothing like that was in the room."

"Did she say why she was here? My sister's a photojournalist, and her specialty is children who need help of some kind or other."

"She did ask when she was checking in if there was an unusually high number of children getting sick in Hope Corner."

That was interesting. "And are there?"

"I don't know what a high number would be, but I know of three children who have leukemia."

If Quinn was asking that question, she had come to Hope Corner for a reason. As he stood by while Betta closed and locked the door, he glanced over, seeing a housekeeping cart outside of a room with an open door. He headed that way.

"Excuse me, miss." He dropped Quinn's food bag in the trash can on the cart.

A young woman carrying sheets out of the room froze at seeing him. "Yes?"

"I'm looking for my sister. She was staying in room nine. Have you seen her?"

The woman's gaze went past his shoulder.

"It's all right, Macy, you can answer him," Betta said, coming up next to him.

Macy's eyes shifted back to him. "The last time I saw her, she was leaving with a man."

Every bone in his body said she hadn't gone freely. "How long ago?"

"It was Wednesday."

That would fit the timeline. "What time did you see

her?" Quinn had missed her Wednesday call. But the good news was that she hadn't been missing since her last phone call on Sunday to her father, so the trail wasn't all that cold.

"Around dinnertime. I was finished for the day and had gotten in my car to leave. She came out of her room with a man, and they got in a car and left. She didn't look exactly happy, but it wasn't my business."

"Macy, this is really important. I need you to describe the man and the car."

"Is something wrong?"

"Macy," Betta snapped. "Answer his question."

"Um, the man was a little taller than her, but not by much. He wasn't skinny, but he wasn't heavy. I guess I'd say he was lean. He had dirty blond hair, and he looked like he needed a haircut."

"How long was it?"

"Past his ears but not touching his shoulder. That's all I remember about him."

It was better than nothing. "What about his car? Make and color?"

She closed her eyes. "It was…um, dark green, but I don't know what kind."

"A sedan or an SUV?"

"Not an SUV. It had four doors because he opened the back door and tossed her backpack in. I know it was hers because it was purple, and she always had it with her. I'm sorry, but that's all I remember."

"You've been a big help. Thank you." He walked over to Quinn's car, tried the door, finding it locked. He peered through the window and didn't see anything inside. There was a sticker on the rear window for a rental car company. Betta had followed him, and he said, "Let's just leave the car here for now. I'll call the rental company if I need them to come pick it up."

"I'm so worried about her now, Mr. Sullivan."

He was concerned, too. "Let's go to the office so I can pay you for another week on the room. I also want to give you my phone number if Quinn should show up or you think of anything else you might remember."

"I hope you find her," Betta said after she took his credit card.

Oh, he was going to. The question was, what shape would she be in when he did?

Chapter 4

Quinn grimaced when she opened her eyes. The sunlight coming in the window hurt. Had she forgotten to close the curtains last night? And her head. A royally pissed off tiny drummer must have taken up residence in her brain. Had she drunk too much wine? That would explain forgetting to close the curtains. She really, really had to pee.

She frowned as she took in the room. Right, this was the cabin where Jasper had taken her. She remembered that he'd hit her when they'd fought for the gun. She wasn't nauseated and her vision wasn't blurry, so she didn't think she had a concussion.

She lifted her hand to see if she could feel a bump on her head. *What?* It took a moment to comprehend what she was seeing. *What the hell?* Manacles attached to heavy chains were fastened around both wrists. Her gaze followed the chains up to the wall where they were secured to one large hook over the bed.

The jackass had chained her up! Now she was furious with him. She stood and tried to yank the chains out of the hook. They wouldn't budge. When the door swung open, she backed up to the wall and pressed against it.

Jasper strode in, a smile on his face as if chaining her to a wall was normal. "You finally woke up. Good."

"What the hell, Jasper?"

"Tell me where my thumb drive is, and you can go home."

"I don't believe a word out of your lying mouth." Would he really let her leave if she gave him the thumb drive, which she might or might not have? She didn't think he was going to pat her on the shoulder if she did have it and gave it back. As long as she kept her mouth shut, she might find a way to get out of this still breathing.

"I have to wonder if you think you can steal my payday for yourself," Jasper said.

"What payday?" Maybe she could get him to tell her what this was all about. She wanted to ask about the children who were getting sick, but that would tell him she'd overheard his phone conversation.

He narrowed his eyes as he studied her. "Why'd you leave without a word, Quinn? Could it be that you had my thumb drive and wanted to leave before I found out?"

Should she tell him the truth or lie? "Take these things off, and I'll tell you."

He laughed. "Nice try. Tell me where my thumb drive is, and you'll be free to go."

"I don't have it. I swear I don't. What's on it that's so important that you'd..." She rattled the chains. "That you would do this to me."

"Don't you know? You looked at what was on it, didn't you?"

"How can I look at something I don't have?" Maybe she could convince him she was really hurt. "I don't feel so great. I think you gave me a concussion." For effect, she rubbed the side of her head. The chain banged against her face, which made her mad all over again. "Seriously, Jasper, I need a doctor. And take these damn chains off me."

He laughed. "Not happening. I have a question for you. If you don't have my thumb drive, and you haven't looked at it, why are you in Hope Corner?"

She couldn't answer that without admitting she'd overheard his phone conversation, so she just stared back at him and said, "You're a bastard. You know that?"

"I do know that, pretty girl." Something dark and dangerous was in his smile and his eyes. "I have to go out. While I'm gone, think real hard about telling me where my thumb drive is if you want to leave this cabin."

She'd told him more than once that she didn't like pet names, and that he'd ignored her and kept calling her things like *babe* and *pretty girl* had been a red flag she'd ignored. Any man who didn't respect a woman's wishes was a jerk.

"What about food and water? I'm hungry."

He walked out without responding.

"Bastard." Although relieved he was gone, what if he never came back? No one knew where she was, and she'd die here. She remembered reading that people died from lack of water before starvation.

How far did the chains reach? There must be water or at least ice in the cooler on the counter. Maybe even food. The chain wasn't long enough to get to it she learned when she reached the end and was a foot from being able to touch it.

She went back to the thick S-hook screwed into the wall, but as hard as she yanked on the chains, the hook wouldn't give. She tried to unscrew it, but that didn't work either. "Damn you, Jasper," she screamed.

Her gaze shifted around the room, landing on her camera bag. If she was able to escape, she'd grab the bag. She was able to reach it, and after putting everything back in it, she zipped it up. There, ready to go.

The closed door next to the bed caught her attention. It

must be the bathroom, and she could reach it. Disappointment that the room was empty almost crushed her, but there was a hand pump over a basin. A well? Maybe water? She eagerly pumped the handle, and at first nothing happened. She almost gave up, then a trickle of rusty water dribbled out. It wasn't anything she wanted to drink, but as she kept pumping, the water cleared up.

Would it make her sick if she drank it? She cupped some in her hand and smelled it. It didn't have an odor so that was good. She stuck her tongue out and tasted it. It seemed fine. As thirsty as she was, she wanted to lap it up, but the last thing she needed was to get sick from drinking it. She'd test a tiny bit, see if she felt okay in an hour or two. Even the little she drank seemed like the best thing she'd ever had in her mouth.

Now for the other thing she needed. She eyed the toilet, recognizing the compost toilet. She'd used one before when she was overseas. "Desperate measures," she muttered as she lifted the lid. There wasn't any toilet paper, but that was the least of her problems. The last thing she wanted was for Jasper to return while she used it, so she made haste.

Better, now that her throat wasn't so dry and her bladder relieved, she left the bathroom and returned to the bed. Bored, she napped for a few hours. When he still wasn't back by dark, and since the water she'd drunk earlier hadn't made her sick, she returned to the bathroom and drank some more. The water in her stomach helped a little with the hunger pains.

How long had he been gone, anyway? Did he plan to starve her until she turned over the thumb drive? She could only assume that she did have it if he didn't. No one else had been in his rental house before she packed up and left.

If she trusted that he'd let her go, she would tell him she might have it at home, but she had a strong feeling that her life depended on denying she had the stupid thing. Or maybe she was being too dramatic, and she should just tell him. She didn't know, and the not knowing was what was going to keep her from saying anything. At least for now.

Movement outside the window caught her eye. A cardinal landed on a branch, a male. She could tell because he was a brighter red than female cardinals. She wished she had her camera in her hand. As she watched him, a female landed close to him. The male chirped his love song, and the female chirped back.

The female cardinal flew off, and Quinn wished for wings so she could do the same. The male continued his song, perhaps begging his lover to come back. After a few minutes, he flew away. Was he chasing his girl bird? Was he fighting off the attentions of other males who wanted her? Was he swooping in like a white knight in a fairy tale, saving her from the evil cardinal trying to steal her away?

She wanted a white knight for her own.

She wanted to be a cardinal and fly free.

Chapter 5

Liam hadn't learned anything helpful from Quinn's father. As far as Mr. Sullivan knew, she didn't have a boyfriend, and no one was stalking her that he was aware of. Grayson had texted Liam the coordinates Quinn's phone was pinging from. Hopefully, it was still with her.

Most people didn't know that you didn't have to have a tracker app on a phone to find it. He wouldn't be able to locate the precise location of her phone without an app, but he would be able to narrow down his search to a few miles in either direction.

The coordinates took him to a rural area of spread-out dirt driveways and KEEP OUT signs posted at their entrances. Unfortunately, whatever structures were at the end of those driveways were hidden by a thick forest of trees. These were the kinds of places where a shotgun awaited any strangers daring to trespass. He'd have to do reconnaissance when it got dark.

While he waited, he cruised around, watching for driveways with recent tire impressions. There were five that showed signs of activity. More than he wished for, but it could have been worse. He had six hours before dark, so he returned to the small town of Hope Corner that he'd passed through earlier. Not wanting to stay at Quinn's motel and face Betta's questions, he found another decent motel and a diner. A few hours' sleep and food in his belly, and he'd be good to go all night if necessary.

At midnight, when most people would be asleep, he did his reconnoitering. He left his BMW SUV at the entrance of the driveways at each location and walked in. The first three cabins were a bust. One was empty; at the second, a man with a white beard halfway down his chest sat on the porch smoking a pipe; and at the third, there were a half dozen junk cars in the yard, along with chickens and pigs. The pigs almost outed him with their squeals when they picked up his scent, and he quickly retreated.

At the fourth place on his list, he turned off his car's lights as he drove up the dirt lane, and as soon as he was no longer visible from the road, he pulled off the dirt driveway. He grabbed his night-vision goggles and exited the car. He made his way through the woods until he came to what looked like an abandoned small cabin. It wasn't abandoned, though. There was a green late model Toyota parked in front of it. Not the kind of vehicle he'd seen at the other places. The hair on the back of his neck tingled.

"This is it," he murmured.

The forest was thick around the cabin, the trees shutting out any moonlight to light his way. He slipped on the goggles, turning everything he was seeing green, yet distinct. There weren't any lights on, and no one was sitting on the porch smoking a pipe, no pigs waiting to squeal on him. He crouched low and ran up to the back of the car. A rental.

"Found you." The question, was she here willingly? He didn't believe so, but he wouldn't go storming in to rescue her until he got the lay of the land. On silent feet, he made a circle around the cabin, listening for voices as he searched for a window without a curtain blocking his view. There wasn't one, and there wasn't any sound until he got to what he thought was the bathroom based on the small, high window.

The cabin was old, the walls were thin, and soft crying had him stopping. That had to be Quinn. Even though she didn't know he was listening to her cry, he couldn't bring himself to leave her. As much as he wanted to rush in and rescue her, she wasn't alone. Until he assessed the situation, and especially learned how much of a danger the man who'd taken her was and if he was armed, he couldn't make a reckless move.

He pressed his palm to the wall. "I'm coming for you, sweetheart," he softly said. He circled the cabin again. There was only one door, so just one way in and one way out. That was unfortunate. He eased onto the stoop and gently tried the doorknob. Not a surprise that it was locked.

Time for a plan. He wished he knew if the man who'd taken her was asleep or awake and if he was armed. If asleep, Liam could easily take him by surprise. If he was awake and had a weapon, different story. That could put Quinn's life in danger. On a special ops team, there was a lot of hurry up and wait, so the military had taught him patience. He'd spent endless hours with his team while holed up near their target, waiting for go time.

As much as it went against his desire to storm in, he still needed intel, so he'd wait. But not too long. He made his way to the back of the house again, stopping where he'd heard her crying. All was quiet now. Unless he heard anything that told him she was being hurt, he'd wait for daylight. If he was lucky, the man would come out without her, and Liam could take him by surprise.

As he stepped to the right, a board creaked. He froze. What was that? He pushed the night goggles to the top of his head, then took his penlight from his pocket and shined it on the ground at his feet. A thin slice of wood was visible through the pile of dead leaves. He crouched down and brushed the leaves away.

"How about that," he murmured at seeing it was a cellar door. Even better, there was no lock on it. He eased it open. His penlight revealed five steps leading down to a small root cellar. With luck, there would be a door giving him entrance into the cabin. He glanced at the sky before he descended. The gray light of dawn was on the horizon, and the sun would be up soon.

The best option would be to sneak Quinn out of the cabin before her captor woke up...assuming the man was asleep. Since he hadn't heard a male voice or footsteps walking around inside the cabin, he thought his chances of safely getting Quinn away were good. They needed to be gone before sunrise.

It was his lucky day. There was a door, and when he turned the knob, it opened. On silent feet, he stepped inside the cabin. Without any light to amplify, night-vision goggles might as well be a blindfold, so he left them off. Loud snores greeted him. Excellent. The man was asleep, and since he was, Liam risked clicking on his penlight. It was black as night in the cabin, and he didn't want to stumble over something and make any noise that would wake him up.

He shined the light at the floor, but it was enough to make out a bed with a man in it. Where was Quinn? She wasn't in the bed, so she must still be in the bathroom. A small kitchen with a cooler on the counter was to his right. A ratty couch was the only other furniture in the room besides the bed. He took a few more steps into the room.

To his left, past the bed, was a closed door. That had to be the bathroom and where she was. The trick was going to be getting to her before she could scream at seeing a strange man. As he aimed for the door, his foot came down on something hard, and he looked down, frowning at what he saw.

Son of a bitch. Two heavy chains trailed along the floor, disappearing under the gap between the door and the floor. She was chained. His gaze followed the chains back to where they were locked to a hook in the wall. This complicated things.

As he quietly moved toward the bathroom, a SEAL saying he'd often heard from Grayson when things got complicated popped into his mind. *The only easy day was yesterday.* That was the damn truth.

When he reached the door, he paused. Should he try to talk to her before he opened it? He needed her to be quiet and not wake up the snoring man. Briefly, he considered returning to the bed and removing the threat of the man waking up by putting him out of commission. Knocking him out with a hit to the head with the barrel of his gun would do it, but again, risky. Sometimes, people didn't react the way you wanted them to, and he liked the idea of the man waking up and finding his captive gone. Vanished into thin air.

He'd leave the man to his snoring. His best bet was to get to Quinn, free her from the chain, and get the hell gone. After she was safe, he'd get her to tell him her story, and then he'd do what needed to be done.

Chapter 6

Jasper didn't return until the next night. Friday? She was pretty sure it was. He walked in the door and threw a white bag at her. Inside was one measly hamburger. Just a burger, bun, and ketchup. *Thanks for nothing, jerk.* But she was starving, and it was better than nothing. She had to force herself to slow down and chew. When she finished, her stomach didn't understand why there wasn't more.

Strangely, he didn't grill her about his stupid thumb drive. After she scarfed down the hamburger, he closed all the curtains, then ordered her to go to sleep. That was all she'd done for the past two days, but she didn't have the energy to argue with him. She rolled over, turning her back to him. He was in a foul mood, and she wondered where he'd been and what had happened.

"Oh, no," she said when he crawled in bed with her. "I'm not sleeping with you."

"Shut up, Quinn."

You shut up. He didn't touch her, and after a few minutes his breathing evened out. An hour later, she realized there was no way she could fall asleep in the same bed with him. That, and she was thirsty. He hadn't given her anything to drink with the burger.

When Jasper started snoring, she eased out of the bed

inch by slow inch. Fortunately, she was on the side closest to the bathroom, so she didn't have to work her way around the bed. Careful to keep the chains tight so they didn't scrape on the floor, she made her way to the bathroom.

She cringed when the pump squeaked, but she needed water. After satisfying her thirst, she braced her hands on the sink, cringing again when the chains scraped across the porcelain. Exhausted, she lowered her body to the floor. It was probably dirty, but she didn't have the energy to care. She couldn't get back in that bed with Jasper, she just couldn't. She was so hungry, her stomach felt like it was eating itself, and she was feeling sorry for herself. For the first time, she cried. And as she quietly cried, her eyes grew heavy, and she closed them.

She shot up from the bathroom floor gasping for air. The nightmare was horrible. Jasper had wrapped the chain holding her prisoner around her neck and was demanding that she give him the thumb drive. When she refused, he twisted the chain so tight that she knew she was going to die.

She breathed in and out until she wasn't gasping. How long had she been asleep? How had she even fallen asleep on the hard floor? She lifted her hands, feeling the weight of the heavy chain. How was she supposed to escape?

The chains moved as the bathroom door opened. Okay. Okay. This was it. Jasper was coming in, and he was going to demand answers. Time to…what? If not for being chained to the wall, she would fight him. Even if she could somehow wrap the chains around his neck, see how he liked it, then what? She'd still be a prisoner.

Except the man dressed all in black wasn't Jasper. Her heart shot up, landing in her throat, and she opened her mouth to scream. The man was unhumanly fast as he reached her and clamped his hand over her mouth.

This was the day she was going to die.

"Shhhh," the man whispered. "Don't scream. Your father sent me. I'm here to rescue you."

She was being rescued?

"You'll be quiet?"

When she nodded, he removed his hand from her mouth. She'd be quieter than a mouse if it meant she was getting out of here. He held a penlight, and he shined it on his face, letting her see him. Jet-black hair, a face sculptured by the gods, and eyes the color of a deep blue ocean stared back at her. Mother Mary, he was beautiful.

"I'm Liam O'Rourke," he whispered after he closed the door behind him. "Nice to meet you, Quinn Sullivan."

A fellow Irishman. Did he believe in love at first sight? Because she suddenly did. "Ah, you, too." But Jasper had taught her to be wary. "What's my father's name?"

"Robert Sullivan. He knew something was wrong when you missed your Wednesday check-in, so he asked me to come find you."

He wouldn't know any of that if he hadn't been sent by her father, and the relief would have brought her down to the floor if she wasn't already on it.

"Are you hurt anywhere?"

"I'm okay. Just hungry. You got a steak on you?"

He chuckled. "Sadly, no."

"Drat. Can we go now?" She wanted to be as far away from Jasper as she could possibly get.

"That's the plan, but first, we have to get you out of these cuffs." He reached into a pocket of his cargo pants and pulled out a small pouch.

"What's that?"

"My breaking-and-entering kit."

They were still whispering, which made this strange encounter feel intimate, like they were the only two people in the world. "Are you a criminal?" Figured her father would find a man talented in getting in and out of places without getting caught. And even if he was a thief, her instincts, honed over her years in war-torn countries, said she could trust this man she'd just met.

"No, ma'am. Just a man helping a lady in distress." He put the penlight between his teeth, aiming it to light up her hands. "Hold still."

"You need to know that Jasper has a gun. He'll use it on you if he wakes up."

"Then let's be gone before he does. Do you know him?"

"Unfortunately." She was too embarrassed to admit she'd had a fling with the bastard.

"Not a stranger then. There, one down."

She blinked at seeing him remove the handcuff from her left wrist. Her arm felt almost weightless without the heavy chain.

He wrapped his fingers around her wrists and lifted her hands so she could see them. "Voilà! All gone."

"Thank you."

"You're welcome. Now let's blow this joint."

She was all for that.

"We need to be very quiet. Walk right behind me."

"Consider me your shadow." He eased the door open, and she slipped her fingers around the back of his belt. No way was he going to leave without her. They were halfway across the room when she tugged him to a stop.

He turned and put his mouth to her ear. "What?"

"My camera bag," she whispered. "I need it." She had thousands of dollars of cameras and equipment that she wasn't going to leave behind.

She expected him to argue that they needed to get out

of the cabin, and they did, but not without the only things that mattered to her. Instead, he surprised her by putting his finger to her lips to hush her, and then he shined the penlight around the room. When he paused the light on the bag that held her cameras, she nodded. Without making a sound, he went to the bag, eased the strap over his shoulder, and returned to her. She slipped her fingers back around his belt, and they started off again.

Where was he going? The door was the other way. She followed him into what she'd assumed was a pantry, but since her chain wouldn't reach that far, she hadn't checked it out. It wasn't a pantry, but a small cellar. He went down first, then shined the light on the steps for her. After she reached the bottom, he went back up and eased the door shut. He led her to another set of stairs, and through the opening, she saw the sky. She saw freedom.

"Stand by a sec," he said after they exited the cellar.

"Okay." Although, it was almost impossible to stand by when she wanted to run away as fast as her legs could carry her.

He closed the outside doors to the cellar, then he took her hand. "Let's go."

They fast walked around the cabin and passed Jasper's car. "Ouch."

He stopped, and she bumped into him. "What's wrong?"

She lifted her foot and brushed away the pebbles sticking to it. "Sorry. I stepped on a rock. I'm okay." Fortunately, she had refused to undress in front of Jasper, so she had on the jeans and T-shirt she was wearing when he'd taken her. Unfortunately, she had taken her shoes off, not wanting to wear them in bed.

He took his penlight out and shined it on her feet. "I should have gotten your shoes."

"I'm fine. Really."

"We have a ways to go." He turned his back to her and crouched. "Get on."

"Your back?" At five-seven, she wasn't a small girl.

He glanced over his shoulder. "Yes. You can't walk to my car without shoes. Get on my back, Quinn."

At the commanding tone in his voice, she almost saluted him. She settled for, "Yes, sir." She climbed onto his back, and he slipped his arms under her legs. When he took off at a jog, she expected him to struggle with the awkwardness of her camera bag bumping against his side and her bouncing against his back, not to mention the strain of her weight. There was no struggle. He wasn't even breathing heavily.

"Are you Superman?"

"Yeah, that's me," he said, still breathing normally.

She almost wouldn't be surprised if he jogged them to a phone booth where he could change into his Superman costume. The driveway was long, and she guessed he'd been running for three or four minutes when they came to a car. She was happy to see it, because it was going to get her far, far away from Jasper.

Liam stopped next to the passenger door and dropped his arms from under her legs. She slid down his body, and boy oh boy, what a body. She doubted he had an ounce of fat on him. She sure hadn't felt any while wrapped around him like a spider monkey.

"Thanks for the ride," she said.

"My pleasure." He opened the door.

No, it was very much her pleasure. She got into the car, and he closed the door. After putting her camera bag into the back seat, he jogged around the hood. When he was seated behind the wheel, he shifted to face her.

"I have to make a decision, and for that, I need intel."

"What decision? Can't we just go?"

"Do we just go, or do I need to take care of the man in the cabin?"

Her jaw dropped. "You mean like, kill him?"

"I guess that's an option, but I'd prefer to hand him over to the police. He did kidnap you. Why, and who is he?"

"His name's Jasper Garrison. And I honestly don't know exactly what's going on. He seems to think I have something of his."

"What's that, and do you?"

"A thumb drive. I might or might not have it. I don't know."

"What's on it?"

"Don't know that either, but whatever's on it, Jasper's planning to trade it to someone for a million dollars."

He whistled. "Okay. I think I need to have a little chat with your friend in there."

"I don't think that's a good idea. I told you, he has a gun. Let's just go."

"And then what? If what you have—"

"Might have."

"He seems to think you do, and for that kind of money, he'll come after you."

She knew that. Of course she did. But she didn't want to be here a minute longer. When she got home, she'd look for the thumb drive, see what was on it if she did have it, then decide what to do with it.

"I just want to go," she said. "Please."

Chapter 7

Liam tapped his fingers on the steering wheel as he glanced up the dirt lane. It went against all his years of military training to turn his back on the enemy and leave him to fight another day, but her father had only hired him to find her and bring her home.

"If we leave now, we're going to the police. You need to file kidnapping charges against him."

"You're right, I do, but I want to go home first and find that thumb drive...if I have it, that is. I need to know what's on it and just what Jasper's gotten himself into. What if he's told someone else I have it? Will that person come looking for me, too?"

She was right. If Garrison thought whatever he had was worth a million dollars to someone, it had to be something big. No offense to the local police, but Hope Corner probably didn't have much of a police department, certainly not anyone with the experience and knowledge this situation might require.

"Okay," he said. "Here's the deal. I'll take you home, we see if you do have what he's looking for, and if you do, decide where to go from there." He wasn't going to just drop her off at her home, not knowing what kind of danger she was in. If it was something she needed to turn over to law enforcement, he'd call his friend in the FBI. And he'd convince her to report the kidnapping.

"Okay."

"Good, but first." He'd noticed the red marks on her wrists when he'd freed her. "We need to get pictures of your wrists. Visible proof that he chained you up. Should've done that before I took the manacles off." He clicked on the car's interior light, then got his phone. "Hold out your hands." He seriously wanted to go back inside that cabin and teach the man a lesson.

The most beautiful green eyes he'd ever seen peered up at him as he snapped the pictures. A need to protect her rose in him, a determination to keep her safe so fierce that it surprised even him. When he finished, he dropped his phone in the cup holder. Unable to stop himself, he wrapped his fingers around her wrists and gently massaged the bruises.

She closed her eyes, and her sigh went straight to his groin. Her long hair was a mess, her T-shirt was wrinkled, and exhaustion lined her face, but she was stunning. He glanced down at her feet, dirty now from walking down the driveway without shoes, and he made a split-second decision. He was going to take her home with him, where he could keep her safe until the threat to her was over.

He eased her hands down to her lap and forced himself to let go of her. "Let's get out of here."

"I'm all for that." She leaned her head back on the seat. "Oh, I have a rental car at the motel. You don't have to take me all the way to Savannah. That's where I live."

"Yeah, your father told me. He said you stay at his house between assignments."

"No reason to pay rent when I'm rarely home. He has a big house, so when he is there, we don't get in each other's way. He also has a log home in Maggie Valley. That's a little west of Asheville. He spends a lot of his time there in the summer because it's cooler. That's where he is now."

Her father hadn't told him that. He picked up his phone and put his finger on it, bringing it to life. He handed it to her. "Call him so he can stop worrying about you."

She took it from him. "Saying thank you isn't close to adequate for getting me out of there."

"It's enough for me." He glanced at her and smiled. As he drove away from the cabin, he listened to Quinn's end of the conversation with her father. It was obvious they were close, and a pang of regret bubbled up from the deep hole where he'd buried his hurt at being disowned. After ten years, he should be over it. Maybe one never got over losing their family.

A few years ago, he'd called his father's office, hoping his dad was ready to put the past behind them.

"May I tell him who's calling?" his father's assistant had said.

"His son."

She'd put him on hold and less than a minute later come back on the line. "I'm really sorry, but he said he doesn't have a son."

And that was that. He'd crushed the ache from missing his family and went on with his life.

"My dad said to tell you thank you, and that he owes you big-time," Quinn said, handing his phone back.

"I'll take a dinner with you and your dad as thanks." He'd very much like to see her again after this was over. At least she didn't live on the other side of the country. Savannah was only about a four-hour drive from Myrtle Beach. Not that she was there much, but maybe they could see each other when she was between assignments.

"Deal."

He almost asked if she could tell him how their fathers knew each other, but he held the question in. That might open the door to her asking questions about his family, and he didn't want to have to explain why he was dead to his father.

The sun was starting its rise over the mountains, and when he glanced at her and saw she was nodding off, something tender settled in his chest. He wanted to protect her from all the bad in the world, wanted to get to know her, to learn what made her laugh.

He didn't know what it was about her that called to him, but from the moment he'd seen her photo, he'd been intrigued. She'd had a rough few days and probably hadn't slept much. It had been near dawn when he'd heard her crying, so she likely hadn't slept last night. He wished he'd brought a pillow for her to rest her head against. He—

He narrowed his eyes as the headlights of a car racing up behind them appeared in his rearview mirror. If the car hadn't been driving that fast, he wouldn't have thought much of it, but the speed the driver was going was dangerous on these mountain roads. As it closed in on them, the sun was up enough to see that it was a green Toyota Corolla, the same model and color car that was at the cabin. Damn.

Liam wasn't worried about outrunning the Toyota. His BMW could leave the Toyota in the dust, but there was nothing but sharp curves and narrow lanes. Too much could go wrong taking these roads at high speed. If the man only followed them, Liam would keep to the speed limit until they came to Hope Corner. The small police department was on the main drag, and he'd go straight there.

He debated letting Quinn continue to sleep but decided to wake her. Better she be aware and ready if the man decided to get foolish and do something reckless.

"Quinn, wake up." When she didn't stir, he put his hand over hers and squeezed. "Quinn, I need you to wake up."

"Hmm?" She stretched her neck.

"Pretty sure Garrison's behind us."

"What?" She shot up and looked back. "Oh, God. What are we going to do?"

"Nothing as long as he doesn't get stupid."

"You can count on him doing something stupid."

As if to prove her point, the bonehead rammed them. How did he know Quinn was even in the car? Was he so desperate that he'd take that kind of chance that she might be? Granted, his was the only car on the road coming from the direction of the cabin and not that far from it, but to risk possibly hurting innocents?

"He's going to kill us," Quinn said, fear in her voice.

"Not under my watch." They were approaching a sharp curve, and Liam slammed his foot down on the gas pedal, trusting the BMW to keep them on the road. And it would have if Garrison hadn't rammed them again before the BMW could outrun him.

The Toyota caught the end of his car's left bumper, spinning it out of control. Tires screeched on the asphalt, the sound of metal against metal filled the car, and the world outside became a blur of trees and pavement. They passed the last of the guardrail going off the road sideways, and at seeing it was her side that would collide with a massive tree, Liam jerked the steering wheel to the right, barely missing the tree that would have killed her. Instead, the front wheels sank into the muddy ditch, and the car came to a shuddering stop. They hadn't impacted with the tree, so the airbags didn't deploy.

The sudden silence seemed out of place after the noise of the crash. Liam took a second to berate himself for not expecting and preparing for Garrison to come after them. The Toyota passed them, and at the squeal of brakes pressed hard as the car came to a grinding halt above them, Liam threw the BMW in Reverse. All he got for the effort was spinning tires.

"He's coming back," Liam said. "We have to get out of the car." He released his seat belt, and Quinn did the same.

Garrison was backing up his car. Quinn had said he had a gun, and they didn't need to sit here and be targets. They only had a few minutes to disappear into the woods. Quinn appeared to be unhurt. He hoped that was the case because he didn't have time to ask.

"Get out and head for the woods."

"What about you?"

"No time to talk. Just go. I'll catch up." She did as he'd asked, and after picking up his phone, he exited the car. He ran to the other side and yanked open the back door. His weapons bag was on the floor, and he grabbed it, his duffel bag, and was backing away when he noticed her camera case. He should leave it, but it was her life, so he grabbed it, too.

He disappeared into the tree line just as the Toyota came to a stop. Quinn poked her head around the tree she was hiding behind, relief on her face at seeing him. He jogged to her.

"Give me something to carry," she said.

"I'm good." He was impressed by how calm she was, but maybe that was because of her experiences and the time she'd spent in war-torn countries as a photojournalist. "Are you hurt anywhere?"

"Just my feet, but that's not from the wreck. I'm good."

That was the reason he'd grabbed his duffel. A car door slammed, and he took his bearings. If he didn't have her to protect, he'd stay and fight, but he wouldn't risk her getting caught in the cross fire. "He's coming this way, so we need to go." As soon as it was safe to stop, he'd take care of her feet. "Stay close to me."

"I'm your shadow."

He chuckled. "You'd make a great Marine."

"Oorah!"

She knew the Marine battle cry? He could only grin at this woman who kept surprising him at every turn. She intrigued him, and he wanted to get to know her better, but first, he had to keep her safe.

This was one mission he wasn't going to accept anything less than success.

Chapter 8

"Whoever you are with Quinn," Jasper called. "It would be better for your health if you sent her back to me." As if to back up his threat, the bark exploded from a nearby tree.

"He shot at us!" Quinn shuddered. That was close. Liam didn't respond to Jasper, just reached back with his hand, found hers, and squeezed. Her feet were screaming in pain, and she wanted to yell at herself for not getting her shoes. At the time, all she'd cared about was her cameras and getting out of the cabin.

If they got lost in this forest, at least she'd be with a man she already liked a lot and who was real easy on the eyes. They could build a cozy cabin, he could hunt for their food, she could grow potatoes, and they could have endless babies with his startling blue eyes.

"Damn it, Quinn, you can't hide from me forever. Just give me my thumb drive, and I'll leave you alone."

Yeah, right. His voice was farther away, now to the left instead of behind them. They were losing him. It amazed her how quiet Liam was compared to Jasper. She could hear leaves and sticks crunching under Jasper's shoes and his grunts as he tried to find them. Liam was a ghost, not a sound coming from him as he took them deeper into the woods on silent feet. He'd told her she'd make a good Marine, and she meant to make that true. She made sure to step exactly where he had, determined to be a ghost, too.

Eventually, any sounds from Jasper were gone. They'd lost him, and knowing that, she could breathe again. She wasn't sure how long they walked before Liam stopped, his head cocked as if he heard something, but what, she didn't know. And although the sun was peeking over the mountain, giving them light, she didn't see anything that might have captured his attention.

"There's a good place just ahead," he said.

"Hope it's a spa." That got her a chuckle. It was a nice chuckle. Strike nice, it was sexy, that low, throaty sound. Even with hurting feet, scared out of her mind, and thirsty, she liked one thing about the mess she found herself in. Liam. The man fascinated her, but even more than mere fascination, there was attraction. And, boy, was she ever attracted to him. Maybe once they were safe and back home—

"No spa here, but I promise you something even better," he said with a wink.

—maybe they could have a little fling. Flings were all she would allow herself because of her job. She never knew where she'd be or for how long, and she'd learned early on even though men claimed they were okay with how much she traveled, they never were.

She liked men, liked their minds, their bodies, the sex. She did not like the jealousy, the demands for more time that she didn't have to give, or even as Aiden—the man she'd been engaged to—had demanded, that she give up the job she loved and her soul needed so she could be there for him every day.

Funny that when she told him he could give up his job and travel with her, he hadn't understood how she could even ask that of him. "Back atcha, pal," she'd said after their worst fight as she handed him back his ring. How could she marry a man who didn't think her career mattered? The love she had for him would have died a miserable death if she'd stayed, giving up her dream. Better that she leave before they ended up hating each other.

After Aiden, she'd adopted a new policy. Flings only with men who were following their own dreams and didn't have the time or the inclination to poke their noses into hers. Pretty much a wham, bam, thank you, sir. Now be off with you. Worked for her.

That was one reason she'd left Jasper. Even though he'd agreed theirs was a temporary thing while they were in California, he'd started to make noises that she should be all about him. The closer she got to finishing up her assignment, the more Jasper pushed her to stay. She refused to even consider it, because she knew exactly how it would go. His career would matter. Hers? Not even.

Then there was his jealousy and possessiveness. It never entered her mind that he'd stalk her, kidnap her, shoot at her. Yeah, that was mind-blowing. Maybe she should consider ditching the flings if her judgment was that whacked. The thought of no more intimate moments with a man, though?

"Do you get possessive and make unreasonable demands of a woman you're dating?" she asked as she followed Liam around a boulder.

He stopped and faced her. "The answer is no. I don't have the right to tell another person how to live their life, man or woman." His brows scrunched together as if he was confused. "What brought that question on?"

Okay, the man was perfect. She shrugged. "Just curious." Obviously, the trick was to be more discerning than she had been. Before allowing any kind of intimacy from here on, maybe she should write up a questionnaire to give to a man she was interested in.

He gave her a quizzical glance before continuing, but she didn't miss the interest in his eyes. She smiled at his back, liking that she had him wondering. A few steps more and then he stopped, stepped to the side, and swung his arm out. "Your 'something even better.'"

"Oh," she murmured at seeing the crystal-clear creek. "Can I put my feet in it?"

"That's the plan."

A few minutes later, she sat on a rock and sighed as she lowered her feet into the cold, foot-numbing water. "Ahhhhh. Heaven."

Liam squatted, zipped open one of his duffels, and rummaged around in it. He brought out a bottle of water, and seeing it, she wanted to kiss him. Next came a box of power bars, then a small first aid kit.

"Good Lord, what all else do you have in there?" She leaned over and peered inside.

"Just a change of clothes and one more bottle of water." He twisted the cap off and handed her the bottle he held. "We have to ration the water, so only drink a little."

Although she wanted to chug the entire bottle, she limited herself to three swallows before handing it back to him. "You're handy to have around when one is lost in the woods."

"I'm not lost."

She laughed at his affronted expression. "Silly me. Of course you aren't."

"Lift your feet out of the water."

"But it feels so good."

"Your superior officer has given you an order, Little Marine. Feet up."

"Aye, aye, sir." She lifted her feet, and he put his hands under her ankles and brought them to his lap.

"That's sailor talk. You would say, 'Sir, yes, sir.'"

"Would I now?" Their eyes met, and she would swear that the air sizzled between them. Would he be bossy in bed? That gleam in his eyes said yes. She imagined him naked beside her, him giving her orders in that commanding voice, and she, being a brat, would resist obeying until he—

"What's going on in that mind of yours right now, Quinn?"

Drat. He interrupted her daydream. It was a good one. "Um, so, what do we do now?"

Amusement danced in his eyes. "A bit of deflection there, but the answer is, we take care of your feet." He lifted the sole of her right foot, frowning as he studied it. "How were you even walking on these?"

"One does what one must." Especially when worried about getting shot. She watched, fascinated, as he tenderly doctored her feet. He used a cotton ball to clean them with antiseptic, then he covered the cuts with a cream that soothed them, and lastly, he wrapped them in gauze. She thought he was done, but no. He took two pairs of socks from his duffel and put them on her.

"Maybe doubling them up will give you more cushion and help you walk."

"Thank you," she whispered, tears burning her eyes at the care he'd given her. Other than her father, no one cared about her. Not really. She didn't do boyfriends, and she wasn't in one place long enough to make girlfriends, so it had always been up to her to take care of herself.

Sometimes, she missed having people in her life, but it was her choice. She couldn't imagine not doing what she loved, even if it meant sacrificing having relationships of any kind. Her work was her passion, but she sometimes got lonely. Thus, the occasional fling. It was a way to touch and be touched by another person, if only for a short time.

He took out his phone, eyed the screen, and frowned. "No signal."

"That's not good."

"Ah, but have faith, my friend." He rummaged around in the other duffel.

"What's in that one?"

He held it open so she could see inside.

She blinked. "Whoa. Are you planning to go to war?"

"I hoped not, but I didn't know what I'd be walking into, so it's always best to be prepared."

"Says the Marine. With all these weapons you have on you, why didn't you shoot back at Jasper? Do you not have a gun on you?" She would've expected him to be armed.

His eyes locked on hers as he lifted his shirt to show her the gun at his waist. "Because you might have been caught in the cross fire, and that was unacceptable. The mission is to keep you safe, not put you at risk. The best way to do that was to lose him. I also have no desire to kill a man if I don't have to."

"Oh." Who was this man who kept surprising her with the things he said? "What's that?" she asked when he removed what looked like a strange phone.

"It's a satellite phone." He punched in some numbers. "It's me. I need an exfil."

Who was he talking to, and what was an exfil?

"I'm in the middle of the woods and can't see where a good LZ is. Get my coordinates and call me back. My rescue's feet are shredded, so find a place not too far. Also, I crashed my car in a ditch and need you to arrange for it to be towed to a repair shop." He gave whoever he was talking to some coordinates, which she assumed was for the car.

"Who was that, what's an exfil, and LZ is a landing zone, right?" she asked when he set the phone next to his side. "How would they know where we are?"

"That was Grayson, one of my teammates, an exfil is an extraction of personnel, and yes, an LZ is a landing zone, and we can all track each other."

"He's sending a helicopter?" When he nodded, she said, "Wow. Who are you guys?"

"The Phoenix Three is me, Grayson Montana, and Cooper Devlin. Our mission is rescuing children from dangerous situations."

Oh, man, he had no idea what hearing that did to her heart. But wait. "I'm not a child, so why did you come to rescue me?"

He chuckled. "To quote your father, 'She is a child, my damn child,' so here I am."

"Sounds like him. Your friend…teammate didn't want to know what happened and why you need extracting?"

"No, if I say I need a ride, a ride I'll get, no questions asked. He'll want to be debriefed when we're back."

"I need to turn my rental car in."

"When we get back, I'll call the rental company and arrange to get it picked up."

She poked his arm.

"What was that for?"

"Just wanted to know if you're real."

He poked her back. "Maybe you're the one who isn't real."

Gah, she liked this man. More than she could remember liking any man, and maybe that was a problem. She could fall for him so easily, but she didn't fall for any man. She had things to do and places to go.

Chapter 9

"You've been surprisingly calm about all this," Liam said as they sat by the creek. She really had been. Most people not trained for dangerous situations would be scared, even falling apart. She'd been calm, had followed his orders without question, and had even teased him.

She stared at the water tumbling over the rocks in the creek. "I don't know. I guess when you've hidden in a basement with families praying the so-called soldiers raiding their village who'll shoot anyone without question don't find you… When you've watched a child die, his belly bloated with hunger, or carried a little girl who had her leg blown off a mile to where you knew Doctors Without Borders were so they could save her life…" She lifted her eyes to his. "I guess in the grand scheme of things it's all relative, you know? Like this crap with Jasper is more like an annoying mosquito buzzing around your face."

"I do know." And right then, that very second, this woman claimed a piece of his heart.

She smiled. "I guess as a former Marine, you do."

He smiled back, then to lighten up the mood again, said, "So, the good news is we won't have to spend the night in the woods. Grayson will have that chopper to us in a few hours. Until we get the coordinates to an LZ, we'll stay put."

He was good with that. It would give him time to get to know her a little. From the first, seeing her photo, her work on behalf of children the world over, reading about her accomplishments and awards, and hearing the love for her in her father's voice—he'd been a little envious of that—he'd been fascinated.

"What got you interested in photography?" he asked as he opened the box of power bars and handed her one.

"Oh, fun, a picnic." She grinned, taking it from him. "With the excitement of being chased, I forgot I was starving."

Even with a dangerous man after her, stranded in the middle of nowhere, and with ruined feet, she remained upbeat. She impressed the hell out of him.

"To answer your question, my mom loved taking pictures, and I wanted a camera like hers so I could take pictures, too. I was nine when she gave me one. It wasn't as fancy as hers, but I loved it. She was killed a few months after giving it to me. An elderly man got confused and went the wrong way on the highway and hit her head-on. After she was…um, gone, the camera made me feel close to her. I still have it."

Her voice caught when speaking of her mom, and instead of hugging her like he wanted to, he put his hand over hers and squeezed. "I'm sorry you lost her." He could relate a little because, although in a different way, he'd lost his family. "What made you want to be a photojournalist and specialize in children?"

"One of my college professors had a sister who was a photojournalist, and he had her come speak to the class. By the time she finished talking about the places she'd been and after watching her incredible slideshow, I wanted to be her. She didn't really focus on any one thing, but she had a section of photographs of children caught in a tribal war, and..." Her eyes watered with unshed tears. "Those children were starving, many of them orphans, yet their too-big eyes for their little faces looked into the camera and they smiled for her. That was the moment I knew what I'd do with my life. Bring the plight of these children and others who are suffering to the attention of the world." She shrugged. "Do my small part in helping them."

Be still my heart. She was perfect, and he fell a little in love with her right then and there. How could he not when she was everything and more that he could want in a woman?

His sat phone chimed with an incoming call. "Liam here." After getting the information from Grayson, he set the phone next to him. "The good news, we only have a mile to get to the LZ, but the helo won't be here for three more hours. We're safe here, so we'll stay put for a while longer. Let your feet rest a little."

"My feet thank you. Your turn."

"For?"

"Your story. You said you rescue children. Why?"

He never talked about his kidnapping, but with her, he wanted to. "Grayson, Cooper, and I were kidnapped when we were in high school. We—"

"Wait." She grabbed his arm. "Did that happen during spring break?"

"Yes."

"I remember that being all over the news when I was in high school, that three boys had been kidnapped. Some SEALs found you and rescued you, right?"

"Former SEALs, and yes. We were very lucky. Grayson's father had been a SEAL, and he called in some favors."

"And that's the reason you all created The Phoenix Three?"

"Pretty much." He told her about those dark days of being held for ransom, their rescue, and how he and his Phoenix Three brothers had come up with the idea of rescuing children. When he finished, he smiled. "We have a lot in common, you know?"

She stared at him without saying anything, her gaze dropping from his eyes to his mouth.

"What?" he said.

"I think you should kiss me."

Well, he wasn't expecting that, but he sure as hell wasn't going to refuse. He decided to turn the tables and challenge her. Why? Because he was learning her, and he thought it was a sure bet that she liked a challenge. "I think you should be the one to kiss me."

"Hmm." She tilted her head and studied him as a smirk appeared on her face. "You think I won't?"

"I'm very much hoping you do."

She leaned toward him, her eyes never leaving his as she closed the distance between them. Her soft, warm lips touched his, and as their mouths pressed together, he committed to memory their first kiss. He never wanted to forget this moment. She was someone special, and he had the feeling that she was going to change his life.

She wrapped her hands around the back of his neck and sighed when their tongues tangled. That sigh went straight to his groin as they kissed.

She lowered her arms and leaned away. "Wow. That was—"

"Earth-shattering?" He was pretty sure the ground shifted under his feet.

"I was going to say *amazing*, but *earth-shattering* works."

He hesitated a moment before saying what he wanted to. He didn't want to come on too strong too soon, but something special was happening here. For him, anyway. He needed to know if she felt it, too. "This thing happening—" he gestured between them "—between us, tell me it's not just me feeling it."

"It's called chemistry."

Yes, there was chemistry, but it was more than that. He didn't believe in love at first sight. How could you love someone you didn't know? But for the first time in his life, he believed he could fall in love with someone, with her. He couldn't know that for sure yet, but he wanted time with her to explore the possibility.

First order of business was to get her safely home, then he'd ask her out on a date. Savannah was a doable drive if she was interested in seeing him. He sure hoped she was.

"Now that we kissed, I want to know more about you," she said. "Did you grow up in Myrtle Beach?"

"No, Kansas City."

"I've never been there. Is that where your family lives?"

"Yes."

"Hmm, I hear tension in your voice. Are you not close to them?"

As much as he didn't want to talk about his father, he wanted her to know him, and the only way for her to do that was to answer her question. And, maybe, sitting here in the woods in the middle of nowhere was the best place for confessions.

"When I was eighteen, right after I graduated high school, I told my father I was joining the Marines. He disowned me. I haven't seen him since."

She stared at him for a moment. "I don't know what to say. I can't imagine a parent disowning their child for any reason. That's really sad, because you're an amazing man, Liam, and he's not around to see that."

"I secretly talk to my mom once a month."

"So, she didn't disown you but isn't allowed to talk to you?"

"Correct." Since he'd told her that much, he told her the rest of his story.

"That's sad for you both that she has to sneak to talk to you," she said when he finished. "I'd like to have a few words with your father."

He grinned as he imagined her doing just that. "I'd love to see that." He glanced at his watch. "It's time to head to the LZ."

Her gaze scanned the area around them. "Do you think Jasper's gone?"

"Probably for now, but he's not going to give up. We're going to talk about that." He packed everything up. "Let's go." He stood and held out his hand to help her up. "We have plenty of time, and we're going to take it slow so you don't ruin your feet even more."

"Why don't you let me carry one of those bags?"

"I'm good. I've carried twice this weight when on an op, so I'm used to it. You just worry about where you step and not hurting your feet."

"You really are a knight in shining armor."

"No, ma'am. Just an ordinary man here."

She snorted. "Right."

Fine. Maybe he wasn't quite ordinary, and if his special skills kept her safe, all the better. Whether she was his future remained to be seen, but for now anyway, she was his to protect.

Trooper that she was, she didn't complain once as they traveled to the LZ even though her feet had to be on fire. When they reached the designated pickup, they had twenty minutes to wait for the bird. The LZ was in a flat meadow surrounded by forest.

After he got her settled inside the tree line where she was hidden from sight, he made a sweep of the area around them. He knew they hadn't been followed, and he didn't expect to find anything of concern, but he wasn't taking any chances where Quinn was concerned. Finding all was quiet, he returned to her.

"Your feet must be in agony," he said as he squatted next to her, dropping the three packs next to him.

"Kind of, but better than they were before you doctored them."

At the sound of a helo in the distance, he said, "I think a kiss would be just the right ending to this little adventure."

She grinned. "Adventures should always end with a kiss."

With permission granted, he covered her mouth with his, and damn, she tasted like the sweetest honey. An addiction he didn't want a cure for. Too soon, the shadow of the bird hovering above and the *whup, whuping* sound of the machine had him breaking the kiss.

When she leaned toward him, eyes dreamy, her mouth seeking his again, he smiled as he brushed her hair away from her face. "I'm going to kiss you again, Quinn. You can count on that, but right now, our transportation is here."

"Why couldn't it be late?"

He laughed. "Not gonna argue with that." He slipped the straps of their bags onto his shoulders, then he scooped her up, laughing again when she yelped.

"Liam! Put me down."

"Nope. I've got you." He ran toward the bird. *I'll always be here for you.*

Chapter 10

After Liam buckled her into the seat, Quinn glanced around. Two pilots were in the seats in front of her, and the one on the left leaned his head around his seat and grinned.

"VIP transport at your service, ma'am. We can't offer you first-class luxury. No champagne or sweet chocolates, but we'll try to give you a smooth ride." He winked.

He was cute, and when she grinned back at him, Liam growled. Well, that was hot. *Liam*. What was she going to do about him? He was mysterious. He excited her. He was a man she would consider fling material without a second thought if...

It was a very big *if*...if he didn't check every single one of her boxes, even boxes she didn't know she had. That made him dangerous to her heart. She didn't risk her heart for any man. Ever.

Yet she wasn't sure she could walk away from him. It was kind of ridiculous actually. She didn't know this man, not really. They'd spent, what, all of a day together? She should be able to walk away. She'd always been able to in the past without a glance back.

Her feet that he'd taken such gentle care of weren't going to be happy leaving him behind. *It's not just your feet, girl.* She laugh-snorted, which the noise of the helicopter thankfully covered up. What a freaking few days. She honestly didn't know if she was going or coming, so no surprise she wasn't thinking clearly.

She leaned her head back against the seat, closed her eyes, and relived kissing him. It might have been the best kiss she'd ever had. Who was she kidding? It was the best kiss she'd ever had. She smiled as she let the dream of Liam's mouth on hers take her.

"Quinn, wake up. Hey, we've landed. Time to go."

"Hmm?" She opened her eyes and stretched. She could probably sleep for days. Of course, she'd gotten very little rest from the time Jasper had kidnapped her, then an escape and a trek through the woods, so it was no surprise that she was exhausted. If only she could blink herself home and into her bed.

Liam moved in front of her and unbuckled the shoulder harness. Gosh, his eyes were beautiful. Indigo blue, she decided. She wished she had her camera in her hand.

"Come on, sleepyhead. Let's get you to a bed."

"Yes, please." With him in it. She glanced out the window. "Are we in Savannah?"

"No, Myrtle Beach."

"I don't live in Myrtle Beach."

"True, but I do." He jumped out of the helicopter with the ease of a man who'd done so many times, then held out his hand.

"Why are we stopping here," she said as she put her hand in his and he helped her down. Once she was standing on the pavement, he reached inside and grabbed their bags, strapping them over his shoulders. She wanted a bath, a glass of wine, and her bed. Her bed was not in Myrtle Beach.

He leaned his head back into the helicopter. "Thanks for

the ride, guys. We owe you." He then took her hand and started walking toward a black SUV. "You need dinner and a good night's sleep. In the morning, we're going to talk."

"And exactly where am I doing this eating and sleeping?"

"My place."

Before she could respond to that, they reached the car where two men built like Liam leaned back against the SUV with their arms crossed over their chests. Two pairs of eyes fell on her, and both men smiled. Double whoa! Where did they grow these hotties?

It was the man holding her hand, though, who did it for her. He stopped them in front of the other two men. "Quinn, these two jokers are my mates. Grayson, meet the lovely Quinn Sullivan."

Both men's gazes dropped to Liam's hand holding hers before exchanging a glance, and it seemed to her that an unspoken message passed between them. The blond man to her left, Grayson, nodded. "A pleasure, Miss Sullivan."

"Just Quinn. Nice to meet you, too."

"He saved the best for last," the man with the chestnut brown hair said with a mischievous grin. "I'm Cooper. The most fun of our little band of brothers."

She didn't doubt that from the playful gleam in his coffee-brown eyes and his flirty smirk. They were both gorgeous men, but she preferred Liam's looks, his black hair and indigo blue eyes, his...well, his everything.

"Feel free to ignore him," Liam said.

It was said with humor, but underneath that humor was a bite. A warning to his friend. Was Liam jealous? She grinned and, unable to resist testing the water, said, "Now why would I want to do that?" He scowled, answering her question. She very much liked that answer.

Grayson's gaze homed in on Liam, and he chuckled as if something amused him.

"This is gonna be fun," Cooper said.

"Why are both of you here?" Liam opened the rear hatch and set their bags inside the SUV. "Don't you have other things to do?"

"Nope," Cooper said. "I for one am curious where you found the lovely Miss Quinn." He winked at her.

"Behave, Coop," Grayson said.

"Where's the fun in that?"

She laughed. She liked both men, but Cooper had an easy way about him that made her feel comfortable with him. Grayson was harder to read.

"It's been a long, exhausting day for Quinn," Liam said. "We'll debrief in the morning, but for now, how about we get this show on the road so she can get off her feet."

"My feet would thank you for that." They loaded up, Grayson driving and Cooper in the front passenger seat. She and Liam got in back, and she sighed as she sank into the soft, buttery leather. She could sleep right here, which she apparently did as sometime later, Liam was waking her again.

She still wasn't home in Savannah where she wanted to be, but right now she didn't care. She just wanted a bed. Once again, Liam played the pack mule and loaded himself up with their bags. She swayed on her aching feet as he had a brief conversation with his teammates. That done, she followed him into a high-rise, where he nodded at a man behind a desk. "How's it going, Wilson?"

"Good, Mr. O'Rourke. All's quiet here."

Wilson's gaze raked over her, ending on her sock-clad feet. She gave him credit for his expression not changing at seeing Liam drag home a dirty, sock-wearing woman.

They continued through a lobby with a beach theme and colors, and into an elevator, where he pushed the button for the fifth floor.

He smiled when she leaned against the wall and sighed. "After what you've been through, I'm impressed you're still upright. We'll have you off those feet and food in your belly soon."

"Not sure I have the energy to eat." She didn't know what he had planned and what tomorrow morning's meeting was about, but if it involved her sticking around, not happening.

"You need something in your stomach, Quinn, and I'm sure you'll feel better after a shower."

"I'm salivating over the thought of a bubble bath and a glass of wine."

"We can make that happen." The elevator door opened, and he gestured for her to walk out first. Halfway down the hall, he stopped in front of a door, unlocked it, and pushed it open. "After you."

She stepped inside, and she didn't know what she was expecting his home to look like, but it wasn't this. "You need to go furniture shopping." There was the biggest flat-screen TV she'd ever seen mounted to the wall, a leather recliner situated in front of it, and a small table next to the recliner. That was it.

His gaze scanned the room, and he frowned as if his lack of furniture was a surprise. "I guess I do." He set her camera bag and his two on the kitchen counter. "I'm not here much, but let me show you where you can find me when I am, unless I'm watching a game or sleeping."

"Oh, this is where I'd be, too." He'd taken her out to the balcony, and his condo was right on the ocean. She spied a comfy-looking lounge chair and headed for it. "I think I'll just crash right here," she said as she stretched out. The sound of the waves lapping onshore and the gentle warm breeze was heaven after the nightmare of the last few days.

"What about that bubble bath?"

Chapter 11

No answer. Liam chuckled. She was out cold already. His gaze traveled over her. Even a mess—clothes dirty, hair tangled, and filthy socks on her feet—she was beautiful. That she needed a bath and a brush but hadn't seemed to care how she looked to him or his teammates was pretty cool. This woman was comfortable in her own skin, even when she wasn't at her best.

He'd let her sleep while he took care of some things. First order of business, a shower and clean clothes. That done, he checked on Quinn. Still sound asleep. There was a grocery store two blocks away. He should be able to make a quick trip there and be back before she woke up. To be safe, he left her a note on the kitchen counter that he'd be back in a few minutes.

The store had a deli where they made subs to go, and not sure what she liked, he got three varieties and added three bags of assorted chips to his order. After picking up a few more items, including bubble bath, he hit the checkout. He was back home twenty minutes after he'd left.

As expected, when he checked on her, she was still asleep. He put the subs in the refrigerator along with the bottle of white wine and the beer. That done, he readied the guest bathroom for her. He'd never had overnight company, never brought women to his condo. It was his sanctuary, his place to retreat to when he needed alone time. It seemed like it should bother him that Quinn was invading his space, but it didn't. Something to think about.

He scanned the guest room with a critical eye. It had never been used. Quinn would be the first to sleep in the bed that he'd bought with the hope that someday, his mother might come for a visit. That was probably never going to happen. Before the hurt of losing his family took him, he walked out.

Back in the kitchen, he noticed the three bags he'd left on the counter, his go bag with extra clothes, his weapons bag, and her camera bag. She didn't have any spare clothes to change into. That needed fixing, and he called Harlow. Arrangements made to fix that problem, he went to his bedroom and found a T-shirt, a hoodie, and a pair of his boxer briefs. Those, he took to the bathroom.

Time to wake Quinn. When he returned to the balcony, she was curled up in a ball. The sight of her vulnerable and at peace stirred something within him. He was a protector, and this woman needed him. She might not like it, but until he was sure she was safe, he wasn't leaving her side.

He leaned over her and shook her shoulder. "Quinn, open your eyes." As if he were a pesky fly, she batted at his hand. Her eyes stayed closed, and she turned over, away from him.

"All right then." He slid his arms under her and lifted her.

She stirred, her eyelids fluttering before slowly opening. Her gaze met his, still hazy with sleep. "Hey."

He smiled down at her. "Hey, yourself."

"Where are you taking me?"

"Bubble bath. Remember that was on your list of must-haves tonight?"

"Are you getting in with me?"

"Not tonight." As much as he wanted to do just that, she was still half-asleep, and he wasn't sure she knew what she was saying. "I'll take a rain check."

"Is it raining?" She closed her eyes and went back to sleep.

This girl had him amused, had him thinking of possibilities, and had him aroused. All those things and wanting to kill anyone who dared to hurt her. He'd been with women he liked a lot, but never had there been one who'd made him feel like a growly, possessive bear ready to swipe deadly claws at anyone with malice on their mind coming near her.

He took her to the guest bedroom, lowered her so that she was sitting on the bed, and had to keep his hands on her shoulders to keep her from falling over. Did she always sleep this deeply, or was it because she was mentally and physically exhausted? Just another thing he wanted to learn about her.

"Quinn, sweetheart, open your eyes."

"Mfff."

He chuckled. "Not sure what that word means."

She blinked her eyes open. "What?"

"There's a bubble bath waiting for you."

"Okay."

"Let's get these socks off you."

She peered down at them. "I ruined your socks." She lifted her feet to show him the holes on the bottom. "I'll buy you new ones."

"I think that's something you don't need to worry about. After your bath, we'll doctor your feet again."

"You're so nice. Are you going to kiss me again?"

Hell yes. "Maybe, if you want me to."

She batted her eyelashes. "Maybe I do."

This girl. "I think you're punch-drunk."

"What does that mean, anyway?"

"It means you're beyond tired and being silly."

"Do you like me silly?"

He lowered her feet to the floor, then let his eyes settle on hers. "I pretty much like you in all the ways I've seen you. Come on." He scooped her up and carried her to the guest bathroom, where a bath was waiting for her. "The bubble bath is a mild formula, so it's not going to sting your feet. There's one of my T-shirts and a pair of boxer briefs you can put on when you're done."

"Oh, goody. I'm getting in your undies."

He laughed as he left her to take her bath and tried not to think about her being naked with only a closed door between them.

After her bath, he doctored her feet, then fed her a sub. She'd only eaten half of it when her head almost fell to the table. She jerked up, giving him a sheepish smile.

"I'm sorry. I don't know why I'm so tired and sleepy."

"Because you're exhausted. You've had a hell of a few days. You want the rest of that sub?"

"No, I don't have the energy to eat it."

"Okay, let's get you to bed." He took her hand and led her to the guest room.

"Will you stay with me until I fall asleep?" she asked softly, her eyes heavy with sleep.

He smiled, brushing a lock of hair away from her face. "Of course, I'll be right here."

"Maybe you could hold me? I feel safe with you."

He toed off his shoes, then slid onto the bed. "Turn your back to me."

She turned, then sighed when he wrapped his arm around her waist. "Thank you for finding me."

"You're welcome." He wanted to thank her for needing him to find her. As she drifted off, he watched over her, his heart full of tenderness. The events of the day replayed in his mind, the way she had trusted him, her vulnerability touching something deep within him.

In the quiet of the room, he realized that his feelings for her had grown beyond simple liking. He would do anything to keep her safe and make her smile.

With a soft sigh, he leaned over and pressed a gentle kiss to the corner of her eye before easing out of bed. "Sleep well, beautiful girl," he whispered.

The next morning, he was up early and gathering ingredients for breakfast when his doorbell rang. He knew who it was, and after opening the door, he smiled as he kissed Harlow's cheek.

"Get your mouth off my woman," Grayson growled from behind her.

Harlow's eyebrows shot up as she scowled at him. *"Your woman?"*

"Yep. Deal with it." He put his hand around her neck, brought her to him, and soundly kissed her.

"When you two finish making out like teenagers, I'll be in the kitchen."

Liam left them to it. His phone buzzed with a text, and he glanced at it. It was from Cooper, telling him he was on the way.

"I have the things you asked for," Harlow said as Grayson set bags from a local department store on the counter.

"Appreciate you shopping for Quinn." He'd given her a list of things he thought Quinn needed until she could get home, and Harlow had gone to the store last night.

"No problem. Is she up yet?"

"I'll go see." At the guest room door, he knocked. "Quinn, you up?"

"Yeah. You can come in."

He opened the door and found her sitting on the edge of the bed wearing his T-shirt with the bottom of his boxer briefs peeking out. "Morning. How are you feeling?" She looked lost, and he wanted to send everyone home, and when they were alone, he'd gather her up and hold her, take care of her.

"Better than yesterday." She frowned down at herself. "I can wash my clothes, but I'm going to need shoes."

"Stand by a sec." He went to the end of the hallway. "Harlow, can you bring the things you got? She seems a little lost today," he quietly told Harlow. "Maybe having something besides my T-shirt to wear will help."

"Can't hurt," Harlow said. "I want to meet the woman who has you sending me to the mall with a list of things most men wouldn't even think of." She grinned. "You like her."

It wasn't a question, so he didn't answer. Harlow followed him into the bedroom.

At seeing her, Quinn's gaze darted between them before stopping on Harlow. "Oh, um… I'm just here until I get some shoes. I slept in here. In his guest room. We're not—" she gestured between her and him "—ah, you know. He didn't tell me he had a girlfriend."

Harlow laughed.

He frowned at Quinn. "What are you talking about?"

"She's afraid I'm going to get mad at my boyfriend because he brought a woman home with him," Harlow said.

Say what now? "I'm not your boyfriend."

"Get lost, Liam. I got this." She smiled at Quinn as she

walked into the room with the department store bags, closing the door in his face.

"Right, I'll get lost," he muttered.

He didn't like...well, whatever just happened. He was the one who was supposed to be a hero in Quinn's eyes, bringing her new clothes and shoes. And panties. He was kind of hoping she would need his help putting on the panties. Guess not.

By the time he returned to the kitchen, Cooper had arrived. "Your fiancée's mean," Liam told Grayson. "She kicked me out and slammed the door in my face." His two friends laughed, and he scowled at them. "Not funny."

"Quit pouting and feed me," Cooper said.

"Dude, are you ever not hungry?" The man was a bottomless pit.

Cooper lifted his gaze to the ceiling, pretending to think about it. He snapped his fingers. "Yup. After dinner last Thanksgiving. You gonna do that again this year, right? It was awesome."

Having grown up working in his father's pub, he was the appointed chef in the group. "If I'm in town, sure." He pushed the plate of bread and the toaster across the counter. "Here, start making toast while I bring you up to speed on what happened."

The bacon was cooked, the hash browns were keeping warm in the oven, and he just needed to scramble the eggs. He was keeping this meal a simple one. The purpose of getting everyone together was to make a plan for keeping Quinn safe and getting his teammates' help in investigating what Jasper Garrison was up to.

"How's Quinn this morning?" Grayson asked.

"Not sure. Didn't really get to talk to her before your woman kicked me out."

Grayson chuckled. "Better not let her hear you call her that."

"Yeah, she's mean." Truthfully, Harlow was one of the nicest people he'd ever known, and Quinn couldn't be in better hands…except for his.

Chapter 12

If not Liam's girlfriend—and funny how happy that made her—who was this beautiful woman smiling at her as if they were besties? Quinn wished she had on something besides an oversize T-shirt and Liam's underwear.

"I'm Harlow Pressley, Grayson's fiancée. I understand you've had a lousy few days."

"Quinn Sullivan. Nice to meet you, and you could say that."

"Well, I have a few things here that might help you feel better." She set several bags bearing a popular department store's logo on the bed.

Quinn peeked in one of them. "You brought me clothes? You're an angel."

"Thank Liam. He sent me shopping with a list of things to get you."

"I'll thank him, but still, thank you for going shopping." She dumped out the items in the bag, revealing two pairs of shorts, two jeans, several T-shirts, and two nice tops. In the next bag were panties and two bras, a nude one and a black one. From the third bag came a brush, hair ties, toothbrush, toothpaste, lip gloss, deodorant, a lady's razor, shampoo, conditioner, body wash, and body lotion. In the last one, she found flip-flops, a pair of white canvas tennis shoes, and a package of socklets.

"All this was on his list?"

"Yep."

"The sizes are right. How did you know?"

"When Liam called me last night and said your clothes were a lost cause and asked me to shop for you, I had him look at the sizes in your clothes to give me some sort of direction." She grinned. "He actually measured your feet since you didn't have any shoes."

"He thought of everything." Not that she needed this much, since she was going home today, but she couldn't imagine another man doing this for her. She was going to miss him, that was for sure.

"Why don't I let you get dressed. Liam's making breakfast, so come on out as soon as you're ready."

"Okay. And, Harlow, I truly appreciate you shopping for me."

Harlow smiled. "Who doesn't love shopping? Found a few things for myself while I was at it."

When she was alone, Quinn gathered up the toiletries and took them to the bathroom. Ten minutes later, she had her hair tamed in a ponytail and was wearing a pair of the shorts and a T-shirt. She decided on the flip-flops as they seemed the best choice for her feet. She then followed the aromas of bacon and coffee to the kitchen.

"Oh, everyone's here. Morning, y'all." She waved her fingers at the guys, getting smiles from Grayson and Cooper. Harlow was pouring coffee into cups.

Liam, standing at the stove, glanced over his shoulder and smiled. "Breakfast is almost ready."

A man who sent someone shopping for her and cooked?

Sign her up. Grayson stood from the bar stool where he was sitting next to Cooper. "Have a seat."

"Thanks." She'd only been on her feet for a few minutes, and already they were hurting from walking on them.

"Coffee?" Harlow asked.

"Lord, yes. About a gallon, please." After adding cream and sugar to the cup Harlow set in front of her, she took a sip. "Ah, perfect." She hadn't had any coffee since the morning of the day Jasper kidnapped her. Another reason to wish him to the devil.

"Breakfast is up," Liam said. "Eat here or on the balcony?"

"I'm good with eating here if the ladies are," Cooper said as he stood. "Harlow, you can have my seat."

"I'm fine here," Quinn said.

"Me, too." Harlow brought her cup of coffee around the island and slid onto the stool Cooper had vacated. She handed Grayson her plate. "Load me up, babe."

"I'll load you up all right." Grayson gave her a wicked grin.

"Hey, no talking dirty in my kitchen," Liam said. His gaze fell on Quinn.

When he winked, she glanced down at her plate, hiding her smile…and the heat that she knew was in her eyes. This man was dangerous to her in all the right ways. As much as he fascinated her, she didn't have time to mess around. She had to find that thumb drive and figure out what Jasper was up to.

"I need to rent a car." She'd considered flying home, but it would actually be easier to drive than deal with airports and flights. She could be home just about as fast. "Oh, crap. I just realized my purse is back at the cabin." That was a problem. She didn't have any money or her credit cards. She'd have to borrow money from him until she got her purse back.

"Let's finish breakfast, and then we'll talk," Liam said.

"Okay."

As she ate, she tuned their conversation out while she tried to think of how to get her purse back. The things in her suitcase, also left behind, could be replaced, but her IDs, credit cards, and cash not so easily. She had about a thousand dollars in her wallet, not a small amount for her.

Few people carried that much money around with them, but it was one of her dad's rules. Call home every Wednesday and Sunday, have enough money in her wallet to get out of a foreign country on the spur of the moment if things went south—which she'd actually had to do once and she'd only accomplished it because she had the cash to bribe a man who could get her on the last plane out—and never drink anything that she hadn't poured herself or watched poured. None of those things were too much to ask of her for her father to not have to worry about her…well, not too much.

"Why don't y'all go talk," Harlow said. "I'll clean up the kitchen, then I need to go home. I have a conference call with a baseball player and his PR person this morning."

"That sounds cool. What do you do?" Quinn asked.

"I design websites, handle social media for celebrities, things like that."

"Girl, we need to talk. My website could use some work. I just never seem to have the time to get to it."

"You have a card?" Harlow said. "I'll take a look at it."

"Not on me." They were in her purse. Oh, wait. She had some in her camera bag. "I'll be right back." From now on, she was going to keep her wallet in her camera bag because that was the one thing she'd never leave behind.

When she returned, she and Harlow traded cards, promising to talk soon. After Harlow left, Quinn said, "I like her."

Grayson grinned. "I kind of like her, too."

She laughed. "Yeah, you'd be a fool not to, and I don't take you as a fool."

"He's a fool in love," Cooper sang.

"That I am," Grayson cheerfully said. "Ready to get down to business?"

"I guess. I could use another cup of coffee, though." When she got up to make it, Liam took her cup from her. While he was refilling it, she glanced out the sliding door. "Can we sit outside?" She loved the beach, but rarely had time to go.

"Sure," Liam said.

Once they were settled around the table for four on his balcony, the guys also with coffee refills, she said, "I'm not sure what there is to talk about except how I'm going to get home. I realized I left my purse at the cabin, which I need to figure out how to get back." Would Liam go back to Hope Corner with her? "Maybe—"

"If you're thinking of going back to get your purse, think again." Liam set down his cup, an unhappy expression on his face.

Men! Why couldn't they discuss things without getting bossy? She had no intention of returning to the cabin by herself, but she didn't like being told what she could and couldn't do. "You're not the boss of me."

"Ruh-roh," Cooper muttered. He poked Liam's arm. "Didn't your mama teach you better than to say things like that?"

Grayson snorted.

"Apparently not." Liam sighed. "I'm not trying to boss you around, Quinn. But—"

"If you'd give me a chance to finish, I was going to ask if you could come with me to get my purse."

"I thought you wanted to go home and look for that thumb drive, see if you have it. That's not your priority?"

"Well, yes." Why did he have to make sense? And as much as she wanted her purse back, it was ridiculous to even think of going back to the cabin.

"Liam filled us in before you came down," Grayson said. "You don't have any idea what's on the thumb drive?"

"All I know is that I overheard his end of a phone conversation where he said children were getting sick because of someone dumping something into the lake, and it sounds like he's blackmailing that person. Apparently, there's a thumb drive with photos on it that I might have accidentally taken when I left." Her gaze scanned each of their faces. "I can't turn my back on that if children are getting sick and it's something I can stop."

"I have a question," Cooper said. "Why don't you just turn all this over to the police? Report the kidnapping?"

"Not yet. I need to find that thumb drive if I do have it, see what's on it. If children are getting sick because of illegal dumping, it's bigger than me being kidnapped."

"I agree with Quinn," Liam said. "The police might not be the best people to bring in on this, depending on what is on the thumb drive. If it's something making children sick, then we're probably talking about the EPA or the Feds."

Grayson nodded. "We need to find that thumb drive."

"Then I have a solution," Cooper said. "Why don't you and Liam go look for the thumb drive, and I'll go to the cabin and get your purse."

"Not a bad idea," Liam said. "You'd be able to nose

around, see if you can pick up anything of interest. You can also check on my car, see if it can be fixed there, or if I need to have it towed to Grayson's dealership."

"You have a dealership?" Quinn asked.

Cooper was the one to snort this time. "The boy has what? Eleven of them? All luxury car dealerships. Need a new car, he's the man to see."

Grayson shrugged as if it wasn't a big deal, but jeez, if he had eleven of them, he must be loaded. She was impressed that he was so down-to-earth, that he came across as just another one of the guys.

"Good to know if I'm ever car shopping." She was relieved that they weren't fighting her and insisting she go to the police. "Thank you for understanding that I can't turn my back on the children."

"Neither can we," Liam said. "Which means you have a team of skilled investigators on your side."

"What he said." That from Grayson. "While you and Liam are looking for the thumb drive and Coop's nosing around Hope Corner, I'll start looking into Jasper. I'd like you to write down everything you know about him before you head home."

Cooper grinned. "We got a plan, folks."

Honestly, she was a bit overwhelmed by these guys who weren't hesitating to help her find out what Jasper was up to. Jasper had no clue who was gunning for him. If he did, he'd make like a rabbit and haul ass.

Chapter 13

"Awesome house," Liam said as he parked the car Grayson had loaned him until his was repaired.

"It's too big for my dad, but he's lived here since he and my mother married, and all his memories of her are here."

Liam guessed the two-story Victorian house was four or five thousand square feet, and it fit the landscape of giant oak trees dripping with Spanish moss. The wide front porch was perfect for sitting in the swing with a book and a sweet iced tea. The ceiling fans would make hot summer days tolerable.

"You said your father's in Asheville?"

"Maggie Valley actually, but that's in the Asheville area. He'll come back to Savannah in early October when it starts to cool down a little. He does come home if I'm here so he can spend time with me. He wanted to be here now, but I told him to stay at his cabin, that I was only going to be here for a day, two at the most."

She unlocked the door, and he held it open for her to step inside. He followed her in and paused to appreciate the entrance. They were in a large foyer, the feature a wide staircase, and he could imagine her walking down it on prom night, her date standing at the bottom, his gaze focused on the beautiful girl floating toward him. In Liam's vision, the girl wore a green gown that fit her curves and matched her eyes. He was jealous of that faceless boy.

"You look a thousand miles away," she said. "What are you thinking?"

"Did you go to the prom?"

"Yes, why?"

"Did you walk down those stairs while your boyfriend tried his best not to drool at seeing you?"

She laughed. "I don't know about the drooling part, but yes."

"What color was your dress?"

"Emerald green. Why are you asking these questions?"

Because he'd seen her clear as day slowly descending the stairs, a soft smile on her face for the boy waiting for her to reach him. "I just wanted to picture it." If he married her, he'd ask her to walk down those stairs in her wedding dress, so he would experience that soft smile meant just for him. He shook his head. Where had that thought even come from?

"You want something to drink?"

"I'm good for now." They walked past the stairs and into a formal living room. "Your home is beautiful."

"Thank you. I think so, too, although I sometimes forget to appreciate it. It's the only home I've ever known."

"Your father's retired I take it?"

"For five years now. He owned a real estate company specializing in commercial property and decided one day he was working too hard, so he sold it. He dabbles in the stock market now, more as a hobby than a job. He seems to have a knack for it, though."

It was obvious father and daughter were close, and he envied that. Even before he'd been declared dead to his father, they hadn't been close. What Patrick O'Rourke saw when he looked at his son was a means to an end, just someone to carry on the O'Rourke legacy. There had never been affection between them, and as hard as the boy he used to be longed for approval from his father, it never came. Yet he still held on to the hope that someday, his father would... well, undead him. That he'd be welcomed back into the family again.

She headed down a hallway. "Come on. I want to look for that thumb drive."

"Right behind you." He took those unwanted thoughts of his father and crammed them back into the box where they belonged.

"Cool room," he said after following her into what he was expecting to be her bedroom but was not. He turned in a circle, taking in the two large monitors sitting on a glass desk, a small blue leather sofa, the photos on the walls, the shelves of awards, and a long, chest-high table in the middle of the room. Scattered across the table were cameras, two closed laptops, and things he couldn't identify.

"Where's your darkroom?"

She walked straight to the table. "You don't know much about photography, do you? With digital cameras, computers, and hundreds of photography software, darkrooms aren't much of a thing anymore."

"Who knew?"

She glanced up from scattering thumb drives over the table and smirked. "I did."

"I want to kiss that smirk right off your face." When she laughed, he stepped around the table. "You find that funny?" He was close enough now to catch her scent, something that made him think of the sea, summer nights, and satiny sheets.

"Are you smelling me?" she asked when he leaned his nose close to her neck and inhaled.

"I am. What's that scent? Makes me want to lick you."

"Harlow brought me coconut-and-vanilla body wash and shampoo." She tilted her head, giving him access to her neck. "You like?"

"*Like* is such a mundane word for what I think." Keeping his lips close to her skin, but not touching, he moved his mouth until it was an inch from hers. "Stop or go?"

"Go?"

"As in can I go ahead and kiss you?"

"If you want."

"Oh, I want." The first time he'd kissed her, he'd committed the taste of her to memory, but maybe his memory was faulty. When his lips met hers this time, it was…different. Their kiss in the woods had been sweet and tentative with a hint of possibilities. This one, man, this one was electric, sending a shock wave of desire through him.

She tasted like sin and a craving only she could satisfy, a dangerous combination that had his head spinning. When they finally broke apart, he was breathless, his heart hammering in his chest. He leaned his forehead against hers. It was in that moment that he realized this wasn't just a passing attraction; there was something deeper between them, something he wanted to explore.

"Wow," she whispered.

"Yeah, that kiss was definitely a wow." He cupped her cheek, her skin soft against his palm. "There's more where that came from. All you have to do is ask."

"I just might do that, but right now, I want to know if I have Jasper's thumb drive."

He picked up one that looked different. "What's this?"

"It's a SanDisk. Sometimes we store our photos on those,

sometimes on a thumb drive. Jasper wants his thumb drive, and he knows the difference, so that's what we're looking for. Purple's my favorite color, so mine are all purple. Jasper's are black, and it's not here."

"So, you don't have it?"

"Don't get excited yet." She got a bigger camera bag. "This is the one I had with me in California. I didn't really go through it when I got back. You'd think if he has photos stored on a drive that are worth a million dollars to someone, he'd keep it safely locked up somewhere. But that's Jasper for you. Never takes care of his things."

"Most people would." He leaned against the table. "Tell me about him."

"He's also a photojournalist. I met him in California when we were both covering the wildfires. He likes to think he's a macho man, gets embedded with teams on the front lines of wars or in California with the hotshots." She stared down at her hands where she rested them on the camera bag. "It embarrasses me to admit that I had a short fling with him."

"Why? You're single, and if you were attracted to him and it was consensual, you have nothing to be embarrassed about." Thinking of her being intimate with another man, though? Not a picture he wanted in his mind. "Did he treat you right?"

"He did in the beginning. Around the time for me to head home, he started getting possessive and talked about me staying even though my assignment was coming to an end. When I reminded him that I didn't do relationships, something I'd been up-front about from the beginning, he just talked over me. By then, I knew I'd made a mistake getting involved with him."

"You don't do relationships at all?" That was not something he wanted to hear.

She lifted her gaze to his. "No."

"How come?" If she wasn't interested in him, he'd walk away, but she was. He could see it in her eyes and in the way she kissed him back. He wasn't a man who let obstacles get in his way. There were always a way around them. To do that, he needed to know what her obstacles were and why they were there.

"Why not, Quinn?"

Chapter 14

Quinn considered her answer. If he were any other man, she'd tell him because that was the way it was, because it was her choice, and she didn't owe anyone an explanation. To explain, she'd have to share her past, talk about Aiden. But Liam wasn't any other man, and she wanted him to understand.

She glanced at her watch. They had all night to look for the thumb drive, and she sensed this was an important conversation to have. "You know what, it's wine time." She didn't want to talk about this while they stood in her photography room at her worktable, looking for Jasper's thumb drive…thinking of Jasper. "Let's go sit out on the patio."

"Is this a diversion tactic?"

"No." She held out her hand, and he took it. "I'm going to bare my soul. I just need a peaceful setting and a glass of wine while I do it."

"All right, then. Lead on."

He was so easy to get along with…now anyway. She knew how that could change if feelings became involved. It was always the woman who was expected to change her life for her man. Even her mother had.

"White or red?" she asked when they reached the kitchen.

"Or maybe you'd like something stronger? Dad's bar is in the butler's pantry if you want to check out what he has."

"I'll have what you're having, but I've never seen a butler's pantry, so I need to check it out."

She gestured to the door past the refrigerator. "It's right over there." After he walked by her, she took a moment to appreciate the rear view. His T-shirt wasn't so tight that his muscles stretched the fabric, but they were there. Broad shoulders, a tapered waist, a mouthwatering butt, and long legs made for a very sexy man. That wasn't even taking into account his face, those blue eyes, and that black hair.

"Yummy, yummy, yummy," she murmured after he disappeared into the pantry. Hopefully, he would be agreeable to a brief fling with the condition that there would be absolutely no feelings involved and they would go their separate ways when their time was up. She ignored the little pang in her chest at the thought of walking away from Liam.

She took a bottle of Pinot Grigio, her favorite wine, from the wine cooler and poured each of them a glass. Was she really going to dredge up memories that still had the power to hurt? After everything went down with Aiden, she'd promised herself never again would she let a man hurt her the way he had. Walls had been erected, and she'd been perfectly happy with life after Aiden.

Aiden had been her first and only love. Although she saw nothing wrong with consensual sex, she was selective and cautious, but she wished she could have a do-over on the last one. She'd like to bleach her brain of any memory of Jasper.

Liam stepped out of the butler's pantry. "If I ever build a house, it's going to have one of these."

She grinned. "Most people want a big walk-in closet or a pool. You just want a pantry."

"Not just any pantry." He took the glass of wine she offered. "One like that."

"Let's take our drinks outside." She started walking toward the sliding door to the patio.

"Can we sit on the front porch instead? I think that swing has my name on it."

"Sure. It's Dad's favorite place to sit in the morning with his cup of coffee." She flipped the switch to turn on the ceiling fans as they walked out.

"Ah, this is nice," he said after they were seated.

She tucked her feet under her so he could push the swing with his long legs. The breeze from the ceiling fans kept it from being too hot, and as he rocked them, she closed her eyes, inhaling the sweet scent of her dad's roses. It was good to be home.

"You're beautiful," he softly said.

She opened her eyes to see his gaze on her, and she smiled. "Thank you."

"Talk to me, Quinn. Why don't you do relationships?"

"Why do you want to know?" She'd kind of hoped he would forget that was why they'd taken a break from looking for Jasper's thumb drive. The weight of his question settled between them, and she wished she hadn't said she'd give him an answer.

"Because I…" He glanced away for a moment before his gaze returned to hers. "I like you, and I think maybe we could have something good between us. Suppose we don't give it a name? We just spend some time together, see how it goes. Would you say yes to that?"

"I'd be more likely to agree to a short fling." If she was ever tempted to be in a relationship again, it would be with him. "Relationships don't work for me because—"

Liam's phone chimed. He pulled it from his pocket and

turned the screen toward her, showing her it was Cooper calling. "Whatcha got for me?" As he listened, his eyes locked on her. "I'm with Quinn now. I'm going to put you on speaker."

"Hi, Quinn," Cooper said.

"Do you have my purse? Oh, and hi."

"I'm sorry to say that I don't have it. We've got a problem. Garrison's dead. Murdered, and—"

"What?" Jasper was dead? Murdered?

"Do you have any details?" Liam asked.

"When I got to the cabin, I found him on the floor, shot in the back of his head, execution style."

Quinn gasped. "Oh, my God." She was furious with Jasper, regretted every moment she spent with him, but she'd never wish that for him. What in the world had he gotten into? What had caused him to kidnap her, chain her up, and in the end get himself killed?

"It gets worse. I have your suitcase, Quinn, but your purse was nowhere to be found."

Her heart fell to her stomach. "What does that mean?"

Liam took her hand and squeezed. "It's not good. Whoever shot Garrison has your purse, knows who you are."

"I think I'm going to be sick." Liam tugged on her hand, pulling her against him. She tucked into him, wishing she could stay wrapped in his arms where she knew she'd be safe.

"Are the police aware?" Liam asked.

"Not yet. I'll make an anonymous call to the local police telling them where to find Garrison as soon as I get back to town. His phone and wallet aren't on him, so I assume whoever took your purse took them, too. I'm going to wipe down anywhere I think your prints might be, Quinn."

"Why not just tell the police I was there?" She didn't kill him. "I could tell them what happened."

"For one, the Hope Corner police department won't have the experience to deal with something like this," Liam said. "They'll want you to go there, and that's not going to happen. We don't know who killed Garrison. Was it someone local? Someone who might have an in with the police? We won't risk it." A fierce light entered his eyes. "I won't risk you."

"He's right," Cooper said.

"So, what do we do?" How in God's name did she end up in the middle of a murder? She never bothered anyone. She just wanted to take pictures of children who needed a helping hand.

"We find that thumb drive, see who Garrison was trying to blackmail and what he had on them. We find out who killed him and how they're involved. Then we fix it and make you safe. Bring in the proper authorities when we know what we're dealing with. Probably the FBI. Until then, I'm not leaving your side."

Her stomach settled a little, knowing he would keep her safe, but still... She was scared, really scared. She didn't want to ask the question in her mind, but she had to. "Does whoever has my purse think I have the thumb drive?"

Liam nodded. "We have to assume that's what they think."

And they knew where she lived. "We have to find it. Right now."

"I'm going to nose around here a little," Cooper said. "See what kind of vibes I can pick up. Keep in touch."

"Will do, and be careful." Liam slipped his phone back into his pocket. "We're not staying here tonight after all. I'm going to get my weapons bag from the car, then let's go see if we can find that thumb drive so we can get out of here."

She waited on the porch for him, and once they were inside, he locked the door while she went to the alarm and set it. Once that was done, she leaned against the wall. "What if you weren't here? I'd be by myself, not knowing what happened after I left the cabin. I wouldn't know someone was looking for me." What she really wanted to do was crawl into the bed and pull the covers over her head.

He dropped the bag to the floor, then wrapped his arms around her. "I am here, so don't even go down that road. You couldn't find anyone better to have your back than the three of us. And I meant it when I said I'm not leaving your side until this is over."

"Thank you," she whispered. She buried her face against his chest. "How did I end up in the middle of a murder?" She stepped away from him. "Come on. Let's find that damn thumb drive." She still wasn't sure she had it.

Back in her office, he set his bag on the sofa. He opened it, took out a holster that he clipped to his belt, then he brought out a gun, slipping it into the holster. At her raised brows, he said, "Best we be prepared for trouble."

"I hate this, but you're right. I'll get mine out of the gun safe and keep it near me."

"Probably not a bad idea."

It gave her the warm fuzzies that he didn't balk at her also arming herself. She'd told him she knew how to use a gun, and he didn't question her, just trusted that she wasn't blowing smoke. He came and stood next to her as she took everything out of her large camera bag, and at the bottom, where she'd hurriedly tossed her own accessories, was one black thumb drive.

"That's it?" Liam asked.

"I think so. I don't have any black ones." She didn't know how she felt about actually having it. A part of her wished she'd never touched it, but if whatever was on it showed why children were getting sick? She would be able to do something about it. At the very least, she could make sure the right someone or agency was made aware.

"Let's see what's on it," Liam said.

"In a way, I don't want to even know, but I guess we need to." She took the thumb drive to her desk computer, logged in, and then slipped the drive into the port.

"It's the only way we'll find out what Garrison got involved in."

She frowned at what they were seeing. "What in the world?"

Chapter 15

"He's dumping something into the lake," Liam said. "That's never good." The video was of a man who had a steel drum turned over on its side, and a colorless liquid was flowing into the lake. The camera panned to where more drums behind the man had either been already dumped or were going to be. "We need to find out what that stuff is."

"Whatever it is, it's making children sick." After the video, there were photos. Still shots of the drums, then one of the lake.

It wasn't a big lake, which also wasn't good, since the liquid didn't have much space to disperse. The next picture was of a section of the lake that had a sandy shore and children playing in the water. There was a playground in the background and picnic pavilions, so the area had been created for people to enjoy the lake.

"That's Black Bear Lake," Quinn said. "I took some photos of it."

He leaned closer to the monitor when she moved on to the next photo. "What's that building?" The picture of a large structure was taken from a distance. "Can you zoom in on the name?"

"Sure."

"Hanson Textiles," he read when the name was enlarged. "We need intel on that business."

"It's a textile mill. I saw it when I was snooping around. It's about a half mile from the lake."

He called Grayson, and when he had his teammate on the phone, he said, "Get Cooper on here with us. I have an update." A minute later, Cooper was on the call with them. Liam told them what they'd found on the thumb drive. "I need you to look into Hanson Textiles," he told Grayson. "We need to know who owns it."

"I'm on it," Grayson said.

"As long as I'm in Hope Corner, I'll see what I can learn on this end," Cooper said. "The big question, if those drums belonged to this textile mill, are they still dumping whatever's in them?"

That was a question Liam wanted an answer to. "And exactly what was in them. Once we find that out, we'll be able to notify the authorities. We know that Garrison was planning to blackmail someone. The question is who. And was this person the one who killed him? Or maybe he sent someone to do his dirty work?"

"I'll do a deep dive on the mill as soon as we hang up," Grayson said. "What's your plan? If our bad guys know about Quinn and think she has the thumb drive, you're not safe there."

"Agreed. Quinn's going to email you a copy of what's on the drive, and then we're going to pack up and come back to Myrtle Beach. It's where she'll be the safest."

Quinn scowled. "Maybe you should ask me what I want to do."

"So, you're good with staying here knowing it's not safe?"

Grayson chuckled. "Sounds like it's time for Coop and me to sign off."

"See you tomorrow." After disconnecting, he crossed his arms and raised a brow. "Back to my question. You want to stay here even knowing someone who's already murdered knows where you live?"

"No, of course not. I just don't like being told what to do. I would appreciate being a part of the decision."

"My bad." He wanted to grin at her disgruntled expression, but he doubted she would appreciate that. He very much liked that she stood up for herself. "Allow me to remedy my blunder. I'm of the opinion that we need to skedaddle ASAP. What would you advise on this situation, Miss Sullivan?"

She scowled at him. "Stop being so entertaining." One corner of her mouth twitched before she caught it.

"Why?"

"Because I don't need to be liking you any more than I already do."

"Sorry, but I can't help myself, sugar pie." He almost laughed when she wrinkled her nose at the endearment. Somehow, he'd known that would rile her up.

"No, no, no. Don't start with the pet names. My name is Quinn. Period."

"Got it. I'll try to refrain from affectionate cute little names. Now that we've got that cleared up, we really need to leave before unwanted visitors show up."

"Give me Grayson's email, so I can send this to him, and then we can do as you advise and skedaddle." After he told her Grayson's email address and she'd sent him copies of the files, she handed him the thumb drive. "You're in charge of keeping this safe."

He put the drive in the front pocket of his jeans. While

she was packing her cameras and accessories, he retrieved his weapons bag. After putting on his shoulder holster, he moved his gun from at his waist to the holster, then slipped a shirt over his T-shirt, leaving it unbuttoned, hiding the gun. With another gun secured in his ankle holster, and a knife in a sheath at his belt, he zipped the bag up.

She'd disappeared into what he assumed was her bedroom, and as he waited for her, he went to a front window and looked out. All seemed quiet outside, but his skin prickled with unease. It was a warning he'd learned to pay heed to.

"We need to go, Quinn," he called.

"Do you see anything?" she asked, coming next to him, carrying her camera bag and a small tote.

"No, but the hair on my neck is standing on end, so I'm uneasy about us walking out to the car. I should've parked it in your garage."

"Would Grayson be unhappy if we left it here?"

"If he has to choose between our safety and the car, he'll pick us. Why? What are you thinking?"

"Get your stuff and come with me."

He followed her through the kitchen and after she set the alarm, they went out to the garage. "Well, well, what do we have here? Is that yours?"

"Yep. And she's fast."

"I just bet she is." He whistled as he eyed the black beauty, a Porsche Cayenne Turbo.

"My dad said I could have any car I wanted for my graduation present from college, and this was what I wanted. It's almost a crime that she sits when I'm gone so much, but Dad does enjoy driving it, too." She tossed him the keys. "You drive."

"Be happy to." They loaded their bags in the back, and

once they were seated in the car, he said, "Do you have your gun on you?" She'd told him she knew how to shoot, and he was going to trust her on that.

"Oh, I was in a hurry and forgot to get it. I'll be right back."

He put his hand on her arm. "No, I don't think we have the time." That sixth sense he was known for was screaming that danger was near. "I can loan you one when we get to Myrtle Beach if need be."

"Okay. Let's get out of here."

"All right, time to see if anyone's waiting for us." He leaned over and caught her eyes. "Listen carefully. If we do have company, or pick up any on our way, you do everything I say when I say, no exceptions."

"Sir, yes, sir." She saluted him. When he narrowed his eyes, she shrugged. "Sorry, couldn't resist. I will obey you without question when it comes to our safety." Her lips ticked up in a grin. "Can't promise that at other times. Just so you know."

"I wouldn't expect otherwise." He glanced up at the visor. "That the garage door opener?"

"Yes."

"I'm going to start the car, then hit the opener. Be ready for anything." He prayed he was wrong and bad guys with guns weren't waiting for them.

"Just try not to let them shoot up my car."

"I'll do my best." Before he started the car, he leaned over and gave her a quick kiss. "That was for good luck. Ready?" She nodded, and after the car was running, he pushed the opener. The door rumbled open. As he was backing the Porsche out, the sound of breaking glass pierced the air, and the house's alarm blared.

"They're breaking in." Fear tinged her voice.

He wished he could take the time to reassure her that he'd keep her safe, but his one goal at the moment was to get her away from danger. He pressed down on the gas pedal, the tires screeching against the garage floor. Clear of the garage, he stopped long enough to throw the gear from Reverse to Drive. Rubber burned as he gave the Porsche gas and spun it around.

"Oh, God," she screamed as a man wearing a black face mask stood in front of them, a gun pointed at their windshield.

"Get down," he ordered, and as she'd promised, she instantly obeyed, lowering her head to her knees.

"Stop or I'll shoot," the man yelled.

It was time to play chicken, as there was no way he was stopping. If he did, they'd both end up dead. He gunned it and headed straight for the man. The man dived out of the way. Shots were fired at them from behind, but he didn't slow down.

Two white SUVs were parked at the end of Quinn's driveway. One was empty, and one had two men in it. Liam managed to get the plate number on one of the cars as he blew by them over the grass. "Sorry about your dad's lawn."

Fortunately, there wasn't anything blocking his view of the road, and not seeing any cars coming, he took the turn onto the street at a speed that if he'd been driving another car, they probably would've fishtailed. The Porsche, though, handled the maneuver as if it had been only waiting to show off what it was capable of.

The occupied SUV tore off after them. He grinned. "Catch me if you can."

"Can I get up now?"

"Yeah."

"Who are they?" she said as she leaned around the headrest and watched the car chasing them.

There was fear in her voice, and he wanted to knock some heads for scaring her. "I don't know, but we'll find out. Sit back and make sure your seat belt is tightened. We're going to see what this baby can do."

"She can do whatever you ask of her."

"Counting on it." The SUV was coming up fast on their bumper, and Liam was sure the intention was to hit them and run them off the road. The Sullivans' house was outside Savannah city limits, in a somewhat rural area. The road they were on was a two-lane and not heavily traveled. He needed to lose the SUV before they got to heavier traffic. The last thing he wanted was to put any innocents in danger.

"Hold on. We're going turbo." He pushed the gas pedal to the floor, and the powerful engine roared to life. As they raced down the narrow road, trees blurred past them in a green-and-brown whirl. The SUV behind them struggled to keep up, and its headlights grew smaller in the rearview mirror with each passing second. The Porsche's tires gripped the road as he took a sharp curve faster than was safe.

An intersection with a four-way stop loomed ahead. "Which way will take us to an area we can get lost in?"

"Left. There's a mall and a bunch of restaurants."

"Perfect." Now the trick was to get lost in traffic.

Chapter 16

Adrenaline rushed through Quinn's veins as Liam wound their way up and down streets, sometimes taking left turns, sometimes right ones. She'd been watching in her side-view mirror and hadn't seen the SUV since they'd taken that first left at the intersection.

"You okay?" Liam asked.

"I'm good." Mostly. That had been scary, though.

"How do we get to I-95 from here?"

"Keep going straight for a few miles. I'll tell you when to turn." As they traveled, she kept her gaze on the mirror. "I think we lost them."

"For now. We just need to hope they don't connect you to me or The Phoenix Three. I'd rather not see them show up in Myrtle Beach."

She definitely didn't want to bring trouble to her new friends. Since they'd lost the men chasing them, she relaxed… somewhat. "Do you think those men are from whoever was dumping that stuff from those barrels?"

"That would be my guess."

Hopefully, Cooper and Grayson would know more by the time they got to Myrtle Beach, but she needed a break from thinking about men out to kill her. His phone chimed, and he pulled it out of his pocket and glanced at the screen.

"It's your dad." He handed the phone to her. "Just hit Accept."

"Hey, Dad."

"Where are you? The alarm company called. Are you okay?"

She told him what had happened, including why they weren't involving the police.

"I'm coming home."

"No, don't. I'm with Liam, and we're going back to Myrtle Beach. It's not safe to be at the house right now. Hold on. I'm putting you on speaker." She turned the phone toward Liam. "Tell him he needs to stay in Maggie Valley."

"Sir, she's right. It's not safe right now, and there's nothing you can do here."

"I don't like it, but I'll stand by for now. All I care about is that you keep my daughter safe."

"That's all I care about, too. Call the alarm company back and tell them it's a false alarm."

Her father loudly sighed. "I'm not liking this. Quinn, get a damn phone so I can call you."

She'd called when they'd returned to Myrtle Beach from Hope Corner to tell him she'd lost her phone and he could reach her through Liam.

"We'll get her a phone as soon as we get back to Myrtle Beach," Liam said.

"Love you, Dad."

"I love you, too, but I need you to stop turning my hair white."

She laughed. "Your hair was already white. Nothing to do with me."

"Humph." Then he disconnected.

She handed Liam his phone. "Can we talk about something besides men with guns and whatever all this is?"

"Sure." He tapped his finger on the steering wheel, then glanced at her. "Cooper's phone call interrupted our conversation, and I want to finish it. You were about to tell me why you don't do relationships."

"Was I?" She was kind of hoping he'd forgotten about that, yet, because he'd said he wanted to explore what this thing between them was, she wanted him to understand.

"You know you were, but if you don't want to talk about it…" He shrugged.

"Okay, here's the thing. Men can't handle my career, and I'm not giving it up to make a man happy."

"You shouldn't have to."

She huffed. "Tell that to Aiden, or even Jasper."

"Who's Aiden?"

His voice had turned growly, and it wasn't the sexy kind of growl. "A man I was in love with. We met right after I graduated college, and I told him right up front that I was going to be a photojournalist and I'd be traveling a lot. He assured me he was fine with that."

"I'm guessing he wasn't?"

"He seemed fine with it until he asked me to marry him. As soon as I said yes, everything changed. At first, it was small things, like couldn't I shorten my assignment to a week instead of the two I'd planned. Then it grew to be all about him. Aiden was a trauma doctor, and his job was stressful to say the least. That was his reason for asking me to give up traveling, that he needed me at home. He said he was saving lives while I was just taking pictures."

"He was wrong. Your work is important. You bring attention to children who need it the most."

"I like to think I make a difference."

He reached over the console, found her hand, and squeezed it. "You do. Never doubt that."

"My mother gave up her career for my father. I didn't know she was unhappy until a few years ago. I don't think my father even knew that. She was never happier than when she had her camera in her hand. A few years ago, I found her diary in a box in the attic. It was an eye-opener. She wrote about how much she loved me and my dad, but she also talked about how something was missing. That if she had it to do over again, she wouldn't have given up her career for my father, but that she hadn't understood back then that she could have both."

"I'd say it was probably a generational thing. That she did what was expected of her and put her marriage first."

"Maybe. In her diary, on my first birthday, she wrote about how much she loved me and how she was going to teach me to go after my dreams, whatever they were. She was going to teach me that my dreams were important, and I should never let anyone come between me and what fed my soul. I found her diary after Aiden, and reading it, I vowed I'd honor her wishes for me. In my experience, it seems that men feel they're the important ones. So, I decided short flings are safe. Relationships for a woman means what you do, what feeds your soul isn't so important."

"I don't think anyone, man or woman, should have to give up something they love for another person," he said. "If you love someone, why would you want them to be less than they are? I can't judge why she gave up a part of herself to make your father happy. Maybe it was because they lived in a different generation, and she didn't know how to speak up for herself. Maybe she loved him so much that she felt like she needed to make him happy, and she wanted to make the sacrifice."

"Didn't sound like it in her diary."

"Maybe not, but I'm not Aiden, Quinn."

"I know." But did she?

After their conversation, they each grew quiet, and she hoped he understood why the only thing between them could be a fling. He might say he wasn't like Aiden or her father, but she wasn't willing to risk it. It was different with her because she was gone so much, so her job wasn't one where she had a career but was home every night.

If she took a chance and, in the end, she fell in love with him and he demanded she give up the one thing that fed her soul, it just might destroy her, because she just knew that given half a chance, she could love Liam so hard.

Sometime later, he shook her. "Wake up, Sleeping Beauty. We're here."

"Hmm?" She stretched. "Sorry. Didn't mean to fall asleep on you."

"That's okay. You needed the rest. Let's unload our stuff, then I want to hide your car. It's too recognizable. We'll get one of Grayson's loaners until I get my car back."

"That's a good idea."

As soon as they dropped their bags inside his condo, they were back on the road. "What about the car we left at my house?"

"I called Gray while you were sleeping, brought him up-to-date. He has a dealership in Savannah. Two of our friends are going to your house to check things out, and then they'll take the car to the dealership."

"Isn't that dangerous for them? What if those men are still there?"

"Doubtful they'll be hanging around. They probably searched your house, and when they didn't find the thumb drive, they would've left. Hopefully, without doing much damage. If they are still around, our friends aren't the kind of men you want to mess with."

"What's this place?" she asked when Liam parked in front of a commercial building.

"Ours. The Phoenix Three's on the top floor. We rent out the other floors."

"Cool." She was curious about their offices.

The lobby was disappointingly plain. Nothing but an elevator straight ahead and two doors, one to the left with a sign for a group of attorneys and the other an insurance agency. She followed Liam into the elevator. As soon as the door closed, he pulled her in front of him, her back to his chest, and he slid his arms around her waist. It was a position she very much liked.

"Hey," he said, his voice next to her ear, his breath warm and tickling. How was one word that sexy?

She leaned against him. "Hey." She glanced up at him and smiled.

His eyes locked on hers. "If I didn't know for a fact that Gray was watching us right now, I'd kiss you senseless, maybe let my fingers go exploring."

"He's watching us?" she squeaked. She'd never kissed a man in an elevator, and the thought of Liam backing her up against the wall did funny things to her stomach and other places. But it was a big no on being watched. She moved to the opposite wall, and the dang man laughed.

The elevator door opened, and she couldn't resist messing with Liam after stepping out. She bent over to retie the laces of her sneaker and threw in a little butt wiggle.

"You're a very naughty girl, Quinn."

"Me? Never." She walked out, exaggerating the sway of her hips and hiding her smile when the man behind her growled. There wasn't anyone in the reception area, and although she didn't know where she was supposed to go, she headed down the hallway. Footsteps on the wood floor sounded behind her, those of a predator stalking his prey, and she, being the prey, felt a rush of excitement.

Suddenly, an arm wrapped around her waist, and she was pulled into an office. He closed the door, and then turned them so that her back was against the wall. A thrill shot through her at his dominance.

He put his hands on the wall, caging her in. "You like playing games, Little Marine?"

The heat in his eyes matched what she knew was in hers. She wanted him in a way that she'd never experienced with another man. And funny in that she hated pet names, but she liked him calling her Little Marine. It was cute.

"Only when I know I'm going to win," she snarked.

A wicked grin appeared on his face, one that made her heart flutter in anticipation. "This is a game where we both win."

His lips crashed down on hers in a fierce kiss that stole the breath from her lungs. The world around them faded away, leaving only the electrifying connection between them. In that moment, there was no one else but the two of them, caught in a whirlwind of desire and unspoken promises. She put her hands on his chest and felt the rapid beat of his heart. He wanted her as much as she wanted him.

He rested his forehead against hers. "You drive me crazy, woman."

"Just so you know, I'm not sorry." She ducked under his arm and walked out.

Chapter 17

Not sorry, eh? Grinning, Liam put his hand on her lower back as he followed her out. "Last door on the left."

"That's your office?"

"No, it's the war room."

She stopped so fast that he almost bowled her over. "War room?"

"Yeah, where all our equipment is. Where we plan our missions."

"Cool. Let's go play with your toys."

He chuckled. "A woman after my own heart."

"Let's keep our hearts out of it. Our mission is to learn who's making children sick and how." She glanced over her shoulder at him and grinned. "But no reason not to have a little fun along the way."

The last thing he wanted was to clue her in that his heart was already in it. That would only scare her away. So, he winked and said, "No reason at all." He'd just have to show her he wasn't like Aiden or any other man of her experience, his own secret mission to win that heart she so closely guarded. He wasn't in love with her...not yet. But he thought he could be if only she'd open her mind to the possibility of a future with him.

At the door to the war room, he put his palm to the security reader, then opened the door.

"That's neat," she said.

"We have some top-grade, expensive equipment in here. Don't want to make it easy for anyone to break in. The door's steel and bulletproof. Gray will be here in a minute."

"Oh, wow. You weren't kidding about having expensive equipment."

He stood back while she explored the room. In the middle was a conference table that would seat ten. In front of each leather chair was a monitor. They'd come in handy when they'd had occasion to have meetings with the police, and twice with the FBI. Everyone in attendance was able to follow along on their own monitor.

The top half of one wall was a flat screen that was connected to the three high-tech computers placed on the three desks along another wall. They could project any location in the world onto the screen as long as their computers could find it on Google Earth or other satellite imagery options such as NASA Worldview.

She stopped at a whiteboard, and her gaze roamed over the photos of the children they'd rescued. There weren't any names identifying the children, but he and his brothers knew every child's name.

"Most of those children were reunited with their families," he told her. "We had to find foster families for the few unfortunate ones who didn't have a family to claim them or that wanted them back." They kept tabs on their rescues, making sure those children were being taken care of and treated right.

"That's awesome, Liam. What all does The Phoenix Three do?"

"Anything that involves the safety and well-being of a child."

She turned to him, looking at him with soft eyes. "You guys are heroes. I'm in awe of you."

"Don't be painting us with something we're not. We're just three guys doing our small part to hopefully make the world a better place."

"Heroes."

Okay, if that was how she wanted to see him, he wouldn't argue. He kind of liked that admiration shining in her eyes. In reality, though, he was just a man sometimes haunted by his past and the resulting invisible scars of his kidnapping. He was a man without a family, and even now, years later, he was still trying to heal from that.

"All this must have cost a fortune."

Beyond what he and Cooper could have come up with. "Gray funded it all." And had refused to accept his and Cooper's offer to repay him over time. Liam headed to the corner where they had a kitchenette with a mini fridge, microwave, and sink. "Do you want something to drink? We've got water, sodas, beer, or I could brew a pot of coffee."

"Water's fine."

"Sorry," Grayson said, walking into the room with his laptop in one hand. "I got held up on the phone. Good to see you again, Quinn."

"Thanks. It's been a bit exciting recently."

Liam snorted. "Only you would think getting shot at by bad guys is exciting." He handed her a bottle of water.

"I didn't say it was fun exciting. I can definitely do without people shooting at me."

"You got shot at?" Grayson said.

"We sure did," she said.

While she told Grayson about the men who'd shown up at her house, Liam pulled out a chair and motioned for her to sit. He took the seat next to her, and Grayson settled across from them. Grayson already knew the men had guns and had used them. Liam had told him that when he'd called in, but his teammate grasped that this was a new experience for Quinn and that she was eager to tell him the story.

"And they didn't even hurt my car, so that was good."

"Sorry about having to leave your car behind," Liam said.

"Not a problem. Vic's already brought it to my Savannah dealership." Regret filled his eyes as he focused on Quinn. "I am sorry to have to tell you that they tore your house apart."

She sighed. "I figured they would. We have a woman who takes care of the house when my dad's away. I'll call her today and get her to go over and clean up as best she can."

"Let us know when she'll be there," Liam said. "We'll have Vic and Mason be there when she is, just in case."

"You think those men might come back? I don't want to put her in danger."

"They probably won't, but we'd rather err on the safe side."

"Y'all are pretty awesome, you know? Thank you."

"We aim to please." He got a little lost in those green eyes shining up at him, and they stared at each other until Grayson cleared his throat. Right, they were here to go over what they had so far. When he glanced across the table at his teammate, Grayson smirked, his amusement obvious. Liam shrugged. What could he say? He wasn't going to deny his interest in Quinn.

It wasn't that long ago that Grayson was falling in love

with Harlow while protecting her and her son from her ex-husband, a man as evil as they came. Maybe Grayson could give him some advice when he got a chance to talk to his friend alone.

Until then, back to business. Liam took the thumb drive from his pocket and slid it across the table to Grayson. "Your turn to keep this safe. What were you able to find out about Garrison?"

"Nothing particularly remarkable about the man. Thirty-two years old, a photojournalist who likes to put himself in his stories. If you look at his published photos, he's in many of them."

"That's true," Quinn said. "He loves the attention."

Liam twirled his chair to the side, facing her. "Unlike you. You're not in any of yours." He knew because he'd deep dived into her published photos, his amazement of her talent growing with each one he viewed.

"Because I'm not the story. The children are."

"You are very good at what you do," Grayson said. "Your photos have a way of tugging at the heart of the viewer."

Liam nodded. "Makes one ask what they can do to help those children."

"That's my goal. Back to Jasper, what else did you learn?"

Grayson's gaze shifted over his laptop screen. "Nothing spectacular about him or his work. He has gotten some good up-close photos of fires, some war zones, and natural disasters, just not anything that's won him any awards."

Quinn frowned. "Really? He told me he's won awards."

"Not any that I could find. He has one DUI arrest from when he was twenty-one. That happened the night of his birthday. Guess he was out celebrating. Other than that, no record. There really isn't anything interesting on him."

"I could've told you that," Quinn said.

Liam didn't like thinking of her with Garrison, but the questions that needed to be asked couldn't be avoided. "How long were you...ah, with him?"

"Almost three weeks. He was fun at first, but then he started getting weird."

"How so?" Grayson asked.

"Demanding. Possessive. Jealous. He thought his work was important, mine not so much. After all, he was getting up-close shots of a massive wildfire while I was just taking pictures of children."

Another man in her life who'd proved her point. "Not all men are like that, Quinn." He wasn't.

"So you say."

They'd veered off onto a road he didn't want to travel, especially not in front of Grayson, who was watching them with curiosity. How hard was she dug in on that belief that all men were alike? Would he ever be able to prove to her that he was different? Was he willing to put in the time and effort if there wasn't hope for mission success? All questions he didn't know the answer to.

"Moving on," Grayson said as he inserted the drive into the computer. "Let's watch what's on here one more time while we're together, then I'll tell you what I learned about the textile mill."

The video appeared on all the monitors around the table. Liam focused on the screen, looking for anything he'd missed the first time around. He hadn't counted the drums, and he did so now. There were sixteen of them. How often did whatever was in the barrels get dumped into the lake?

"We need to find out if this is a onetime thing or something they do on the regular," he said. "Although, with Garrison attempting to blackmail someone with what's on this thumb drive, I'd say it's something they do on the regular."

"Agreed," Grayson said. "Cooper's bringing us samples from the lake we can send to a lab. Find out if the lake is contaminated and if so, by what."

"These drums are from that textile mill?" Quinn asked.

"Probably. We'll find out for sure." Liam watched the man on the video roll the empty drum aside, then he pushed over another one. "Who do you think Garrison was talking to on that conversation you overheard?"

She lifted her shoulders in a shrug. "I don't know who he expected to get money from or who he was talking to. It did sound like he was talking to a friend."

"The question is, is that who killed Garrison, maybe didn't want to share a million dollars?" Grayson said.

Liam shook his head. "That doesn't feel right. The men who showed up at Quinn's were professionals, and there were four of them in two Chevy Suburbans. Bodyguard cars. Going on the assumption that only Garrison and a friend, or maybe a family member, were working together—"

"Professionals? Like hit men?" Quinn said. "Unbelievable. This is like a bad movie."

Liam smiled. "Just keep in mind that the bad guys always lose, and the good guys live to see another day."

"I think Garrison and whoever was in this with him got in over their heads," Grayson said. "Messed with someone more powerful and dangerous than they could imagine."

Liam nodded. "That's my thinking. Anything on that license plate number I gave you?"

"Not yet. It belongs to what appears to be a shell company. It might take a little time to follow the trail back to whoever's behind it."

"I kind of know the concept of a shell company, but what is it exactly?" Quinn asked.

"Easy answer," Liam said, "it's a company or companies within companies set up to mask the true identity of the individual or individuals behind it."

"Is that legal?"

"Sometimes they're legit, sometimes not. I wouldn't be surprised to find this one isn't." He glanced at Grayson. "What did you find out about Hanson Textiles?"

"Something interesting. Hanson Textiles is owned by Senator Charles Hanson's family. The mill is the biggest employer in the county. The senator sits on numerous committees, is serving his fourth term, and is on the short list of vice presidential candidates in the upcoming election."

Liam whistled. "In other words, powerful and has much to protect. He'd also have the connections and money to hire the kind of men who showed up at Quinn's house."

"Exactly," Grayson said.

Quinn groaned. "This just gets worse and worse."

No, it just got more interesting. From the expression on Grayson's face, his teammate agreed. They'd never gone after anyone as powerful as Hanson, not in civilian life, but they were trained to beat the odds. With careful planning and execution, they could win this battle…if it was indeed the senator at the wheel of a murder. More than that to Liam was they'd scared Quinn. The senator would go down for that alone if those men were his hired guns.

Chapter 18

Like Cher, Quinn wished she could turn back time. But would she do anything differently, knowing whatever was being dumped in that lake was making children sick? What if children started dying? No, she'd do the same thing all over again.

If she hadn't accidentally taken the thumb drive and hadn't heard Jasper's phone conversation, there would be no one to stop the illegal dumping. Because both those things had happened, she'd ended up with three formidable men at her back, one of whom had probably saved her life.

Whoever was hurting those children had to be stopped, even if it was a powerful senator. "So, what do we do now?" She didn't miss the glance exchanged between Liam and Grayson, and if they thought they were going to keep her out of this, they could think again.

"I understand your father's in Asheville, where he has a vacation home?" Grayson said.

"Maggie Valley, actually, but close enough." She knew where he was going with this, but she'd let him say it before she told him what he could do with his suggestion.

Grayson tapped a finger against his lips, then said, "I don't suppose you'd consider staying with him for a while?"

When Liam snorted, she almost smiled. That he got her gave her the warm fuzzies. "I don't suppose I will. So, again I ask, what do we do now?"

"Now we take your car to Grayson's dealership, where they'll keep it until this is over, pick up another car, and then go get some dinner," Liam said.

Grayson scowled. "You need to stop losing my cars, brother."

"He loves me," Liam whispered loudly enough for Grayson to hear.

"So you say." Grayson removed the thumb drive from his laptop. "I'll put this in the safe." He stood. "Cooper's coming back tonight. Let's plan to meet at my house for breakfast in the morning. Nine o'clock good?"

Liam glanced at her, his brows raised.

"Sounds good." She eased out of her chair. "Thanks for hiding my car. She's my baby."

Grayson walked to the window and peered down at the parking lot. "Is it that Porsche?"

"Yes, a present from my dad."

"Nice. I'll call the dealership and tell them to have a car ready for you." He lifted a hand as he walked out. "See you kids in the morning."

"He's really nice," she said when they were alone.

"Yep." Liam stepped in front of her. "But I'm even nicer."

"And sexier." She trailed her finger down the front of his shirt. "Maybe."

"Maybe?"

"Well, that's my impression, but I could be wrong." She shrugged as if she wasn't sure, then walked out of the war room.

"Where're you going?" he said from close behind her.

"To hide my car so you can get busy proving I'm not wrong." She inwardly smiled when he grabbed her hand and urged her to walk faster.

They traded her car for a used white Mercedes SUV that would blend in with other cars on the road. The sales manager assured them that the Porsche would be hidden in a warehouse they had on the property.

Since they didn't feel like eating out, they stopped at a small, hole-in-the-wall Italian place that Liam promised had the best pizzas in town and ordered a large one to go. When she asked for a meat lover's with extra cheese, Liam declared her the best date in the world.

After quick showers—him in his bathroom and her in the guest bath—because they both felt grimy, they were now sitting on his balcony. Each with a craft beer and the large pizza on the table in front of them, they were eating as if they hadn't had a meal in a week. In all the excitement of getting shot at, they had missed lunch and were starving.

"You're right. This pizza is soooo good. I can't believe I ate four pieces." She licked her fingers.

"I'm done, too." He closed the lid on the pizza box. "Another beer?"

"No, thanks." She held up her bottle. "Mine's still half-full."

"Hold on to your beer."

"Eeep," she squeaked when he scooped her up from the balcony table where they'd sat to eat their dinner. He carried her over to a chaise longue with no more effort than it took her to carry a sack of groceries. Who knew a man carrying her would be such a turn-on? "You Tarzan, me Jane," she said with a giggle when he let her feet fall to the floor.

His eyes gleamed with amusement as he stared down at her. "Should I be wearing a loincloth?"

"Yes, please."

He laughed as he settled onto the chaise, then he pulled her down so that she was sitting in front of him, her back to his chest. "I'd wear one for you." He kissed the side of her neck.

Shivers traveled across her skin at the touch of his lips, and she arched her neck, giving him access. She'd wanted him from the day they'd sat by the stream and he'd gently doctored her feet. With all that had happened since then, it felt like that was ages ago. But finally, he was going to be hers for as long as this thing between them lasted.

He sat back, taking his mouth away. She wanted to protest, to beg him to go on with what he was doing. "Don't stop," she said.

"Watch the sunset." He slid his arms around her waist and rested his chin on her head.

She'd rather have his mouth back on her, but she lifted her gaze to the sky. "Oh, wow."

"Hmm," he hummed next to her ear. "Beautiful."

Without even looking at him, she knew that his eyes were on her and he didn't mean the sunset. She smiled, loving this moment with his arms around her, the gentle sound of the waves lapping onshore, and the soft breeze caressing her face. It struck her that Liam was romancing her, and it was a new experience. She'd never been romanced before, not even by Aiden. He'd been too busy with his medical career to think about romancing her.

As they watched the sun set to the west, the sky a brilliant painting of pinks, blues, and yellows, she changed her mind about living in the woods with Liam and growing potatoes. Instead, they'd live on a deserted island. He'd build them a hut house and fish for their dinner while she gathered coconuts and made coconut pies. After watching the sunset, they'd make love each night under a sky filled with glittering stars that looked like diamonds on black velvet.

Liam slipped his hands under her T-shirt, and as the sky grew dark and the scent of salt was heavy in the air, he danced his fingers over her stomach and up to the curve of her breasts. She softly sighed as she closed her eyes.

"You like that?" His mouth was next to her ear, his breath a warm tickle that gave her goose bumps.

"Yes." A thousand yeses.

"Give me your mouth."

She lifted her face.

"Such an obedient Little Marine," he said.

"Only for you."

"Good answer."

He kissed her then, softly, his lips brushing over hers, teasing, a little playful. Then the kiss grew demanding, possessive, and when his tongue sought entrance, she welcomed him in. He tasted delicious, and she lost herself in the desire for him building inside her. His hands covered her breasts, toying with them, igniting a fire that burned hotter with each touch of his fingers on her skin.

Suddenly, without Quinn quite knowing how he did it, he lifted her and turned her to face him. "Much better," he said as he positioned her legs so that she was straddling him. He took the bottle from her hand and set it on the table next to them. "Now kiss me."

"You're a bossy one. I like it." He'd told her to kiss him, so she did. He kept his hands on her hips but made no other move to try and control her. When she sucked his lower lip into her mouth, he groaned, and the sound of that low groan rippled through her.

His fingers tightened on her hips, and something about that possessive hold thrilled her. Heat coursed through her veins, fueled by the raw passion radiating from him.

"You're driving me crazy," he whispered, his voice low and husky, before capturing her mouth in another searing kiss.

"Good."

He chuckled, then surged up, bringing her with him. "Need a bed."

"A bed sounds lovely." She wrapped her arms around his neck as he carried her to his bedroom. When he began to lower her, she said, "Throw me."

He stilled, his eyes locking on hers. "Throw you?"

She nodded. "Like you're a barbarian about to take his spoils of battle…that would be me. The barbarian, that would be you, finds me hiding in a corner of my thatched-roof house, and your eyes light up at seeing such a pretty girl that is yours for the taking. So, take me you do. You bring me back to your home, throw me on the bed, and ravage me."

His mouth slowly curved up in a grin. "Your mind is…"

"Weird?" Sure, her imagination often ran wild, but she didn't like him thinking she was strange. Even if she was.

"I was going to say *fascinating*."

Okay. *Fascinating* was so much better than *weird*. She'd take it. She really hadn't meant to give voice to the movie playing in her mind. She'd never before given a man even a hint that she created these little scenarios in her head. They just appeared through no effort on her part. She did think she was a little weird.

His grin grew sly, and… He threw her!

She bounced on the bed, laughing and ridiculously happy. He came down on top of her, catching his weight on his elbows. "Hi," she whispered as she stared up into his beautiful blue eyes.

"Hi," he whispered back. "Did I pass the barbarian test?"

"You get a five-star review on Yelp."

"So, what does a barbarian do next?"

"Well, ravish me, of course."

"I can so do that."

And he did. Magnificently, in fact.

Chapter 19

Liam awoke to the feel of Quinn's body wrapped around his with her head on his chest. She was mumbling in her sleep, something about coconut pies. Smiling, he pressed his lips against the top of her head. Lord only knew what she was dreaming.

He tried to think of something he didn't like about her or that annoyed him, but he couldn't think of a thing. She was brave, funny, incredibly talented, and sexy as hell. They'd made love, and it had been amazing. She was comfortable in her body and her sexuality. She preferred to sleep in the nude. She loved pizza and beer. Pretty much the perfect woman, and he didn't want to give her up when what she insisted was only a *fling* came to an end. He didn't want to think of her not being in his life.

What he did want to think about...losing himself in her body again. He slid his hand down her bare back to one round butt cheek. "Sweet," he murmured. He shifted his body toward her and brought his other hand to her breast. They were on the small side, but they fit perfectly in his hands. He flicked his thumb over a nipple and got a soft moan.

The gray light of dawn chased away the night. He turned his head and eyed the clock. It was only six in the morning. He should let her sleep another hour, but he wanted... no, needed to bury himself inside her.

She stirred, her eyelids fluttering a little, then her eyes opened and met his. She smiled. "Good morning."

"Yes, it is, and it's about to get even better." He trailed kisses down her neck to her shoulders. "Do you want this? Me?"

She rubbed against him. "Morning sex is the best."

The perfect woman. He dipped his fingers between her legs. "I love how wet you are, and it's just for me."

She lowered her hand to his erection and wrapped her fingers around him. "I love how hard you are, and it's just for me."

"You got that right." He nuzzled her neck. "I want to be inside you right now, but if you need a little foreplay, we can start with that."

"You foreplayed me enough last night to carry some over to this morning. Just slide right on in, hot stuff."

How could he not laugh? This woman was something else. She checked all his boxes and some boxes he didn't even know to wish for. He reached over to the night table where there were still a few condom packages left from the night before.

"Let me." She took the condom from him and scooted to her knees between his legs.

He put his hands behind his head and watched her. Her tongue stuck out to the side as she concentrated on rolling the condom on him, and when she finished, she looked up at him and grinned.

"All covered up and ready for me."

Was he ever. "Ride me, Quinn."

Her eyes lit with pleasure, and she lifted and moved up

until she was positioned over him. "Giddyap," she cried out as she slid down on him.

When they'd made love earlier, it had been deep and emotional, both of them stunned by the hot and heavy chemistry between them. Well, he had been anyway, and he was pretty sure she'd felt it, too.

This morning, she was full of fun with mischief shining in her eyes. He let her play until he was on the verge of climaxing. When he was close, he flipped them so that his body covered hers. "Playtime's over." He rested on his elbows and put his hands along the sides of her face. "Beautiful girl." And for now, his.

Her eyes softened, and she ran her fingers through his hair. "Beautiful boy."

"Let's make some magic." He kissed one corner of her mouth, and then the other. When she parted her lips, he slid his tongue inside, and with their bodies joined, he began to move. Their rhythm built, and their movements became more frenzied, their hearts beating in sync, their lovemaking raw and untamed.

Her fingers dug into his back as she gasped his name, and he let go, joining her as she arched up, her body trembling with the aftershocks of her climax. He buried his face against her neck, put his mouth on her throbbing pulse, and felt his heart pounding as hard as hers.

"Wow," she said. She gave him a soft smile as she nestled her head against his chest. "Did you see stars?"

"Still seeing them." He wrapped his arms around her and rolled them over so they were on their sides. As his heart slowed back to its normal rhythm, contentment washed over him. Surely she felt this connection between them, but he didn't ask, too afraid she'd dig in on her insistence that this was nothing more than a fling, soon to be over.

The trick was to consider this a mission, the end result being to win her heart. He would not fail.

They arrived at Grayson's ten minutes late. He blamed their lateness on the shower they'd taken together. Not that he was going to share that with Grayson.

"Good to see you again, Quinn," Grayson said after opening the door to them. "Harlow's dropping Tyler off at school and should return any minute. Come on back."

"What about me?" Liam asked.

Grayson raised his brows. "What about you what?"

"Isn't it good to see me again?"

"You're a needy one this morning, but if it makes you happy, sure, it's good to see you again." Grayson smirked. "Happy now?"

"Ecstatically so," Liam answered with a silly grin. "Love you, too, bro."

Grayson leaned close to Quinn. "The boy's a cute one, isn't he?" he stage-whispered.

"He is, but don't tell him I said so," she said, also stage-whispering. "It might go to his head."

"You two are hilarious." He slung his arm around Quinn's shoulders. "Come here, you." She tucked herself into his side, right where he liked her. If she didn't have a dangerous threat hanging over her that they needed to discuss and make a plan for keeping her safe, he'd turn her right around and take her back home, where he'd spend the day loving on her. But keeping her safe was the only thing that mattered, so he didn't throw her over his shoulder like a caveman and carry her off to his lair.

Grayson's phone dinged, and after reading what was on the screen, he said, "Cooper's on the way. You two go on out to the deck while I finish up breakfast."

"Can I help?" Quinn asked.

"Thanks, but it's pretty much done. Go enjoy a morning on the beach."

"Well, hello. Who are you?" She bent over to pet the cat winding around her feet and talking up a storm.

"That's Einstein," Liam said. "He always has a lot to say."

"Nice to meet you, Einstein. You're a fine-looking boy."

"And he knows it," Grayson said. "He'll talk to you all day if you let him. Go on out to the deck and enjoy the beautiful morning."

Quinn gave him one last pet. "I'll come talk to you later."

"This is awesome," she said when they stepped out on the large deck. "I want to live on the beach."

His place was on the beach. She could come live with him. A few minutes after he and Quinn were seated, Cooper came around to the back of the house. "What's that?" Liam asked as Cooper walked up the stairs to the deck.

Cooper glanced down at the creature that was glued to his leg. "Have you never seen a dog before?"

"Yes, but not one that looks like it was patched together like a quilt of many colors." The dog was seriously weird. Long-haired with a patch of black, another of brown, one golden, with some red and white thrown in. He'd never seen anything like it.

"Aww, he's strangely cute," Quinn said.

"She." Cooper put his hand on the top of the large dog's head. "She's on the lam and a bit afraid of everything."

"Who's on the lam?" Grayson said, joining them on the deck.

"Ruby."

"Who?" His gaze fell to the dog trying to hide behind Cooper's legs. "What the hell is that?"

Cooper rolled his eyes. "Has no one ever seen a dog before?"

"Are you sure that's a dog?" Grayson said. "And why is it on the lam?"

"Yes, it's a dog, and if you'll give me a minute to get a cup of coffee, I'll tell you Ruby's story. It's a good one."

"Harlow's here now and bringing out the coffeepot in a minute, as soon as she takes the breakfast casserole out of the oven."

"I'll go help her," Quinn said.

"That's why I came out, to tell everyone to come help." He pointed a finger at Cooper. "You, though, can stay out here with whatever that is, because that is not a dog."

"You're hurting Ruby's feelings. Tell her you're sorry."

Liam laughed when Grayson rolled his eyes before walking inside.

With everyone helping, it only took a few minutes to have the table on the deck set and the food and coffee brought out. Once they all had their coffee cups filled and food on their plates, Liam said, "Story time." He leaned back and glanced under the table, where Ruby was curled up in a tight ball next to Cooper's feet. "Why is Ruby on the lam?"

"Not sure, but I suspect she was being terribly mistreated. She's not in bad shape physically, no ribs showing or anything like that. I'm taking her to the vet this afternoon and getting her checked out to be sure. But I think she's been mentally abused, maybe even used to being hit. She shies away if you make a sudden move."

"Poor girl," Quinn said.

Grayson pointed his fork at Cooper. "How'd you come to have her?"

"Funny story. I was gassing the car up, getting ready to

leave Hope Corner. I'd left my door open, and here comes this animal..." He grinned. "At first glance, I honestly thought it was a wild boar or something. Then I saw the chain she was dragging and realized it was a dog. She jumped into the car and parked herself right on the passenger seat."

Harlow put her hand on her chest. "A chain? Like she'd been chained up?"

Cooper nodded. "Yeah. It was around her neck, and she was dragging about three feet of the chain. It wasn't a heavy one, and it looked like she'd pulled on it hard enough to break one of the links."

"Thinking of her chained up like that makes me want to cry," Quinn said.

Liam reached over and clasped her hand. She had to be thinking of being chained up herself and the fear and helplessness she'd experienced.

"I was trying to urge her to get out of the car when her ears suddenly perked up," Cooper said. "I looked up and saw a piece-of-junk pickup truck in dire need of a new muffler coming down the street. She whimpered, and let me tell you, it was about the saddest sound I've ever heard. She scrambled to the floor and tried to crawl under the seat. She could only fit her face just past her eyes under there, but I guess she thought she was hidden."

Liam glanced around the table and guessed that, like him, everyone was on the edge of their seat, waiting for the rest of the story.

"I got in the car and closed the door. As I was leaving, the pickup stopped next to me, and this dude with the meanest eyes I've ever seen wanted to know if I'd seen an ugly-assed dog. At the sound of his voice, Ruby whimpered, and afraid he was going to hear her, I told him I hadn't seen any dog, then took off."

"You saved her," Quinn said.

Cooper shrugged. "I guess I did. About a mile down the road, I pulled over. She was violently shaking, and I started softly talking to her. The Stones' 'Ruby Tuesday' came on the radio, and I just started calling her Ruby. She seemed to like it, so I guess that's her name now."

"I think it fits her," Quinn said.

Cooper nodded. "I looked up the lyrics to 'Ruby Tuesday' last night. There's a line in it, 'She just can't be chained,' and Ruby felt like the right name for her."

"What are you going to do with her?" Liam asked as he set his silverware on his empty plate.

"The only thing I can do. Keep her."

Quinn smiled at him. "You're a softy, Cooper."

"Only for pretty girls in dire need of a bath. She's getting the works at the vet, an exam, a bath, and toenails clipped. It's going to be traumatic for her, so I'm going to hang there with her." He looked at Quinn. "I need to leave for her appointment in about an hour, which leads to let's talk about your situation."

Harlow stood. "I'll clear the table while you guys talk."

"I can help," Quinn said.

Grayson pushed his chair back. "We all can."

"No," Harlow said. "Cooper needs to leave soon, and this is important. Sit. It won't take me long."

Quinn picked up her plate, handing it to Harlow. "Thank you. Breakfast was delicious."

"Yes, it was," Liam said, handing Harlow his plate. He sat back, thinking about how easily Quinn fit in with his friends. They all liked her, but then, she was easy to like. He was pretty sure she'd be easy to love, too.

Chapter 20

Quinn wished she didn't have to ruin a perfect morning with her new friends by talking about anything to do with Jasper. Temporary friends that was. When this was over, they'd go their way, and she'd go hers. She would miss them when that time came, especially Liam. If she was a different person, one who could be happy staying put and taking wedding photos or whatever, she'd open her mind to a possible future with him. But that wasn't who she was.

"I stopped by the office and left the water samples on your desk," Cooper said.

She pushed her musings aside and glanced up to see that Cooper was talking to Grayson. Getting the water samples was a big step forward. "How soon do you think it will take to find out if the water is contaminated, and if so, what's in those barrels?"

"Normally one to two weeks," Grayson said. "But I pulled in a favor, and we'll get the results back in a few days."

"I hate the waiting part," she said. "I really want to know what they're dumping in that lake. If it's something that's making children in that area sick, we need to notify the Environmental Protection Agency as soon as possible. They'll be able to find any sick kids."

"While we wait, we need to find out if there's a connection between the men who showed up at Quinn's and Senator Hanson," Liam said.

"I want to go back to Hope Corner and get some more pictures. We have the photos from Jasper, but what if we can get photos with those kinds of drums located at the mill? It would be another link to who the drums belonged to."

"That's not a bad idea," Liam said.

She beamed at him. She'd expected him and the others to tell her that it was in fact a bad idea. He kept surprising her in the best kind of way.

"You do plan to go with her?" Grayson said, his gaze on Liam.

Liam scowled as if the question was ridiculous. "Do you really have to ask?"

Wow, no pushback from any of them on her returning to Hope Corner. Who were these guys?

"I really did," Grayson said with a smile as he looked at her. "I was just checking that I was reading the room right."

"Huh?" What did he mean?

"You're reading the room perfectly," Liam said.

Both men exchanged a smile she didn't understand, but they weren't fighting her on going back, and that was all she cared about.

Harlow returned, taking her seat next to Grayson. "What'd I miss?"

"An interesting development." Grayson leaned over and gave her a quick kiss. "I'll fill you in later."

She still didn't know what they were talking about, but her mind was on the things she wanted to do when she returned to Hope Corner. Along with the photos she wanted of the drums and their locations, she'd like to get pictures of children playing in the lake.

"Ruby and I are off to the vet," Cooper said as he stood. Ruby moved with him as he stepped away from the table.

"Oh, Einstein got out," Harlow said, jumping up. "No, Einstein, no!"

The cat swerved to stay out of Harlow's reach as she tried to grab him. He ran straight to Ruby. Quinn held her breath, fearing they were about to witness a fight in which poor Ruby had no chance of winning.

Seeing the cat coming at her, Ruby dropped her belly and chin to the deck, closed her eyes, and made a sound of distress. Before anyone could get to Einstein, he stopped right in front of Ruby and sat. Then he started chattering to the dog. As he talked, he gently lowered a paw to the top of Ruby's nose and patted it.

Ruby opened one eye, then the other, and Quinn could swear she saw relief on Ruby's face that she wasn't being clawed to death.

"I'll be damned," Cooper said when Ruby lifted her head and stretched her leg out until she was touching Einstein's fur. She tentatively sniffed Einstein's outstretched paw as her tail made a slow sweep over the deck.

"Someone has a new friend." Quinn wished she'd brought her camera. Einstein was still talking to Ruby, and Ruby appeared to be raptly listening as her tail continued to swish across the deck. Didn't dogs wag their tails when they were happy? She'd never had a pet, so she didn't really know anything about them.

"Why don't you bring her back here after you finish at the vet's," Harlow said. "I think time with Einstein might be just what she needs."

"I'll do that." Cooper took a few steps back. "The question right now is, who will she choose? Me or Einstein?"

"I'd pick the cat," Liam said, making everyone laugh.

Cooper slapped his hand over his heart. "Harsh, brother."

Ruby's gaze swiveled from Einstein to Cooper, and then after one last look at the cat, she rose and hurried to Cooper's side.

"That's my girl," Cooper said. "Although, she might regret her choice when she finds out where she's going."

Einstein tried to follow them as they walked down the steps, and Harlow grabbed him. "You really don't want to go to the vet."

Two hours later, after a stop at The Phoenix Three for Liam to get some weapons and equipment he wanted and then back to his condo to pack, they were on the road to Hope Corner.

"This is nice," Quinn said when they arrived at the cabin Liam had rented. They hadn't wanted to stay at the same motel she had when she'd been here before or any motel, preferring to keep a low profile while in Hope Corner.

"I would never bring you to a not nice place." Liam set their bags down. "I'll get the groceries if you'll put everything away."

"Deal." They'd made a stop at the grocery store one town over so they wouldn't have to go out to eat. He brought in the cold food first, and she put everything in the refrigerator.

"That's the last of it," he said as he set three bags on the counter.

He unloaded the bags, and she put everything away in the pantry. For a cabin in the middle of nowhere, the kitchen was really nice with new stainless steel appliances and granite countertops. The first floor was an open concept with a view of the mountains out the floor-to-ceiling windows. The stone fireplace that went all the way up to the vaulted ceilings was stunning.

"Is that a creek?" She walked to the French doors. "It is. And a small waterfall."

Liam came up behind her and slipped his arms around her waist. "There's a grill and a table on the deck. Let's have our dinner out there."

"I'd love that."

He nuzzled her neck. "Are you in a hurry for dinner?"

"Depends on what you have in mind." She tilted her head, loving the feel of his mouth on her.

"I have in mind having you for a predinner treat."

"Hmm, I could be on board with that."

"Good answer." He scooped her up in his arms and carried her up the stairs without a single gasp for air. "Do you want me to throw you?" he said when he stopped at the bed.

"Yes, please." They'd need an air mattress on their deserted island so that after she finished making their coconut pies, he could toss her on it like a barbarian setting about the business of claiming his spoils, her being the spoils, of course.

"Commence throwing." He tossed her into the air.

She laughed as she bounced on the mattress. Liam O'Rourke might be the coolest guy on the planet to humor her in her secret fantasy of being dominated by a really hot guy. Maybe she'd eventually get up the nerve to tell him the rest of her fantasy.

Also, dinner was very late, but she wasn't complaining.

Chapter 21

The sun was peeking over the top of the mountain when Liam woke up. He then spent the next twenty minutes watching Quinn sleep. She was on her side facing him, both hands tucked up under her chin. Her hair was a wild mess covering her pillow, and he took satisfaction knowing that he was the cause of that wild mess.

She had a smattering of freckles across her nose she said she hated. Why, he didn't understand because he thought they were adorable. A slight smile was on her face, and her lips were moving as she murmured something unintelligible. Maybe she was dreaming about him.

He thought about waking her up for a little morning sex, but they'd been up half the night making love. She needed her sleep. He placed a soft kiss on her cheek, then eased out of bed. By the time she came downstairs an hour later, he had coffee brewed, scrambled eggs ready to cook, and bread in the toaster.

"Do I smell coffee?"

"You sure do." He poured a cup and doctored it just the way she liked it, one sugar and enough cream to turn the coffee milky white.

She took the cup from him and brought it to her nose, inhaling the aroma. "You're awesome."

He was trying to be. "What's the agenda for the day?" This was her trip, and he wanted to show her that he was cool with her being the boss.

"Since it's summer and the kids are out of school, I'm hoping we can get some photos of kids playing in the lake. This afternoon is probably better for that. Let's start with checking out the mill, get some pictures there, and if we're lucky, of some of those drums."

"Sounds like a plan."

After breakfast, he googled the mill's address, and when they got in the car, entered the address in the GPS. "Twelve miles from here. We'll do a drive-by, get the lay of the land."

The drive to the mill took them through Hope Corner. Because they'd both been here, to help disguise their appearances, they wore ball caps—her hair tucked up under hers—and sunglasses. Just tourists out to see the sights. Not that there was a lot to see. But there were a dozen or so cabins for rent on the town's only Realtor's website, so they did get tourists.

"If we're questioned, our cover story is that we're on our honeymoon," he said.

"Well, hello, husband." She grinned at him.

"Hello, wifey." He winked at her.

"Don't you dare call me wifey in front of anyone."

He laughed. "But I can in private?"

"No, you cannot. I have a name. Use it."

"Yes, ma'am. Just curious, but what's your aversion to pet names."

"They're silly. Like you'd want to be called a silly name."

"I wouldn't mind it so much if it was you doing it."

"So you'd be okay with love nugget or pookie?"

He laugh-snorted. "I'd hope you'd come up with ones better than that."

"What was your Marine nickname?"

"Irish, not very original."

"Maybe that's what I'll call you."

She could call him anything she wanted as long as she called him. "I guess I should stop calling you Little Marine."

"For some reason I can't comprehend since I have such strong feelings about pet names, I kind of like that one."

"Good to know. Target coming up on the left."

"It's bigger than I expected," she whispered.

"You do know you don't have to whisper right now?" He grinned when she punched his arm. "Little Marine's got muscles."

"Damn straight." She flexed her arm, showing off her muscles.

"We'll drive by it. Maybe there's a place to park nearby where the car won't stand out." A few blocks past the mill, they came to a strip shopping center, and he pulled in. "There's a diner. Let's get coffees to go and walk around." He parked between two other cars at the end of the lot, closest to the mill.

They walked past an insurance agency and a Laundromat before reaching the diner. When they entered, the five people scattered around stared at them. He tagged them as breakfast regulars not used to seeing strangers in their restaurant. They would be remembered, but that was okay. No one would be asking about them.

"Good morning," he said to the woman behind the counter. She looked to be in her sixties with gray hair held back in a tight bun and kind but tired eyes.

She smiled. "Good morning. Do you want a table?"

"No, ma'am. We'd like two coffees to go, and maybe a couple of those breakfast pastries. They look delicious."

"I can rightly say they are, since I baked them fresh only a few hours ago."

He put his arm around Quinn's shoulders. "What would you like, sugar?" She ground her heel on his toe, and he bit back a laugh.

"Well, that cheese Danish looks amazing, but so does the apple muffin."

"Then let's just get you both, sweetie." She elbowed his side, and he snorted, then coughed to cover the snort. "My wife will have those two, and is that a cinnamon coffee cake?"

"Cinnamon and walnuts, and it's a favorite."

"Awesome. I'll have one of those and a dozen assorted doughnut holes." He glanced out the window. "It's a beautiful morning. Is there a park nearby where we can enjoy our breakfast?"

"There's one at the lake," the woman said as she poured their coffee. "You just go about a half mile past the mill, and you'll see a sign on your left directing you to the park. You folks on vacation?"

He smiled at his lovely wife. "My honey bear and I are on our honeymoon." He smirked, and she glared back at him. He was going to pay for this, but he did love that riled-up fire in her eyes.

"Isn't my pookie the cutest thing ever?" She beamed at the woman as she stomped on his foot again.

The woman handed over their coffee and pastries. "The cutest thing ever is a puppy." She studied him for a moment. "Now, if you said he was a handful, I'd have to agree with you. Good luck with him."

Quinn laughed, and after they exited the diner, said, "You got that right, lady."

"Hey now. Don't be talking about your husband like that. Besides, you can't be mad I called you honey bear. That wasn't you I was talking to. It was my imaginary wife who happens to love my little pet names for her."

"You're ridiculous."

"What I am is the best pretend husband you'll ever have, who just happens to be hot in bed. Go ahead. Try to deny that."

She rolled her eyes but couldn't stop a grin. "You have me there."

"Here's a secret." He leaned his mouth close to her ear. "I'd like to have you here, there, and everywhere."

"You're starting to sound like Dr. Seuss."

"Dr. Seuss wishes he could come up with lines like mine. But hey, if you're not into cheesy rhymes, I can always switch to Shakespearean sonnets. 'Shall I compare thee to a summer's day?'"

She was trying to pretend he wasn't amusing her, but he could see the laughter in her eyes. He'd read somewhere that women loved a man who could make them laugh, and he'd take all the help he could get.

Chapter 22

It wasn't the first time that Quinn thought the man needed to stop being so amusing. It hadn't been easy, but she'd managed not to give him the satisfaction of laughing. She liked him so much it wasn't funny.

The day really was beautiful. Much cooler in the mountains than at home in Savannah or even in Myrtle Beach. "Are we going to walk awhile or drive to the park?"

He shrugged. "It's your operation. Just waiting for my orders."

This man just kept surprising her. "Let's walk awhile. See how close we can get to the mill without being noticed."

A high school was between the strip center and the mill, and a group of teens were playing a game of volleyball. She'd finished eating the cheese pastry and only had her coffee in her hand.

Liam held out the white bag. "Want the muffin now or some doughnut holes?"

"Maybe later. Hold this a sec." She handed him her coffee so she could get her Nikon out of her purse. She took back the cup, drank the last of her coffee, and then crushed the cup.

"Here, I'll hold that while you do your thing."

She gave it to him. "You're a great photographer's assistant."

"Totally indispensable, eh?"

"For now."

"Tough crowd," he muttered, making her laugh.

She glanced around and, seeing no one was paying attention to them, she snapped some photos of the school, the kids, and in the far background, the mill.

His phone chimed, and after taking it out of his pocket, he showed her the screen before answering Grayson's call. "You got me." As he listened, his expression hardened, and his eyes turned cold.

That was his warrior face, and fascinated by the sudden change in him from a goofy pretend husband to a battle-ready Marine, she lifted her camera to her eye and snapped pictures of him.

After a lengthy call where he mostly listened, he put his phone back in his pocket. His gaze was distant, as if he was mulling things over.

"What was that about?"

"That was Gray. His car that we left at your house when we ran, his service manager found a tracking device on it."

"How did that happen?"

"We assume they put it on before they broke in, before we left."

"So, what does that mean?"

"Right now, only that they know the car was taken to Gray's Savannah dealership, but we can't discount that they made a note of the license plate number. That means they'll learn the car is a dealer's loaner out of his Myrtle Beach dealership."

"That's not good. That's all they can find out, though, right? That it belongs to the dealership."

"Depends on how smart they are. It won't take much to connect the dealership to Gray and Gray to The Phoenix Three.

"He also said he did a deep dive on Garrison. Turns out Garrison has a cousin who lives in Hope Corner. Name's Joey Garrison. Their fathers were brothers. My guess is that Garrison was visiting his cousin and stumbled on the illegal dumping."

"Oh. And you think the conversation I overheard was Jasper talking to Joey?"

"Exactly." He put his hand on her lower back. "Let's start walking before we draw attention just standing here."

Were people already watching them? The mill was just ahead, and she slowed. The sidewalk they were walking on ended on this side of the street. "Will we look suspicious walking past it?"

"Not if we play it right."

"What do you mean?"

He handed her the muffin. "Who's going to suspect an infatuated couple out for a stroll while eating their goodies?"

"I'd like to get a picture of the mill."

"Wait until we're across from the entrance."

"Okay." She bit into the muffin. "This is delicious. Want a bite?"

"I'd rather have a bite of you, but I'll settle for your muffin."

She giggled as she held it out to him. "That almost sounds dirty."

"You want dirty? All you have to do is ask."

"I just might do that."

After taking a bite, he put his arm around her shoulders.

"That is good. Let's stop and get a selfie. Is your camera set where I can just push a button?"

She changed the setting to auto mode, then pointed to the button he needed to press. "It's that one."

"Okay, turn your back to the mill."

He held the Nikon up. "Smile." The camera wasn't aiming at them, but just over their shoulders. After taking several pictures, each time slightly moving the camera angle to get different parts of the mill, he said, "There's a man standing at the entrance watching us." Before she could answer and still clicking the button, he kissed her.

Chapter 23

Liam angled the camera to get a picture of the man watching them, and then he took one of him kissing Quinn. That one he took for himself. It was time to move on, though, before they drew any more attention. "Don't look at the man or the mill," he murmured against her lips. He lifted his head and smiled at her. "We need to go."

"Is he still watching us?"

"Yep." It could be nothing, but his gut said the man had more interest in them than normal. From the corner of his eye, he could see that the man watched them until they disappeared. Just curiosity or suspicion? He risked a glance at the windows on the side of the mill. Good, no one inside the building seemed to be paying them any attention.

"Liam," she said.

The urgency in her voice had him looking around them for the threat. "What?"

"Look over there. Are those the same two cars that showed up at my house?"

There was a parking lot behind the mill, probably for employees, and parked side by side in front of an entrance door were two white Suburbans. "I'm guessing so, but we need to get pictures of the tags to be sure."

"If I can get a clear shot from behind them, I can zoom in."

The lot was fenced in, so they couldn't just mosey over. He scanned the area around them. "Let's go over there." He pointed to a tree that was just outside the corner of the fence.

"I can't see the license plates from here," she said.

"Show me how to zoom in." After she did, he said, "Keep an eye out." The tree had a low branch, and he pulled himself up to it. "Hand me the camera." From his vantage point, he was able to zoom in over the top of the other cars and get a clear shot of both plates. He jumped down and gave her back the camera. "The car on the left has the plate number I memorized when we were being chased."

"Wow," she said. "We did it. We connected what's going on to the mill."

"And maybe a powerful senator."

"Yeah, that part makes me nervous. Like what have I gotten myself into?"

"Whatever it all turns out to be, you're not alone in this, Quinn. Let's head down to the lake before someone notices us hanging around here." At the entrance to the park, he tossed their empty coffee cups into a trash can.

"Do you think it would be safe to look for those drums?"

"The mill probably operates overnight shifts, but it should be safe enough to nose around after it gets dark." He slipped his hand around hers and walked them to a picnic table. They sat, facing the lake.

"It's pretty here." She lifted her camera and started snapping pictures of the lake and the surrounding area.

"Very pretty," he agreed, his eyes on her. He thought about standing on Grayson's deck and feeling envious of his relationship with Harlow. That he wanted someone special in his life, and that he just needed to find *her*. Had he? Was Quinn the one?

What was it about her that called so strongly to him? He thought about that for a minute and what he liked about her. It was nice that she really was pretty but *needs to be pretty* wasn't at the top of his list. She was feisty and would challenge him, keep him on his toes. He very much liked that about her. He admired her and what she stood for and who she was. When they made love, he had the sense that he'd found his home, something he'd never felt with another woman. He loved her smile and how her eyes would light up like glittering emeralds when she was happy or when she teased him. She was fearless but not reckless. She always smelled so damn good.

Things he didn't like about her... He drew a blank.

"No one's at the lake this morning," she said. "We need to come back this afternoon, see if there are any kids playing in the water I can get pictures of."

"Okay. Why don't we drive around a little, then go back to the cabin and have lunch. Come back here—" A white Suburban came into view, driving slowly. He put his hand on Quinn's cheek, turned her to face him, and kissed her. "We've got company," he said against her lips. Without trying to see for herself, she put her arms around his neck and kissed him back.

He had on sunglasses, so his eyes were hidden, and he was able to watch the car. Two men were in it, and both were looking their way. *Keep going. Nothing to see here.* The driver said something and both men laughed, then the car picked up speed and disappeared down the street.

He lingered for a moment with his mouth on hers, then reluctantly pulled away. "Let's go before they decide to come back."

It was a ten-minute walk back to the car, and they reached the Mercedes without incident. He needed to call

Grayson and let him know they'd confirmed the Suburbans were connected to the mill. He'd do that when they got back to the cabin.

Speaking of phone calls... "Did you have time to call and cancel your credit cards?"

"My dad's canceling my credit cards. I did call the DMV and reported my driver's license stolen. They're sending me another one."

"Should've known you'd be on top of things." He reached over and put his hand on her leg. "Want to be on top of me?" That got him an eye roll and a grin.

"You have a one-track mind, sir."

"Appears so where you're concerned. All your fault, Miss Sullivan."

"Well, maybe a little playtime after lunch before we go back to the lake would interest you?"

"The answer is yes, yes it would." He might've exceeded the speed limit to get back to the cabin.

Kids were playing in the water when they returned later that afternoon. To look like they were here to enjoy the lake, they'd changed into shorts and had brought towels to set on the sand.

"It's hard to sit here and stay quiet," Quinn said. "I want to tell them to get out of that water."

"Since we can't do that and risk the mission, we just have to prove the lake is contaminated so we can warn the town." There were five families enjoying a summer afternoon at the lake. He guessed the kids ranged in age from two or three years to sixteen or so. It was hard to stand by and not say anything. It was also possible there wasn't anything wrong with the water.

Quinn lifted her camera and started taking pictures. He

couldn't take his eyes off her. When her camera came up, she was in her element, and he didn't doubt that anything not in that viewfinder ceased to exist for her. He could take pictures that were just that, a picture, nothing special. He'd studied her work, and she had a keen eye for detail and composition that set her photos apart from those of an amateur. She impressed the hell out of him.

Since he'd forgotten to call Grayson when they returned to the cabin because a certain woman had wanted to play, he called his teammate while she took her pictures. Liam updated him on finding the Suburbans at the mill, then got an update from Grayson.

"Anything new?" she asked after he finished his call.

"Gray's still trying to trace the shell company back to the owner or owners. He said it's sophisticated and that there are layers and layers, which tells us it isn't a run-of-the-mill operation. There are powerful people behind it."

"Like a certain senator?"

"Quite possibly. He has made progress on developing a profile on Joey Garrison. He was a mechanic in the Army for three years until he was dishonorably discharged for stealing Humvee parts."

"Doesn't surprise me then that he and Jasper are cousins. Do you think he's the one who killed Jasper?"

"Hard to say at this point, but I don't feel like he's the one. From what Gray said, Joey doesn't have the smarts to pull their scheme off by himself. I think he needed his cousin for their plan to be successful, so he wouldn't have killed him. Or he wanted all the money for himself and did kill his cousin. Did you get all the pictures you wanted?"

"For now. Until we can come back tonight and see if we can find those drums."

"Good. Gray texted me Joey's address, so I thought we might do a drive-by."

They gathered their things and headed to the parking lot. Once in the car, he put in the address Grayson had sent him. "It's not far from here."

"How do you guys find these things out?"

"If I told you, I'd have to kill you." He gave her a sad face. "I'd miss you."

"I'd come back and haunt you."

"Now I'm afraid." Following the GPS's instructions, he turned onto Cow Creek Road.

"Fun name for a road."

"Small rural towns have some great road names." The GPS announced that they'd reached their destination, and he slowed as they drove by. The neighborhood was run-down, the small houses close together.

"Doesn't even look like anyone lives there," she said.

The yard was overgrown, and an old car missing its tires and back bumper was up on blocks in the driveway. "The windows are open, so someone must be around."

A man talking on a phone came around from the back of the house. The man had a full beard that could use a good trim, and he could also use a haircut and some clean clothes.

"Looks like he's been mud wrestling," Quinn said. "Do you think that's Joey?"

"Joey's twenty-seven. This guy looks like he's in his forties, so I'm thinking maybe not. Still want to go drum searching tonight?"

"Definitely. I wonder if there's a box store close by. I need to go shopping."

"What for?"

"You'll see." She got out her phone and after a few minutes of searching said, "There's one about thirty minutes from here. We've got time to go there."

What was she up to? At the store, she told him she'd meet him back at the front of the store in twenty minutes. Guess whatever she was up to would remain a mystery for now. When they returned to the cabin, she spent the evening getting her cameras and what she called her spy outfit ready. He spent it getting his weapons ready and worrying about keeping Quinn safe.

Chapter 24

"You look like a cat burglar." Liam's gaze traveled over her. "A very sexy one."

Quinn bowed. "Thank you, kind sir." She'd found everything she wanted on her shopping trip: a black, long-sleeved T-shirt, black leggings, black socks and running shoes (she sure hoped she didn't have to do any running, though), and a black knit beanie to hide her hair under. That had been her most important purchase since her red hair was memorable. Overkill maybe, but this was her first spy operation, and she wanted to be an invisible spy.

"Did you shop for black clothes, too?" He wore a black T-shirt and black jeans.

"No, brought them with me. Never know when you might need to blend into the shadows. Open your phone and give it to me."

She handed it to him. "What are you doing?"

"Adding a tracking app. I'm not going to let it happen, but I'm trained to prepare for the unexpected. If we should get separated, I want to be able to find you."

"Oh, good idea."

He handed her back the new phone he'd gotten her before they'd left Myrtle Beach. "You ready for this?"

"As ready as I can be. Do you have your gun?"

"Let's hope we don't need it, but..." He lifted his T-shirt to show her the gun holster on the right side of his belt and a knife holster on the left side. Then he lifted a pant leg to show her his ankle holster.

"You forgot to give me a gun when we were in Myrtle Beach."

"You just worry about taking pictures, and I'll worry about keeping you safe. Deal?"

"Deal." She held her hand up for a high five. Instead of high-fiving back, he wrapped his hand around hers and pulled her to him.

"I think a kiss for good luck is necessary."

"Is that so?"

"Yes, ma'am."

He lifted his hand to the back of her neck and lowered his mouth to hers. No one had ever kissed her the way Liam did. He had a way of kissing her that was soft yet demanding and possessive. It wasn't just that he was a great kisser, which he was, it was that he made her feel as if nothing and no one in this world mattered to him but her.

He pulled away and pressed his forehead to hers. "Want to blow off this op, get naked with me, and let me kiss my way from your toes to your nose?"

"Hmm." She gave him a quick peck on his lips. "Save that thought for later."

"You're no fun," he grumbled as he followed her to the car.

She only smiled because she had her back to him and he couldn't see.

Liam found a secluded stretch of land a mile from the mill where he was able to park the car so that it was hidden from the road. It took them fifteen minutes to fast walk to the mill, and Liam was right, they did operate a night shift. She stood next to him at the tree line, scanning the area around them.

All the windows were lit up, and there were cars in the parking lot. A small group of men and women were standing outside the entrance smoking cigarettes. "It must be break time."

"Yeah." He put his hand on her back. "Let's circle around the building."

It was dark, they were dressed in black, and were far enough away that no one noticed them. Even knowing that, Quinn's heart raced. If someone did see them, what would they do? Chase them? Call the police? "How do you stay so calm?"

"Training. It also helps knowing there's not an enemy sniper or two out there with me in their sights."

"Well, when you put it that way." There weren't any drums in the back that they could see, which was a disappointment. "Maybe they keep them inside." If so, it would be impossible to get photos of them.

"Maybe, but it appears like they have a good bit of property back here. Let's look around."

It took about ten minutes, but behind a shed set back in the trees, they found the drums. She counted sixteen of them. "Yes!" She pumped her fist in the air. "It feels like we found gold."

He chuckled. "Most women want flowers and candy. My girl just wants rusty barrels."

She should take umbrage at being called his girl, but she kind of liked it. She got her camera out of the fanny pack she'd bought with her spying outfit.

"You don't need light to take your pictures?"

"It would be nice to have light, but I don't need it, thanks to the light posts in the parking lot. I can work with that." She adjusted her camera settings, and when they were to her liking, she took her pictures. She got shots of all of the drums together, then up-close ones of several of them. For the last few, she backed up, wanting to get the drums with the mill in the background.

"All done," she said after she finished. "What are you doing?" He was prying open the lid on the top of a drum.

"This one's full. We can get a sample of what's in it to send to the lab. If the lake is contaminated, and the chemicals in here match, that's pretty good proof, don't you think?"

"You're so smart. You even thought to bring a vial. Where'd you get that?"

"At the store today while you were getting your spy clothes. Thought if we did find the drums, we might get lucky and find one that was full." After filling the vial, he stoppered it then handed it to her. "Put that in your pack."

As soon as her camera and the sample were put away, she said, "Let's get out of here before our luck runs out."

"Roger that."

They hadn't taken ten steps when their luck ran out.

"Stop unless you want to be shot," a man said, stepping around the shed, his gun aimed at them.

Oh, God. It was the man who'd shot at them when they were fleeing her home.

Liam shoved her behind him. "We don't want any trouble. We were down at the lake and got a little turned around trying to find our car."

"You think I fell off a turnip truck? I know who you are, and the little lady has something that doesn't belong to her. We want it back. There's no getting out of this."

She peeked around Liam's shoulder. "How would I have something of yours? I don't even know you."

"I'm not playing games here. Jasper said you have the thumb drive. I want it and the camera you had in your hands a few minutes ago."

What he didn't know was that she had her Nikon set to automatically store any photos she took in the cloud, so they'd still have the proof that the drums were here. He also didn't seem to know that they had a sample of what was in the drums.

Since she wasn't going to argue with a man pointing a gun at her, she unzipped her fanny pack, removed her camera, and tossed her very expensive Nikon to him. "It's all yours, but I can't give you what I don't have, and I don't have your thumb drive."

As the man reached his hand out, his attention on catching the camera with his free hand, Liam did some kind of body twist in midair and slammed his foot against the hand holding the gun. The weapon went flying, landing ten feet away. She rushed to it and grabbed it.

The two men were circling each other, but then Liam stopped and dropped his hands to his sides. He smirked at the man. "I'll give you a chance to walk away without a broken nose or worse. You should take it."

What was Liam doing? That man wasn't going to just walk away.

The man laughed. "You're a dead man. You just don't know it." He glanced at her. "And you and me, pretty lady, we're gonna have a little fun before I send you to hell with him."

Should she shoot him? She'd never wanted to shoot a person before, but she sure wasn't up for the kind of fun the man insinuated, and also, she'd do it to protect Liam.

As if he knew what she was thinking, he positioned himself between her and the man, taking away her chance to pull the trigger.

"You touch her, you die," Liam said in the coldest, deadliest voice she'd ever heard in her life.

The man growled and launched himself at Liam, aiming her Nikon at Liam's face.

"Liam," she gasped. He was going to let the man hit him with her camera, and that was going to hurt. Just as the Nikon was inches away from connecting with Liam's jaw, he ducked, and at the same time, he brought his fist up, landing an uppercut right into the man's gut. The man doubled over, wheezing as he tried to get air into his lungs. He dropped her camera, and Liam picked it up, tossing it to her. One hard hit to the man's jaw and he crumpled to the ground, out cold.

"Let's go," Liam said.

She was all for that. She handed Liam the man's gun, then dropped her camera into her fanny pack. He grabbed her hand, and they ran through the woods.

At the car, she put her hands on the hood and tried to catch her breath. "Not fair. You're not even breathing hard," she said.

He grinned. "I could give you mouth-to-mouth."

Did nothing faze this man? "We almost got killed and all you can think about is kissing me?" He'd been magnificent and seeing him in his element had been hot. She could have done without having a gun pointed at her, though.

"I think about kissing you all the time, and trust me, you didn't come close to getting killed. I wouldn't have allowed that to happen on my watch. Now, get in the car and let's get out of here before they come looking for us."

As they drove back to the cabin, he took her hand and put

it on his leg. "I'm proud of you. You did good back there. You need a reward."

"I think so, too, and I know just what I want."

"And what's that?"

"You. You're my reward."

"Oh, the sacrifices I make." He grinned at her. "But if you insist…"

Chapter 25

Liam recognized that Quinn was high on adrenaline, a common feeling after a tense or dangerous event, like having a gun pointed at her by a man who'd threatened to kill them. When the bastard said he would play with her first before killing her, he'd had to use every bit of his discipline not to tear the man's tongue out of his mouth.

He wasn't complaining, though. That adrenaline had turned her into a wildcat. Within seconds of entering the cabin, she turned to him, put her hands on his chest, and pushed him against the wall. He raised his brows. "Want something?"

She tugged on the hem of his T-shirt. "My reward and this off."

"Yes, ma'am." He pulled his shirt over his head and dropped it on the floor. "Now what?" Indecision was in her eyes, but he wasn't going to help her. He liked this game and wanted to see how far she'd take it.

"Now you ravish me."

"There's a word I can get behind. Tell me a fantasy you've had but never experienced."

"I have lots of fantasies I've never experienced."

"You stick with me long enough, and I'll give them all to you. For right now, tell me just one of them." He brushed his thumb over her bottom lip. "Make it one that really excites you."

"I've always wanted to be taken against the wall. The idea of it sounds hot, but I just don't see how it could really work. I think all those romance novels exaggerate how sexy it really is. I want to know if it's even possible."

"Stop talking." He crashed his mouth down on hers. He'd never had sex against the wall either, but he was determined to live up to those scenes in romance books. And yes, he'd read quite a few. When on deployment, during downtimes, when he was bored, he'd read anything he could get his hands on. Many of the guys would, and the women on base thought that was cool and would pass their romance books around.

He put his hands on the wall above her head and pressed his body against hers, trapping her between him and the wall. Her throaty moan went straight to his groin, and when she scraped her nails down his back, he growled and deepened the kiss. She arched against him, and damn, he'd never been this hot for a woman in his life.

"I need to feel your skin against mine," he said.

"Yes. Naked is good."

They shed their clothes with frantic haste, and thankfully, he was still coherent enough to remember to get a condom out of his wallet before dropping it and his pants to the floor. She watched him put the condom on, and seeing her eyes on him as she swiped her tongue over her lips almost sent him over the edge.

"You're the sexiest, most beautiful woman on the planet, Quinn. Are you ready for me?"

"I've been ready."

"Good, because I'm going to bury myself so deep inside

you, you're going to think we're one person. Wrap your legs around my hips."

She did, and he slid his arms under her bottom and held her close to him as he pressed her against the wall again. In this position, it was on him to do all the work since she didn't have room to move, and he was good with that. He thrust into her, pulled back, and did it again. Nothing in his life had felt this good. *Good* wasn't even the right word. Amazing. Incredible. Mind-blowing. Those were so much better words for how being inside her felt, and underneath those words was a feeling he never wanted to lose. He'd found his home, and it was with her.

She scraped her teeth along his shoulder. "I want to bite you."

"Do it." When her teeth clamped down on his skin, he almost lost it then and there. Only by sheer will did he hold off. "Can't wait much longer. Come for me, little vampire."

"Liam."

That was all she said, but it was how she whispered his name, as if he meant more to her than just the fling she kept insisting this thing between them was. He was done for. "Now, Quinn." He found her mouth and stroked his tongue over hers. Her body tensed, then shook as her climax crashed through her, driving his own release.

He let go of her mouth and buried his face against her neck as he struggled to get air back into his lungs. What just happened? He'd never come that hard, and before his legs—the same ones that could walk miles across the desert with eighty pounds of gear on his back without a quiver—threatened to quiver him right down to the floor in a heap with her on top of him... Before that could happen, he managed to get them to the couch, where he fell back, still holding her. He might never let her go. Never wanted to.

"You okay?" he said. She'd snuggled against his chest with her head resting in the crook of his neck.

"Better than." She gave a sigh of contentment. "You zapped all my energy. I think I'll sleep right here."

He refused to sound needy, so he didn't ask if what just happened was as good for her as it had been for him. But he wanted to because, eff him, he was feeling pretty damn needy right now.

When her breaths slowed and he realized she was asleep, he rose with her still wrapped around him and carried her to the bedroom. Lowering her to the bed, he pulled the cover over her, then kissed her cheek. "We have some talking to do," he quietly said. After what just happened between them, there was no way she could deny there was something between them. They were not going their separate ways when this was over because it would never be over.

He let her sleep for two hours while he gathered their things and had all but her bag set at the front door, waiting to be put in the car. That done, he made some sandwiches and packed them along with apples, chips, and bottles of water. He didn't want to make any stops on the road where their route home could be tracked. The remaining groceries they'd bought went into a trash bag. There was a bear-proof can at the end of the driveway, and he took the bag out to it.

They hadn't planned to leave for another day, but the men after her would be out looking for them even now. He had no intention of sticking around long enough for them to find her. It was time to wake her up, and he went into the bedroom. She was still asleep, all that magnificent red hair that he'd had wrapped around his fist spread over her pillow. One leg was out from under the covers, something he'd noticed before that she did when sleeping.

His girl did love her sleep. Affection for this woman

swelled in his chest, and he wanted nothing more than to crawl back into that bed and spend the day loving on her. The risk of being found was too high to stay any longer, though.

He sat on the edge of the mattress near her waist. "Quinn, wake up." He shook her shoulder. She mumbled something and burrowed deeper into the covers. He shook her again. "Up and at 'em."

She squinted her eyes open. "Still dark."

"I know, but it's not safe to stay here any longer. We need to go."

"'Kay." She closed her eyes and went back to sleep.

"Sorry about this." He pulled the covers off her, then the pillow out from under her head. "Up, Quinn." And…he'd forgotten she was naked. He briefly considered risking a few more hours at the cabin, but she was too important to take that kind of chance.

"I don't like you." She stuck her tongue out at him.

He grinned at that. "That's not what you were saying a few hours ago. In fact, I seem to recall these exact words. 'Oh, Liam, you're amazing. You're the best thing that's ever happened to me, Liam.' Admit it, you really like me."

"I never said any of that."

"Maybe not, but I know you thought it." He stood. "Up. We really do need to go."

"You're no fun," she grumbled as she rolled out of the bed.

"Not true. I'm the funnest guy you know. The bag with your clothes and girlie stuff is on the counter in the bathroom. I'll make us coffees to go while you get dressed."

He had their coffees made and in travel mugs he'd found in a cabinet by the time she walked into the kitchen. "Ready to go?"

"If we have to. I wish we could stay a few more days."

"Too risky. We got what we came for, pictures of the drums and the lake with children playing in it. Even got a sample of what's in the drums, which is a great bonus." He handed her the coffee mugs. "Carry these. I'll load our bags in the car."

It was a little after midnight when they drove away from the cabin, and there were only a few cars on the road. Liam tensed each time a car passed them, but no one paid any attention to them. He only relaxed when they made it to I-95 without incident.

"What if they move the drums before we can get the proper authorities involved?"

He pulled over to the left lane to pass a slower moving car. "Won't matter. We have plenty of proof with the thumb drive, your photos, and the samples from the drum and the lake."

"I'm ready for this to be over. I want my life back."

Did she include him in that picture? He wanted to talk to her about where they went from here, and the long trip home would give them plenty of time. Before he could bring up the subject of a future, she yawned. "Why don't you sleep for a little while," he said instead. "We've got about four hours before we get home."

"You don't mind?"

"Not at all."

"Thanks. I can barely keep my eyes open."

She reclined her seat, and within minutes, she was sound asleep. Although disappointed that he wasn't going to learn where they stood, maybe it was for the best. A better idea would be to bring it up at his condo. Tomorrow night, he'd romance her, make her a nice dinner, and then after, they could sit on his deck, drink a little wine, and talk. It was a much better plan.

Chapter 26

It was the morning after they'd arrived back in Myrtle Beach, and they were in The Phoenix Three's war room again. "The lab results came back on the lake water," Grayson said as he held up the vial containing the sample they'd taken from the drum. He eyed the colorless liquid. "The lab found concerning levels of PERC in the water."

"What's that?" Quinn asked.

Grayson set the vial on the table. "Tetrachloroethylene, a chemical commonly used by textile mills and dry cleaners. The chemical has been linked to several kinds of cancer both in adults and children. The EPA has proposed a ten-year phaseout of the chemical. It's definitely not anything a town wants to find in their lake water, and with the thumb drive, we can prove the mill dumped those barrels into the lake. That means serious trouble for them. Another concern is whether it's gotten into Hope Corner's drinking water."

"Wow, that's unconscionable that they would risk the lives of people like that, especially the children." No wonder whoever was after that thumb drive was desperate to get it back. She knew there were evil people in this world, but the thought of what the mill was doing made her sick to her stomach.

As if sensing her thoughts, Liam reached for her hand.

"With the lake water results and the sample we got from the drum—assuming the chemicals will be a match, which we do—along with your photos and the thumb drive, we have the proof we need to bring in the authorities."

"We can do that today?" She didn't want to wait another minute.

Grayson tapped the vial. "Let's get a report back from the lab on what's in the drums first. But we have another problem. You're wanted for questioning by the Hope Corner sheriff."

"Me? Why? Cooper got my suitcase, and he said my purse wasn't there for the police to find. He was going to wipe the cabin down so my fingerprints wouldn't be there. And how would they know to call you?"

"They didn't, the county sheriff put out an APB on you as a person of interest in a murder. I've been expecting something like that, so I have a friend in our police department who's been keeping an eye out for me should something like this happen."

"I still don't understand why they're looking for me if they don't know I was in the cabin."

"Since I wondered the same thing, I had your lawyer call the sheriff."

"My lawyer?"

"John Fowler, your attorney for dealing with the sheriff. He's one of the best criminal attorneys in the state."

"I'm not a criminal." She wasn't liking this at all.

"We know that, the sheriff doesn't. According to the sheriff, he received an anonymous phone call that you were in the cabin with Jasper. We have to assume the call was made by whoever killed Jasper."

"Do I have to talk to him?"

"It would be best to before they issue a warrant for your

arrest, which the sheriff threatened to do if you don't go in for questioning," Grayson said. "John told him you'll talk to him here, and he'll be with you for the interview."

"They'll want to talk to me, too, since I was there," Liam said.

She frowned. "They don't need to know that. What if they think you killed him?"

"We'll have to explain how you got away, so there's no way around involving me. Besides, you're my witness that I didn't kill him." Liam squeezed her hand. He glanced at Grayson. "I'm thinking we don't mention the contaminated water and drums. I hope not, but it's always possible someone in the sheriff's department there is…let's just say favorable to the mill and its owners. We say that Quinn had a short relationship with Garrison and after she broke it off, he stalked her and then kidnapped her."

"I agree," Grayson said. "I'll tell John to contact the sheriff today and make the arrangements."

"What if they insist I go there?"

"The answer will be no, and if they have a problem with that, I'll involve a friend of ours from the FBI."

"I don't like putting you guys in the middle of this. Maybe it would be better to meet somewhere besides here."

Grayson shook his head. "No, we want him to see that you're not alone and without protection. We want him to see us and The Phoenix Three. We're not a fly-by-night operation, and that's obvious to anyone who sees this place."

"A little intimidation isn't a bad thing," Liam said.

"I guess. So, why was I in Hope Corner if I'm not going to tell them the real reason?" Surely, they would ask her that.

"Easy," Liam said. "Your job is taking photos of children in need of help. You were there documenting the poverty the children of coal miners who've lost their jobs were living under. There is a coal mine that has been shut down not far from Hope Corner, so that story holds weight."

"Okay." Honestly, she didn't care about any of this. She just wanted the people making children sick brought to justice. And she wanted her life back. She was scheduled to leave for Ukraine in two weeks, and with everything going on, she'd almost forgotten about it and hadn't thought to tell Liam. It was a trip she had no intention of canceling.

The warmth of his hand still holding hers felt good, too good. As much as she wished otherwise, she wouldn't change her mind on no relationships. Her life wasn't one any man would put up with for long, even Liam, no matter how much he said otherwise.

There was regret, though, that it had to be this way. Men went off to war, some spent weeks working on oil rigs, smoke jumpers were gone during fire season, et cetera, et cetera. They all expected their women to be waiting for them back home. It wasn't fair, but it was the way it was.

"Where's Cooper?" Liam asked.

Grayson chuckled as he glanced at his watch. "Right about now, he's pacing the floor at the vet's office. Ruby's getting spayed today, and Coop's freaking out, afraid it's going to traumatize her."

Liam grimaced. "It would sure as hell traumatize me."

She laughed. Men were such wimps with anything that had to do with the family jewels. If they had to be the ones to push babies out of a tiny hole, there would be no babies.

"I've got some other news," Grayson said. "Harlow and I have set a date for our wedding. The first week of November. You all will, of course, be there. She wants a small beach wedding, just us and our friends. I'm taking her and Tyler to Hawaii for our honeymoon."

"Because surfing," Liam said.

Grayson shrugged. "It would just be wrong not to surf while we're there, but she's always wanted to go to Hawaii, and I live to make her happy."

That soft look in his eyes when he talked about his fiancée almost had Quinn envious. She'd never have a man live to make her happy, but then that was her choice, so no feeling sorry for herself.

"Congratulations," Liam said. "You're a lucky man."

"And well I know it." He pushed his chair back. "Anything else we need to discuss this morning?"

"Not from me," Liam said, and she shook her head when he glanced at her. "It's been an exhausting few days, so Quinn and I are just going to hang out at my place for the rest of the day. If anything new pops up, give me a call."

"Will do." Grayson nodded at her, then left.

"Want to go have a beach day with a little hanky-panky thrown in?"

She grinned. "Where do I sign up?"

After they ate lunch, Liam talked her into playing in the ocean for a bit, and when they came back inside, they showered together. There was hanky-panky involved. "You really know how to treat a lady," she said after they got out and he took the towel from her and dried her off.

"There's only one lady I'm interested in impressing."

"Oh? Who would that be?"

He wrapped the towel around her and tucked in the end, and then he tapped her on the nose. "Such a silly question. After you get dressed, let's sit out on the deck and watch the sunset."

"I'd like that. Give me a few minutes to get the tangles out of my hair."

"While you're doing that, I'm going to pour us some wine and make us a snack. Meet you on the deck."

He'd wrapped a towel around his waist, and as he walked out of the bathroom, she sighed at the view. She'd had her hands all over that amazing body, had pressed her fingers into those muscles, finding them as rock-hard as they looked. He was funny and kind, and an amazing lover. He was setting the bar high for any man who came after him. She looked into the foggy mirror and frowned at herself. After him, would she even want another man?

Chapter 27

Liam chickened out. It was the perfect time and place to bring up wanting to see where this thing between them could go. The sky was an artist's abstract painting of yellows and pinks. The soft slap of the ocean against the sand was music floating in the air, and his gaze was drawn to Quinn as she closed her eyes and lifted her face to the gentle breeze.

It was the perfect evening for having that talk, but what if she wasn't ready to admit, to accept that they were past having a simple fling? If he tried and she shut him down, dug her heels in and closed her mind to the possibility of them, he would lose any chance he had with her.

So, instead of that talk he wanted to have, he decided they would have a quiet, romantic night. The situation she'd found herself in was close to breaking open, and this might be their last chance to spend time alone. At the moment, she was staring out at the ocean and seemed miles away.

"Penny for your thoughts." She didn't respond. Had she even heard him? "Quinn?"

She startled. "Sorry, what?"

"Where'd you go? In your mind?" Why was she blushing?

"Oh, just...um, you'll think I'm weird."

"I already think you're weird, so no problem there." He

winked to let her know he was teasing her. She had his curiosity going, though. When she just stared at him, he said, "You can tell me anything."

"You know, you're the first person I've felt I could tell about this little quirk I have."

"Now you have my attention." It had to be a good thing that she trusted him with something she'd never told anyone else.

She picked up her wineglass and took a healthy swallow. After setting it back down, she cleared her throat. "Okay, here goes. Just now, I was imagining us living on an island in the South Pacific. No one else lives on that island but us. Well, along with these cute little monkeys that swam ashore after a shipwreck a hundred years ago. They showed us where there was fresh, pure water. There were mango trees and banana trees and coconuts, and all the fish we could eat. So we had plenty of food, but I was getting kind of tired of eating nothing but fish. We…ah, we didn't wear clothes." She was blushing again. "See, I'm weird."

"That's very detailed." He ignored the weird part for a moment.

She shrugged. "All my fantasies are."

"Do you have these fantasies often?" Quinn Sullivan was more fascinating by the minute.

"I don't know. Just sometimes my mind creates these pictures. Mostly when I'm stressed and want to escape. It started after my mom died. I missed her so much and cried a lot. One day, my dad took me out to her favorite spot in the garden. He had a picnic spread out on a blanket the same way she used to. He told me to imagine she was with us, and we talked about her. It made me feel better.

"After that, when I would cry, he'd tell me to create a

story in my mind with her in it. Like someplace special we might be, and he'd ask where we were, what we were doing, what we were eating. I was ten years old, and those stories I'd make up with Mom in them were a comfort. As time went on, the stories would get more creative, more detailed. At some point, I started creating fantasies that didn't have her in it. I've had a few with you in them."

"Yeah? More than this one?" She nodded. "Tell me another one about us."

"The first one I had with you in it was when we were in the woods and Jasper was shooting at us. I was a bit stressed out, so my mind made up a story that took me away from the danger we were in."

"I want to hear it."

"Well, we built a cabin in the woods. You hunted for our food, and I grew potatoes. We...ah, we had babies with your blue eyes."

"Maybe we could have one or two with your green eyes." He was suddenly imagining her pregnant with their baby and his male brain liked that picture.

She laughed. "I guess that would only be fair."

"Right now, I'm having my own fantasy. Want to hear it?" He loved how her eyes lit up when she was happy.

"Tell me."

"I'd rather show you." He stood and held out his hand, pleased when she didn't hesitate to take it.

"Where are we going?"

"Someplace we don't need clothes." He took her to his bedroom, where he tried to show her without words how much she meant to him. He wanted to tell her he was falling for her, but he was afraid that would scare her off. She hadn't given him any indication that he meant more to her than that fling she insisted they were having.

Fling. He hated that word.

* * *

The next morning, Liam was enjoying a cup of coffee on his balcony while he waited for Quinn to wake up. He thought about how he should proceed with her. She hadn't said anything about her next assignment. He didn't doubt she had one scheduled, probably had her next year booked out. He frowned. Did she intend to tell him her plans or just leave when the time came?

Should he push for some kind of commitment from her or let things play out? He couldn't decide, and he hated being hesitant to do so. His military training had programmed him to be decisive. She'd told him the reason for her no-relationship rule, and he got why she felt that way after her experiences with other men. He wasn't other men, but how could he prove to her that he would never come between her and the career that she loved?

His phone chirped, Grayson's name on the screen. "What's up?"

"The West Virginia sheriff and one of his deputies are on the way here to interview Quinn. They expect to arrive around one."

"Did they give any pushback on coming here?"

"Big-time. Threatened to issue an arrest warrant if she didn't appear at the sheriff's office by noon tomorrow. John told them she wasn't returning to Hope Corner, so if they wanted to talk to her, it was here or nowhere. Then he dropped the big bomb. Said since she was kidnapped, she wanted to call the FBI to report what Garrison had done. He told the sheriff that he was advising her to do just that."

Liam chuckled. "That must have gone over big."

"It went over like a lead balloon. John said he got about a full minute of sputtering before the sheriff grumbled his agreement to talk to her here."

"Interesting that they don't want the FBI involved."

"John's vibe from the sheriff is that he doesn't want another agency encroaching on his territory, especially the Feds. John wants to meet with Quinn before they get here, so why don't you bring her over to my place for an early lunch. John will be here, and she can talk to him then."

"Sounds like a plan." Their lawyer was soft-spoken and kind to those he liked, and he would like Quinn and she him. Underneath that gentle nature was a man as sharp as a whip and a formidable opponent to any who came up against him. She would be in good hands. "What was his impression of the sheriff?"

"That he doesn't have any other suspects, so he's going to try to pin Garrison's murder on Quinn. This isn't going to be fun for her, so let's make sure she's well prepped before the interview. Since you're going to surprise him with the story that you rescued her, John's also meeting with you. I don't think the sheriff's going to be happy when he finds out you're involved in all this."

"Because he'll realize he can't bully me. Not to mention that I'm a decorated Marine, giving his suspect an alibi."

"Exactly. See you in a few hours."

Liam hadn't even met the sheriff yet, but his hackles were already up. He was going to have to work hard to keep his temper in check if the man tried to terrorize Quinn into making a false confession. Under no condition were they taking Quinn back to Hope Corner with them. If he had to spirit her away and hide her, he would.

Chapter 28

Quinn chewed on her thumbnail—a nervous habit she'd broken years ago—as she waited with John in a small conference room at The Phoenix Three, a room she'd never been in. Grayson had told her it was where they met prospective clients.

It was an impressive room. She wasn't sure what the small table that sat six was made from, but the finish was a glossy black lacquer. The walls were painted a soft gray, and the six cushiony leather chairs around the table were slate gray. Abstract paintings in subdued colors hung on the walls, and a mini fridge was tucked under a counter that matched the table. A fancy coffee maker sat on the counter, and cups and glasses filled two open shelves about the counter.

Grayson was right. The sheriff would see that The Phoenix Three wasn't a fly-by-night operation, but would that matter? She'd be the first to admit she was terrified. What if the sheriff manufactured evidence against her? She so did not want to go to prison.

John reached over and pulled her arm, taking her finger away from her mouth. "It's going to be all right, Quinn. You've got three of the most formidable men I've ever met circling the wagons around you, protecting you, especially

Liam." He smiled, and it was such a sweet smile. "Then you have me. They might be the muscle you need right now, but I'm the brains, and I take no prisoners. We got you, okay?"

Something about his quiet assurance calmed her. "Okay." When she and Liam had met with him earlier, they'd told him everything. He knew about Jasper's conversation she'd overheard, the thumb drive, the contaminated water, Jasper kidnapping her...all of it. He'd agreed that the sheriff didn't need to know about all of it at this point, only that Jasper had fixated on her and had kidnapped her after she'd ended things with him. She didn't like having to lie, even if it was only by omission, but agreed it was necessary for now.

Liam came into the room and put his hands on her shoulders. "The sheriff's coming up in the elevator now. I'm going to insist that he interview me first so that you have an established alibi before he meets with you." He leaned down and kissed her cheek. "You got this, but if you feel threatened at any time, walk out. I'll be right outside, and I'll get you out of here."

"Liam," John said, a warning in his voice.

"I don't care," Liam said, staring John down. "She needs to leave, she's leaving. End of discussion."

John let out an exasperated sigh before he smiled at her. "Didn't I tell you they'd protect you, especially this one?"

"You stay in here." Liam squeezed her shoulders. "I'll come to you as soon as I'm done."

"Okay. Where are you meeting him?"

"In the war room. We're giving him a kind of tour by me meeting him in there, and then bringing him here to talk to you." He winked at her, then left.

"I have to go with Liam," John said. He touched her arm. "It really is going to be okay."

Alone now, she dropped her head down on the conference table. How could they know it was going to be okay? What if the sheriff didn't believe Liam? Even worse, what if both she and Liam were arrested for Jasper's murder?

"You hanging in there?"

She lifted her head and forced herself to smile at Grayson. "Yeah. Everyone keeps telling me it's going to be okay, so I'm going to believe it. Do you think Liam's going to get in trouble?" All he'd done was rescue her, and she couldn't bear the thought that he'd be in trouble because of her.

"He's going to be fine."

"I hope so. Did you meet the sheriff?" When he nodded, she said, "What was your impression?"

He slid into a chair across from her. "I don't want to scare you, but I've always believed it's better to be prepared than not."

"Oh, God, that bad?"

"'Fraid so. He's got an attitude, so be ready for that. John will be with you and will put a stop to any questions you don't want to answer. Just keep to the script we've already gone over."

"What if they arrest me?"

"They won't. They can't, not today anyway. First, they don't have any evidence that you killed Garrison other than an anonymous phone call that you were in that cabin. Second, they personally can't arrest you. They'd have to go through our local police with a warrant for your extradition to West Virginia. If they had that, they'd have gone straight to the Myrtle Beach police. Should that happen at some point, we'll fight it with every tool available."

"I can't thank you guys enough for what you're doing for me."

He tsked at her. "Not necessary. You mean something

to Liam, and we protect those we care about. Would you like a cup of coffee while you wait?"

"No thanks. I'm jittery enough as it is. I wouldn't mind some water."

"Coming your way." He stood and went to the mini fridge, grabbed a bottle and brought it to her. "Help yourself if you want more. There are also sodas if you'd prefer one of those."

"Thanks. You don't have to babysit me," she said when he sat back down.

"How about we just sit here and talk until it's your turn. Maybe take your mind off things for a while?"

"If you don't have other things you need to be doing, I'd like that."

"Nothing pressing. Anything you'd like to know about The Phoenix Three?"

"Lots of things. Liam told me about you guys being kidnapped when you were teens, and that was why y'all joined the military. Were the three of you all Marines, serving together?"

"No, we each joined a different branch of the military. Liam the Marines, Coop the Army, and I was in the Navy."

"Liam said he was a Marine Raider. Were you and Cooper also in special ops?"

"Yes. Coop was an Army Ranger, and I was a Navy SEAL."

"I would've thought you'd want to serve together after what you went through."

"That was the plan at first, but then we decided we could learn different things if we each joined a different branch, then come back together and start The Phoenix Three."

"Liam told me what Phoenix Three does, and I have to say that I'm in awe of you guys."

"Pretty sure Liam is in awe of you." He grinned. "He showed me some of your photos that are out there, and I see why he's impressed. The attention you bring to children in need is something the three of us can fully support."

"Thank you. It's—"

Liam came in, followed by John. She jumped up. "Are you okay?"

He held up his hands. "No handcuffs, so I'd say yes. Are you?"

"I was freaking out, but then Grayson came in and talked to me. He took my mind away from what might be happening to you. I guess that was on purpose." She gave Grayson a grateful smile, and he winked, confirming that was why he'd stayed with her.

"The sheriff made a pit stop, but will be here in a minute," John said. "Liam's laid the groundwork, and all you have to do is tell the story we talked about."

"Did he believe you?" she asked Liam.

"He doesn't want to, but he doesn't really have a choice. We're each other's alibi, and unless he can prove we're lying, which we aren't, he's got no case against you." He wrapped his arms around her, hugging her. "I'll be in my office waiting for you."

"I wish you could stay in here with me."

"Me, too, but I won't be far away." Liam kissed her forehead, then left.

"Please excuse me, as well. I need to check for our visitors," Grayson said, exiting the conference room.

She dropped back into her chair. She should've asked Liam to run away with her, go to the Highlands in Scotland, where a county sheriff couldn't find her. They could raise those adorable Highland cows with the long bangs.

John slid into the seat next to her. "Don't let the sheriff

rattle you. If he tries to intimidate you, I'll step in. Anytime you're not sure what to answer, you can say 'I don't know,' or 'I don't remember.' Don't let him make you feel guilty for anything. You didn't do anything wrong. He has one of his deputies with him, and he'll try to make you uncomfortable by staring you down. Ignore him."

"I'll be happy to."

The door opened, and Grayson stepped inside. "Miss Sullivan is waiting for you in here," he said as a uniformed man walked in, followed by a younger man, also in uniform.

The sheriff wasn't what she'd expected. She'd formed a picture of a good old boy, maybe a little overweight, average height, and going bald. He wasn't any of that; instead, he was tall and lean, with a full head of salt-and-pepper hair cut short and icy blue eyes. Although there wasn't any warmth in those eyes, they were sharp with intelligence as they raked over her in a calculating way. She needed to be careful with this man.

"I'm Sheriff Lamott, Miss Sullivan. Before we start, I'm going to read you your rights."

"Why? Is Miss Sullivan a suspect?" John said.

"At this time, she is a person of interest."

"Then you're just here to interview her, not interrogate her, correct?"

"For now."

"Then no need to Mirandize Miss Sullivan if this is only an interview and she isn't a suspect."

John had told her that he'd do little things to throw the sheriff off his game, and he was doing just that if the sheriff's obvious annoyance was any indication.

"Fine." The sheriff glared at John, then turned his attention to her. "Miss Sullivan...may I call you Quinn?"

"No. I only let my friends call me Quinn, and I don't think you're my friend, sir."

"Very well. Do you know why we're here to talk to you?"

The deputy standing against the wall crossed his arms, drawing her attention. She pointed her finger at him. "Who's that?"

Sheriff Lamott narrowed his eyes, apparently not appreciating her question. "That's Deputy Dough. Don't concern yourself with him."

"Deputy Dog?" She grinned at the deputy, who was scowling at her. "Sorry." Out of the corner of her eye, she saw John smile, while the sheriff joined his deputy in scowling at her. Good, they weren't liking that she wasn't cowering in fear as she should be doing if she had in fact killed Jasper.

"It's D-o-u-g-h," Deputy Dog said, emphasizing each letter as he spelled it for her.

"Gotcha." Sorry, he would always be Deputy Dog to her.

The sheriff tapped his finger on the table. "I asked you a question, Miss Sullivan."

"Yes, I know why you're here. Someone killed Jasper, and you think I know something about that. I don't, but ask your questions."

"Do you have any idea who that someone is? You were the last to see him."

"Not true. Whoever killed him was the last to see him. That wasn't me."

"Mr. O'Rourke stated that Garrison kidnapped you. Tell me about that."

After she related the story, she sat back in her chair. "And that's it. After Liam and I escaped into the woods *because Jasper was shooting at us*, I never saw him again. You can verify with the garage that picked up Liam's car that it had been wrecked. That was also because of Jasper crashing into us."

"Why didn't you report him to the police?"

Thankfully, John had prepared her and Liam for this question. "Liam wanted me to, but I was afraid Jasper would find us if we stuck around Hope Corner, and I just wanted to go home. Plus, I felt sorry for Jasper. I mean, I know he chained me up, but it was a case of misguided love... No, *love* isn't the right word. *Obsession*'s a better one. Liam wasn't happy about not telling the police what had happened, so promised that I'd consider reporting him after I was home where I felt safe. Sadly, Jasper was killed before I could do that."

Liam hadn't been happy about letting her take the blame, but John had convinced him that it was the best answer. She was good with her being the reason Jasper wasn't reported to the police. She'd do whatever she could to keep Liam out of trouble.

The sheriff stared at her for a long minute before speaking. "What aren't you telling me, Miss Sullivan?"

"I have no idea what you're referring to. Jasper stalked me, kidnapped me, chained me up, all because I broke up with him and his tiny ego couldn't handle the rejection." She sighed. "Men. Such babies, yeah?"

"Miss Sullivan, this is your chance to help yourself by telling the truth. If... No, *when* I find out what you're hiding, it will be worse for you. See, there are reports of a man and woman fitting your and Mr. O'Rourke's descriptions seen in Hope Corner after Mr. Garrison was killed, yet both of you claim you left prior to his death."

Oh, boy. That wasn't good. Too late to change their story now. Had this question come up with Liam? If so, why hadn't he warned her? She had no choice but to stick to her guns, so she met the sheriff's gaze. "Listen, my father hired Liam to find me. He did, and he rescued me. Neither one of us saw Jasper again. End of story."

"Sheriff Lamott, unless you have an arrest warrant for Miss Sullivan's extradition to West Virginia that you've presented to the Myrtle Beach police department, Miss Sullivan is done here," John said. "Do you?"

"Not yet."

"Great. Nice talking to you, Sheriff Lamott." *Not*. She stood. "I hope you find who killed Jasper. He turned out not to be a nice man, but he didn't deserve to die." She felt Deputy Dog's eyes on her as she walked out of the room. The man made her uneasy.

"I'm not in handcuffs either," she exclaimed as soon as she saw Liam.

He grabbed her hand and pulled her into his office, closing the door behind them. He put his hands on her cheeks and roamed his eyes over her. "You're okay?"

"Yeah. Just happy it's over. Well, over for now. I'm sure we haven't heard the last from Sheriff Lamott. He asked—"

Someone knocked on the door, and Liam stepped away to open it. Grayson walked in, followed by John.

"John said you did great," Grayson said.

"I was fine until the sheriff told me a couple matching my and Liam's description was seen in Hope Corner after Jasper was killed. It took everything in me not to react to that."

"He didn't ask me that," Liam said. "I wonder why."

"It was an ambush," John said. "He didn't ask Liam that question on purpose. He didn't want you warned that he knew you were back in Hope Corner. You did good not to react, because he was hoping it would rattle you."

"Well, it did. I'm amazed my voice didn't quiver. It was

a mistake to go back. I just really wanted those pictures to prove the barrels belonged to the mill."

"What's done is done," Liam said. "He can't prove it was us, so he still has nothing."

"And if he does prove it was us?"

"Just because you returned to Hope Corner isn't evidence that you were involved in Jasper Garrison's murder," John said. "According to Liam and Grayson, this situation will be resolved soon, and the sheriff can turn his focus from you to the actual murderer."

"I'm supposed to leave for Ukraine in two weeks. Will that be a problem if whoever killed Jasper hasn't been arrested?"

Liam frowned. "You're leaving?"

Chapter 29

"I didn't mean to tell you like that."

"How did you mean to tell me?" Grayson and John had quickly excused themselves. Liam figured it was his scowl at hearing Quinn's news that sent them running.

"When we were alone. I've had this trip scheduled for months, Liam, before I met you. It has nothing to do with you."

"Nothing to do with me? I thought…" He swiped his hand through his hair.

"You thought what?"

"Maybe that I meant something to you. Enough of a something that you would tell me you had plans to leave the country. Guess I was wrong." He was being an ass. He knew it, but he plowed on anyway. "Did you plan to wait until the last minute to tell me, like when you were packing to leave? Or were you just going to walk away without looking back?"

"This is why I don't do relationships." She turned her back on him, walked to the window, and looked out. Her shoulders were stiff, her frustration visible. "Why do men think they have a right to dictate how a woman lives her life?"

"I'm not trying to—"

She faced him. "I thought maybe you were different.

My career is my life, Liam. It's what I live for. I've been up front with you about that."

"Meaning you don't have room for me." It wasn't a question because he got it. He was, after all, exactly what she'd said. A brief fling. He should have listened to her from the start.

"I wish..." She shook her head. "Never mind."

"You wish what?" He was close to begging her to make room for him in that life of hers that she guarded so fiercely, but stubborn pride kept his mouth shut.

"That I'd never met Jasper. Then I wouldn't be standing in this room worrying about men after me, children getting sick, and doing my best not to cry because I feel like I just lost a friend."

She wished she'd never met him. That hurt. It also made him feel mean. He held up his thumb and index finger an inch apart. "I was this close to falling in love with you, but I guess I should thank you for showing me the error of my ways."

Tears filled her eyes. "You're welcome." Without another word, she walked out of his office.

Eff him, he was an ass. A pissed-off ass, but an ass all the same. How had it come to this? He scrubbed his hand over his face. If she never intended to include him in her life, it was better this way. Yes, he was hurt. And yes, he was falling in love with her, but he should thank her for saving him from being all in.

His office suddenly felt empty without her in it. If only she had given him a chance, he would have shown her that he wasn't like her ex...whatever the hell his name was, or any other man in her life who didn't encourage her to fly free. He would have been there for her, been her number one cheerleader. He would have never stopped her from doing what, as she'd said, "fed her soul" no matter where in the world it took her. He would have been her safe haven whenever she came home to him.

"Guess that's that," he muttered. He walked to the window, stood where she had, and looked out at the view she'd seen. The Phoenix Three was on the top floor of a three-story building that Grayson's father had bought and rented back to them when they'd started their company. It was two blocks from the beach, and over the tops of the buildings, he could see the Atlantic Ocean.

Was it only last night that he'd sat out on his balcony with her, enjoying that same ocean and feeling so much hope for the future? Her coconut vanilla scent was still in the air, and he breathed deep. He'd almost handed over his heart, not knowing she'd be taking it to Ukraine with her but not bringing it back to him. Good thing he hadn't.

He'd lost his family, and now he'd lost the woman he could love, make a life with. Even years later, he still missed his family, and since losing them, he'd longed to make a new family of his own. A woman who loved him and a home filled with the laughter of children. Maybe the universe was sending him a message that he was meant to be alone. Yeah, he was feeling sorry for himself. He was entitled to a little self-pity, wasn't he? If only for tonight? Tomorrow, he would pick up the pieces and move on.

Too bad he wasn't much of a drinker. If he was, he could go home and drink his misery away. Sadly, a beer in the evenings while sitting on his balcony and decompressing from the day or wine with dinner occasionally when on a date was about the extent of his alcohol consumption.

Where was she? He walked out to the hallway. The small conference room had an all-glass wall, and seeing that she was sitting at the table where she was safe, he returned to his office.

He went to his desk, hesitated for a moment, then picked up his cell phone and called his mother. He needed to hear the voice of the one person in the world who unconditionally loved him and hadn't abandoned him. The name Lisa would show up on her screen, a fictional book club friend. If his father was around, she'd let it go to voicemail and call him back later.

"Hello, son. This isn't our usual day to talk. Is everything okay?"

"I was thinking about family and missing you." She worried about him as it was, so he wasn't going to tell her he was nursing a broken heart and give her more reason to be troubled on his account.

"I wish…"

"Yeah, me, too. But he's never going to change, Mama. I did get an interesting phone call. Do you know a Robert Sullivan?"

"If it's the same man, he's the Realtor your father used when he was looking for property in Savannah some years ago. I met him at dinner a few times when I went down there with your father. Nice man. Why are you asking?"

He remembered his parents going to Savannah to scout a location for a new pub back when he was in high school. "It's the same man. His daughter went missing, and he asked me to find her. Here's the shocker, though. He said Dad gave him my name, said that if anyone could find her, it was me."

There was a long silence, then, "Your father gave him your name? Actually said your name after swearing he never would again?"

"That's what Mr. Sullivan said."

"Oh, Liam. That's wonderful. It means there's hope he'll forgive you."

He crushed the anger heating his neck, swallowed the words she'd wash his mouth out with soap if he uttered them. This was his mother. "I did nothing wrong to be forgiven for, Mama. I'm doing good things, you know, like saving children. Why can't he see that?"

"I don't know, son. I've tried to talk to him about this, but the stubborn ass refuses to listen. I thought for sure he'd eventually come around."

He didn't have to see her to know that tears were running down her cheeks. "He's too hardheaded to back down. You know that. Once he takes a stand, that's it for him." He blew out a breath. "Listen, it's not your job to fix this. Only he can, so don't take this weight on your shoulders." Grayson came to the door. "I need to go. I'll call you on our usual day."

"Liam."

"Yeah?"

"I'm proud of you. I want you to believe that."

"Thanks, Mama. That means a lot to me. I love you."

"I love you, too, my precious boy."

"How's your mother?" Grayson asked after Liam disconnected the call.

"Missing her boy and wishing my father wasn't a stubborn ass." Both Grayson and Cooper knew he'd been declared dead by his father.

Grayson came in and took a seat in front of Liam's desk. "Think he'll ever come around?"

"No. If he was going to, he'd have done it by now."

"I say it's his loss. What was that between you and Quinn?"

"Hell if I know."

"As an objective observer, it seemed like you overreacted."

"I guess I really messed up. She insists we're nothing more than a fling."

"And you want more, I take it."

"Yeah. I think she's the one, Gray. Unfortunately for me, from her past experiences, she has it in her head that men want to control her life. I can't seem to get her to understand I'm not like those other men."

"Don't take this wrong because I'm on your side, but your reaction to learning she has a trip to Ukraine planned didn't help your case."

"I know. I didn't handle that well. She just caught me by surprise, and I reacted. Where is she? I'll go talk to her. See if I can repair the damage." It was going to be awkward with her staying with him if he couldn't, but she couldn't go home. Not yet. It still wasn't safe for her.

"Give her a few minutes to calm down. She called Harlow and asked if she'd come pick her up."

At least she would be safe with Harlow.

Chapter 30

Had she overreacted to Liam's reaction to learning about her trip? Maybe. Okay, she had, but his questioning her was a trigger from her time with Aiden. She'd learned to be defensive whenever Aiden started on her about her job and travels as if her career wasn't important. Even now, years later, those old wounds put her on the defensive, thus reacting the way she had.

Harlow would be here to pick her up in a few minutes, and Quinn decided to wait downstairs in the lobby to avoid talking to Liam. Pretty immature behavior on her part. He didn't deserve the way she'd treated him. Not that she'd changed her mind about their time together being more than a fling…maybe. The idea of a possible future with him if they could come to an understanding about her career had already been hovering in the edges of her mind.

She should've stayed and talked to him, and that thought had her returning to the elevator to go back up and do just that. He would understand when she explained that she'd heard Aiden's voice in her head telling her that her *pictures* weren't important. Just as she pushed the button, someone walked up behind her.

"We're going to quietly walk out of here, Miss Sullivan."

She gasped as she spun around, her eyes widening at seeing the man invading her space.

"One sound out of you, and it will be the last one you'll ever make." He turned his hand up, showing her the knife he held. "Don't for a minute think I won't cut you and leave your body for your boyfriend to find if you don't do exactly as I say."

Deputy Dog! She hadn't liked the vibes coming from him as he'd stared at her in the conference room. She should have paid attention to her instincts. "You'll regret this if you make me leave with you. Those men upstairs won't stop until they find me, and when they do, they'll make you sorry you came anywhere near me."

"Stop talking." He put his arm around her and pulled her next to him. "Feel that?"

"Yes." He was pushing the tip of the knife into her side hard enough to hurt. How could she get out of this?

"Start walking or I really will cut you."

"I'm not going anywhere with you."

He pushed the tip of the knife into her hard enough to pierce her skin. "Ow. That hurt."

"That's nothing compared to what I will do if you don't start walking."

Did she have a choice? It had been stupid of her to come down to the lobby by herself, but she'd thought she was safe as long as she stayed in the building, which she'd planned to do until Harlow arrived. She'd just been so angry at Liam that she hadn't been thinking about anything but getting away from him. It had been misplaced anger, and now she was paying the price for overreacting.

When Deputy Dog poked her again, she started walking. Maybe Harlow would drive up when they stepped outside. She wasn't that lucky. When they reached his car, he pulled her hands behind her back and handcuffed her. "Is that necessary?"

"Can't have you trying to jump out of a moving car." He pushed her onto the seat, then belted her in.

She wouldn't hesitate to jump out when she thought she could do it without killing herself, but now that she was handcuffed, she couldn't open the door. "Where are you taking me?" she asked as he drove away from the safety of The Phoenix Three.

"Someone wants to talk to you."

"Who?"

"Just someone." He glanced at her. "Why aren't you scared? You should be."

"Are you planning to kill me?"

"Me? No, but you should still be scared."

She wasn't because Liam would find her. He had before, and he would again. And knowing that, the truth stared right back at her. Liam wasn't Aiden. How many times had he told her he wasn't, but she hadn't been able to quite believe him. "My bad," she murmured.

"What did you say?"

"Just talking to myself, calling you vile names."

He laughed. "It's too bad we met under these circumstances, Quinn. I have a feeling you and I could've had some fun together."

In your dreams, Deputy Dog asshat. And really, not even then. What she could do was get information that would help them expose what the mill was doing. "So, is Sheriff Lamott involved in whatever this is?"

"That Boy Scout?" He snorted. "The good sheriff won't even take a free doughnut. What were you and your boyfriend doing in Hope Corner?"

"I assumed you rode down to Myrtle Beach with him,"

she said, ignoring his question. "Where does he think you are right now?"

"Obviously I didn't ride with him, and I had some time off due me, so I'm officially on a beach vacation."

"Could've fooled me, since it appears we're leaving the beach." If she had to guess, he was taking her back to Hope Corner. That was the first place Liam would look for her. Oh, how could she forget? He'd put a tracking app on her phone, so he'd easily find her...as long as Deputy Dog didn't take it away from her. What if someone called her? That would remind him to take it away from her. She was surprised he hadn't already. *Please, no one call me.*

"Are we going back to Hope Corner?"

Clearly losing his patience, he scowled at her. "Anyone ever tell you that you talk too much?"

"Nope, my friends love listening to me. So, who made that anonymous phone call about me to the sheriff? I bet it was you."

"How about you shut up."

"No problem. I don't like talking to you anyway." It was him, she just knew it. Why? So he could find her? That had to be it.

What she didn't understand was why they—whoever *they* were behind this—didn't think that if she did have the thumb drive, she wouldn't have made copies. Or shown it to someone. They had to have considered that, so why were they kidnapping her? What was their end game?

Chapter 31

"Is she planning to stay with you and Harlow tonight?" Liam asked. Would she need to get her things from his condo? He rubbed his hand over his chest, right where there was an ache in the vicinity of his heart. His place was going to feel empty without her in it. He didn't have to be there to already know that.

Grayson lifted from the chair. "I think so. Don't give up hope, Liam. Most relationships experience a bump along the way."

"Not fond of bumps." And he wasn't so sure this was a simple bump. Instead of hearing her, he'd closed his ears to what she'd said from the beginning, thinking he could change her mind. All he'd done was prove her point.

"Hey," Harlow said as she walked into his office.

She went straight to Grayson, and Liam glanced out the window when she lifted on her toes to give him a kiss. He'd never kiss Quinn again, never wake up next to her again. The sooner he accepted that… He didn't want to accept it. Maybe she just needed time, and with that time, maybe she'd miss him.

"Is Quinn ready to go?" Harlow asked.

"She's in the conference room," Grayson said.

"No, I just looked in there."

Liam frowned. "I saw her in there, too." He stood, telling himself not to panic. "She's around here somewhere." She had to be. He walked past Grayson and Harlow out into the hallway. "Quinn?" She didn't answer.

"I'll look in the bathroom," Harlow said.

"Where is she?" She wouldn't take off on her own, would she? Grayson disappeared into his office while Liam's search for her grew more frantic. She wasn't in the war room or any other room he checked.

"Liam, come here," Grayson said.

The urgency in Grayson's voice had Liam hurrying to his office. "You find her?"

"Unfortunately."

Liam's heart dropped to his stomach. What did *unfortunately* mean? "Where is she?"

"Come look at this."

He walked around Grayson's desk. The security camera feed from the lobby was frozen on the screen. "What are we looking at?"

Grayson hit Play, and they both watched as the elevator door opened into the lobby. Quinn stepped out, and it seemed she was deep in thought. A minute later, she turned back to the elevator and pushed the button. Was she coming back up? Hope beat in his heart that she hadn't been any happier than he with the way they'd left things, and she was coming back to talk.

"Who's that?" A man was walking up behind her, and Liam frowned when he recognized the face. "That's Lamott's deputy. I thought they left."

"Watch," Grayson said. "I've turned the volume up on the sound."

When they'd outfitted the building with security cameras, they'd included audio. The deputy stopped behind Quinn, crowding her body.

"We're going to quietly walk out of here, Miss Sullivan," he said, startling her. "One sound out of you, and it will be the last one you'll ever make." The deputy showed her the knife he held. "Don't for a minute think I won't cut you and leave your body for your boyfriend to find if you don't do exactly as I say."

Liam growled. "He's a dead man." He stared hard at the screen as the video continued. She should have been safe in their building, but they'd unknowingly invited the devil into their midst. They didn't have security personnel in the lobby, hadn't thought they needed it. That was going to change.

"Ow. That hurt," Quinn cried as she tried to pull away, but the man held on to her.

"The fucker cut her." When the deputy walked her out of the building, Liam wanted to punch his hands through the screen and snatch her back. "She has to be so scared. I was supposed to protect her, and I let my ego—"

"Stop right now," Grayson said. "That shit's not helping her." He pushed away from his desk.

"Yeah, okay. We need a plan." He was going to tear the deputy apart with his bare hands when he caught up with them.

"First we have to figure out where he's taking her."

"Back to Hope Corner?" Liam said. "We can't call her phone. If he hasn't thought to take it away from her, calling her will remind him to do that."

"Let's hope she still has it on her. She'll call you if she gets a chance to."

"She… Wait, I put a tracking app on her phone." With the shock of her being taken, he'd forgotten he'd done that.

Thank God he had. He logged into the app. "Looks like they're heading toward I-95. If they go north, then he probably is going back to Hope Corner. Let's go. I'll drive." He was halfway out of the room when Grayson stopped him.

"Hold up, O'Rourke. You were a Marine Raider. You wouldn't have gone on a mission with a half-cocked plan."

Liam fisted his hands as he turned to his friend. "And if it was Harlow in that car? Where would you be right now? I'll tell you where. Chasing them down, just like I'm going to do."

"True, and you would have stopped me, like I'm doing now. And I would thank you for it."

He was right. Liam knew it, but that didn't mean he liked hearing it. "They've got a good thirty-minute head start on us, and the longer we delay leaving, the bigger that lead is."

"So, we get our helicopter friends to pick us up. I'll call Brant and put them on standby so they're ready to go when we are. We need to get Coop in here, too."

"Let's hope they're available. I'll call Coop while you call Brant." Somewhat mollified that they'd be able to catch up with Quinn in a helicopter, he got Cooper on the line. "We need you here stat."

"On the way."

No question on Cooper's part as to why they wanted him here immediately. That was what it meant to be on a team, to be a band of brothers who would always have each other's backs no matter what.

"Bad news on the helo," Grayson said. "It's out on a charter. Brant said it'll be back in three hours, and he can have it refueled and ready to go thirty minutes after that."

Not what he wanted to hear. "Coop's on his way in." He checked the tracking app. "They're still heading toward I-95. Should reach it in about twenty minutes, then we'll know which way they go. We're only an hour behind them now. If we drive, we can make up some of that time, more than waiting three hours for a chopper."

"I still think the helo's our best option." Grayson headed for the door. "Let's go in the war room."

Liam followed him out. "We'll need transportation when we land if we take the helo. We drive, that problem's solved." He couldn't handle twiddling his thumbs while they waited for the helicopter to return. If they drove, they could leave as soon as Cooper arrived.

Grayson put an aerial view of Hope Corner on the large wall screen. They were studying the map for possible landing sites if they helicoptered in when Cooper arrived. "Sitrep?"

"Quinn's been taken." It was hard to even say that without putting his fist through the wall.

"Shit. How'd that happen?"

He brought Cooper up to date. "So, drive or wait for the helo?"

"Drive. We'll lose another three hours waiting for the helo, then add the time it'll take to fly us close to Hope Corner?"

Liam nodded. "We take the car, we're only an hour behind if we leave now."

"That's if they're going to Hope Corner," Grayson said. "If we take the helo, no matter where they go, we can..." He stared at the aerial view on the screen. "No, you're both right. We'll be too far behind taking the helo. We drive. Let's gear up."

"Good thing you put that tracker app on her phone," Cooper said as the three of them were putting enough weapons on their bodies and in their duffel bags to start a small war.

"I agree, because now I don't have to shoot myself for not doing it."

As they rode the elevator down, Grayson called Brant and canceled the helicopter. "He said if we need backup, they'll be on standby."

Brant and his partner, Zed, were former SEALs who'd served together before opting out of the Navy and starting their security company. They were good people, men who would always have a brother's back.

Grayson took the driver's seat, Liam the passenger's, and Cooper the back. The Range Rover's 626 horsepower twin-turbocharged V-8 was fast, with plenty of legroom for big men.

It was a car Grayson kept for missions like this. Liam pulled up the tracking app. "They're on I-95 North. Looks like Hope Corner is their destination.

"Do you think the sheriff's involved?" he asked.

Grayson passed three slower-moving cars. "I didn't get bad-guy vibes from him, but he could just be a good actor."

"I didn't get any either. The deputy, though, whole nother story."

"Yeah, I didn't like him either," Grayson said.

"When we catch up with them, the deputy's mine."

Chapter 32

Quinn stared out the window at…pretty much nothing. I-95 was a boring highway. She'd given up trying to get information out of Deputy Dog since he'd stopped answering any of her questions. She was trying hard not to panic. Liam would find her, but until then, she had to be smart. She just needed to figure out how to do that.

So far, no one had tried to call her, so her phone hadn't chimed. That was a relief, but how long was that going to last? She'd talked to her father last night, so he wouldn't call. Liam hadn't called either, which was something of a surprise. Although, Liam was smart, and maybe he'd realized it was better not to.

"I need to stop for gas," Deputy Dog said as he exited the highway. "You try anything, you call out to anyone, I'll shoot you on the spot." He lifted the hem of his T-shirt to show her the gun in a holster strapped to his belt. "Then I'll shoot whoever you try to get help from. Understood?"

"Yes." He knew exactly what threat to use to keep her from trying to escape.

After he was out of the car, she managed to reach her purse and pull it behind her back. After a bit of fumbling, her fingers grasped her phone, and she felt around until she found the button to silence it. Instead of putting it back in her purse, she pushed it under the waistband of her jeans. Hopefully, no one would frisk her.

When they were back on the road, she tried again to find out where they were going. "I'm thirsty and have to go to the bathroom. How much longer before we get wherever we're going?"

"We'll get there when we get there."

"And there is where?" He ignored her. *Jerk.*

She was bored, her shoulders hurt, and her arms felt like a thousand needles were poking them. She was also scared. Why had she been kidnapped? Deputy Dog hadn't once asked about the thumb drive. Wasn't that what he, or whoever was involved in this, wanted? What were they going to do with her? Maybe she didn't want to know the answer to that question.

"There's the exit for Hope Corner." She frowned when he drove right past it.

She guessed they drove for another hour, and she was seeing mileage signs for Washington. "Are we going to DC?" Again, nothing. He was making her mad. If the capital was their destination, were they going to see Senator Hanson? She couldn't think of any other reason to go to DC.

He exited the highway some miles later. Before long, the four-lane road turned into a two-lane, and they were out in the country. The area was beautiful with big, sprawling homes on one- and two-acre lots. People with money lived out here, and that made her think she'd be meeting the senator soon. She didn't want to. Without ever having laid eyes on him, she had the sense he was a man she should be afraid of.

Deputy Dog pulled over to the side of the road. He reached into the console compartment and pulled out a sleeping mask and put it on her, covering her eyes. The car started moving, and she tried to ignore the panic rising up. Not being able to see, combined with her hands cuffed behind her back, made her feel like a caged animal. She focused on her breathing in an effort to calm her nerves. It didn't work.

After what seemed an eternity, but was probably twenty or thirty minutes, the car came to a stop. She heard his door open, and a moment later, hers. Deputy Dog roughly grabbed her arm, pulling her out of the car. She stumbled slightly, disoriented by the sudden change in movement.

"Where are we?" she demanded, the fear creeping into her voice despite her efforts to remain calm.

"Shut up and walk." He guided her with his hand on her elbow, and she'd only walked for a minute when he said, "Three steps up."

"This would be easier if you'd take off this damn mask."

"I said shut up."

Touchy. She tentatively lifted her foot, feeling for the first step, then did the same for the next two. It wasn't easy to keep her balance with her arms bound behind her back. Something creaked, and she thought it might be a door opening. When the temperature dropped, she knew they were inside an air-conditioned house. The strong smell of lemon oil permeated the air, telling her it was probably like one of the well-kept houses they'd passed before she was blindfolded. Deputy Dog pushed on her elbow, forcing her to keep walking.

"Can't you take these handcuffs off me? My hands and arms feel like someone's sticking a thousand needles in them. It's not like I'm going anywhere."

"Sit." She was pushed down on something soft, a sofa she guessed.

"Take the blindfold off," a man said.

He's someone who expects to be obeyed, she thought. Suddenly, she didn't want to see whoever it was. If she didn't see his face, he wouldn't have to kill her. "That's okay, you can leave the blindfold on, but I'd appreciate the cuffs coming off."

Despite her wishes, the blindfold was removed, and she blinked against the sunlight coming in through the window. Her gaze fell on the man sitting behind a chrome-and-glass desk. Behind him was a full wall of bookshelves, what looked like law books filling them. An attorney then? Was Senator Hanson a lawyer? She should've learned more about the man...if this was him.

The man wore a COVID-type face mask, only his eyes and hair visible. His hair was a dirty blond and expensively cut, and although she couldn't see his full face, from what she could see, she guessed him to be in his sixties. She had a photographer's eye for detail, and because she did, she noticed something about one of his, something most people wouldn't see. There was a gray ring around the pupil of his left eye but not the right one.

If she ever saw that eye again, she could point her finger at him and say, "He's the one who had me kidnapped." She made a mental note not to forget to tell the authorities about that gray ring. It would make a difference if she gave that description before she ever saw him again.

If she lived through this, that was.

"Where's her phone?" the man said.

Her gazed narrowed in on her purse that he was rummaging through. Not that there was much in there, since she hadn't replaced most of what used to be in her lost purse. "My phone was in my purse at the cabin, which I assume you people have. I'd sure love to have it back." She was getting mad, and she welcomed that anger because she wasn't quivering before this bully of a man.

"Frisk her," the masked man said.

Deputy Dog yanked her up, and when his hands slid over her, she gritted her teeth. As much as she'd wanted the cuffs off, she was glad they weren't for this. She was able to keep her bound hands over where she'd slid her phone to hide it. She almost sagged with relief when the deputy didn't find it.

"She's good."

"Uncuff her and then leave," the masked man said.

Okay, as much as she didn't like the deputy, she didn't want to be left alone with the man she was sure was the senator. Was that pity in Deputy Dog's eyes as he pulled her up to take the handcuffs off? Her stomach took a sickening roll when the door closed behind the deputy, leaving her alone with the man.

"Sit," he said in that intimidating voice.

As much as she wanted to refuse, to laugh in his face and tell him to go to hell, her legs decided sitting was a grand idea. Her body gracelessly crumpled in on itself. At least there was a sofa behind her to land on and she didn't end up a heap on the floor. Small favors.

Her hands and arms were tingling as if they were waking up from a long sleep, and she laced her fingers together and waited. When he did nothing but sit there and stare at her, she wanted to squirm. She managed not to.

When she couldn't take his staring with those cold eyes any longer, words she couldn't stop tumbled out of her mouth. "Who are you? What do you want from me? I—"

He held up a hand, palm out, and as if she was a puppet obeying the master, her mouth snapped closed.

"It matters not who I am. As for why you're here, it's

called damage control, Miss Sullivan. Who have you shown the thumb drive to? How many copies did you make? Where are they? You honestly answer those questions, and then we'll talk about how you get to live another day."

Okay, what was the next level of fear? Petrified? *Buy some time to think, Quinn.* "Your deputy kidnapped me hours ago and didn't let me have a restroom break. I really, really need to pee, so unless you want me to piddle on your sofa, you'll—"

A disgusted expression crossed his face. "Through there." He pointed to a door to the right of him.

His eyes stayed on her until she closed the bathroom door. That was just creepy. It was a powder room, only a toilet and sink. She did really need to pee, and she pulled her phone out and set it on the corner of the sink. After relieving herself, she washed her hands, and after drinking some, she splashed cold water on her face. She picked up her phone, intending to put it back in the same place, but what if... She checked the charge, finding it almost full. They'd already searched her, so they wouldn't do it again. Leaving it in silent mode, she hit Record, then stuffed it inside her bra.

It wasn't until she returned to the sofa that it occurred to her that she should've texted Liam when she had the chance. Disgusted with herself, she wanted to slap her head for not thinking smart. She folded her hands in her lap and waited for the man to speak.

Chapter 33

"They passed the exit for Hope Corner without getting off," Liam said as he tracked Quinn's phone.

"How far behind are we?" Grayson asked.

"About eighty minutes." They'd lost more time when traffic came to a dead stop because of a wreck that closed both northbound lanes shortly after they got on I-95. Sitting still, unable to move, had been torture.

They were speeding and making up the lost time now, and he hoped they didn't get stopped. Considering the number of weapons in the car, it would take a lot of explaining. The Range Rover had a top-of-the-line built-in radar detector, so hopefully they'd have adequate warning to avoid getting stopped.

"Where the hell is he taking her?"

"You have considered the possibility that the deputy tossed the phone in the bed of a passing pickup truck, right?" Cooper said. "That we're on a wild-goose chase?"

Liam turned and glared at him. "Don't even go there. If that phone's not with her..." He couldn't let himself think that they had no clue where she was.

Cooper raised his hands. "Don't shoot the messenger, brother, but it's something we need to consider. What's

Plan B if we catch up with the phone and it's not with Quinn?"

"We could make a detour to Hope Corner and talk to the sheriff," Grayson said. "He might know where his deputy has a hidey-hole. That would also let us get a bead on Sheriff Lamott, determine if he's a part of this." Grayson glanced at him. "It's your call."

Liam closed his eyes and drew in a deep breath. It was an almost impossible decision to make. What was the right one? Was the phone still with her? What if it wasn't? He opened his mind to that place inside him that he'd learned to trust, that had kept him alive on dangerous operations. Every instinct he had said the phone was still with her.

"We follow the phone. Think about it. If the deputy had found it, he most likely would have destroyed it. That's what people tend to do." Although not a religious man, he sent a prayer to the Man above that he'd made the right decision. *And just keep her safe until I can get to her.*

"We'll find her," Grayson said as he pressed down on the gas pedal, picking up speed.

They would, but would it be in time?

"So, it's serious, you and Quinn," Cooper asked.

"On my part."

"Not on hers? Could've fooled me."

"How so?" Cooper hadn't been around the last few days, so he'd missed the blowup of any relationship Liam had hoped for with her. He was going to rescue her, and then he'd do as she wished and send her on her way. It was going to hurt to lose her, but he'd do it for her.

"The way she would look at you, like she had real feelings for you. What happened?"

"Based on prior experiences, she has it in her head that men and the career she loves don't mix."

"You have to show her it will be different with you."

If only.

"Move over, dude," Grayson grouched when a car in the passing lane stayed at the same speed as the car next to it. He flashed his lights, and the car finally moved into the right lane. "There's always hope, Liam. Look at me and Harlow. She was adamant that as soon as she had her son back it was over for us. She lasted a week, and now we're getting married."

"I guess anything could happen." But he didn't believe it. Harlow didn't have a career that took her all over the world, a career that she'd learned the hard way that men couldn't deal with. Quinn was wrong about that. He could, but she wasn't going to give him a chance to show her.

"What'd you do with Ruby?" Grayson asked Cooper.

"She's at your house, playing with Tyler and Einstein."

Grayson sighed. "Now Tyler's going to want a dog."

As the two of them talked about Cooper's new dog, Liam stared out the window, a battle brewing in him. He would respect Quinn's condition for their fling, but that wouldn't stop him from feeling angry that she refused to give them a chance.

"You still following Quinn's whereabouts?" Grayson asked.

Right. Get your mind on the mission, O'Rourke. He pulled up the tracking app and frowned. "They exited the highway about five minutes ago, now heading west. We've gained forty minutes on them." He gave Grayson the exit number. They were still forty minutes behind. Anything could happen in forty minutes. He pushed that thought out of his mind. Finding her safe and unharmed was the only acceptable ending to this operation.

He kept his gaze on the tracking app, following the moving dot that was Quinn's phone. "Looks like they're out in the country now." Where was he taking her? Twenty minutes later, the dot stopped moving. "Coop, pull up Google Maps." He held up his phone so Cooper could see the coordinates for where the phone was. "See what's there."

"Lakeside Estates. Stand by a minute. I'll do a search for that area."

"They're still not moving," Liam said as he watched his phone screen.

"Lakeside Estates is a community of million-dollar-and-up homes."

"What the hell are they doing there?" That didn't make any sense. Unless… "This is close to the capital. Do we know where Senator Hanson has a home?"

"Let me see if I can find out," Cooper said.

If anyone could, it was Cooper. He could tease information out of a computer that would make a hacker jealous. "They're still at the same location. We're thirty minutes from the exit, then about twenty from where her phone is." He refused to consider that the phone wasn't with her. If it wasn't, then he'd made a big mistake in insisting they drive instead of taking the helicopter.

"Got it," Cooper said. "Hanson has a condo in DC and a home in Lakeside Estates."

"Bingo. It is surprising that he'd risk bringing her to his home."

"I'm thinking he's arrogant enough to think no one will ever know she was there," Grayson said.

All he cared about was getting to her, and they'd just confirmed they weren't on a wild-goose chase. He blew out a relieved breath. "Does he think no one will come looking for her?"

"He's desperate to get that thumb drive," Cooper said.

Desperate enough to hurt her? They finally exited the highway and were soon on a two-lane country road. They'd be at the location in twenty minutes. *Hang in there, Quinn. We're almost there.*

Chapter 34

"Here's what you need to understand, Quinn... May I call you Quinn?"

"I prefer Miss Sullivan." What was with all these people she didn't like wanting to get familiar and call her Quinn?

A beam of sunlight from the sun now low in the sky touched her face, and she turned toward it. The view outside the tall windows was beautiful. There weren't any buildings behind his house, and the word that came to mind as she took in the meadow of rich green grass, wildflowers, and rolling hills was *pastoral*. Behind a split rail fence, a herd of Arabian horses grazed. She wished she had her camera.

She wished Liam was here. He'd carry her away from this horrid man. Her gaze fell on a beautiful stark white horse. That was the one Liam would toss her on and then jump on behind her. She'd laugh with joy as they rode away, over those hills filled with wildflowers.

When he finally stopped the horse, he whispered in her ear, "This is my secret waterfall. I've never brought a woman here before." He lifted her from the horse, and they shed their clothes.

"Are you listening, Miss Sullivan?"

She reluctantly tore her gaze from the distant hill where

she was frolicking in the pool of the secret waterfall with Liam. "Not really."

"Well, you should if you care at all for your friends at The Phoenix Three."

He had her attention now.

"As I was saying, I want that thumb drive and any copies you've made. I want to know who you've told of its existence. I want your assurance that you'll convince the men helping you to forget anything to do with what's on that thumb drive."

"Or?" She really didn't want to know, but she needed him to say it for the recording. God, she hoped her phone was still recording.

"Or they'll lose their company and will be investigated nine ways to Sunday by every alphabet agency you can think of. And believe me, Miss Sullivan, I can make that happen. Do you want your friends ruined?"

"Who are you?" With that particular threat, she was certain now that it was the senator, but maybe he was one of the senator's minions.

"I'm someone you and your friends don't want to mess with."

She didn't doubt it, but not much she could do except keep denying, denying, denying. "I don't know what thumb drive you're talking about. All the Phoenix Three men have done for me is help me fight being accused of killing Jasper. I have a feeling you know for a fact that I didn't."

"Careful, Miss Sullivan. To imply I know anything about a murder doesn't please me."

She sighed. "Yes, I know, you're not a man I want to displease." She was poking the bear, but his threats toward the guys made her angry.

"Need I remind you that no one knows where you are?

There is no one coming to rescue you." He sat back in his chair and stared at her a moment before saying, "Your attitude needs improvement. I think a time-out for you to think about the situation you're in will do much to adjust your unfortunate attitude." He pressed a button on the landline on his desk. "Return," was all he said.

A minute later, Deputy Dog walked in. "Sir?"

"Take Miss Sullivan to spend time with our friend. Perhaps she'll rethink the wisdom of refusing to cooperate."

She didn't like the sound of that, and what friend? "I'm fine just sitting here. I promise I'll keep my mouth shut and not bother you."

Amusement filled his eyes, and she sensed that he was smiling behind that mask. "I'm beginning to be sorry we didn't meet under better circumstances, Miss Sullivan. I think we could have enjoyed each other's company."

When hell freezes over. Deputy Dog yanked her up, pulled her hands behind her back, and handcuffed her again. As he forced her to walk out of the room, she cast a glance over her shoulder at the horses, then lifted her gaze to the hills where Liam's secret waterfall was.

Tears filled her eyes that she wasn't truly playing in the water with him. If she had one wish, it would be to turn back the clock and not have ended things with him the way she had. What if he was mad enough at her to not search for her? That thought almost crushed her, but no, that wasn't Liam. No matter what he thought of her now, he was out there looking for her.

Deputy Dog blindfolded her again before taking her back to his car. "Where are we going?" she asked when they were on the road. He didn't answer her. The man was still ignoring her, and that made her want to snarl. "Aren't you worried about what's going to happen to you when this whole thing blows up? Like you'll be the one in handcuffs?" Still no response from him, but maybe she'd given him something to think about.

Her best guess was that they'd traveled twenty or so minutes before the car came to a stop. Deputy Dog opened her door, hooked his hand under her elbow, and pulled her out of the car. Rough gravel under her feet and the blindfold had her stumbling, and the deputy tightened his grip on her arm.

They stepped into a building, and she wrinkled her nose at the musty smell. He walked her deeper into the building before stopping her and removing the blindfold. "Enjoy your new home," he said, then walked out, closing the door behind him.

"You forgot to take off the handcuffs," she yelled.

"I doubt he forgot," a man said, the voice familiar.

She spun around and screamed at seeing a dead man. "Jasper?" she gasped. She fell back against the door. "You're dead." Well, obviously, he wasn't, but he sure looked like someone had tried to make him dead by beating him to a pulp. Both eyes were bruised black, his nose looked broken, and one arm hung limply by his side. He was sitting in a hard-back wooden chair, and blood stained his white T-shirt.

"As you can see, I'm still among the living."

He sounded like someone who had a very sore throat, rough and raspy. "Then who was the dead man in the cabin?"

"My cousin."

"Oh, I'm sorry." Well, she was sorry someone died, but everything that was happening was all on Jasper. She almost told him his cousin was dead, he was beat up, and she had been kidnapped because of his greed, but caught herself in time. She needed to continue to claim she knew nothing about the thumb drive, besides... She scanned the room, and yes, there was a blinking red light in a corner of the room. They were being recorded and listened to.

"How long have you been in here?"

"What do you care?"

Because they were being recorded, she needed to be careful about what she said. "Just because it didn't work between us doesn't mean I like seeing you like this. I have no idea why these people keep asking me about a thumb drive. Why would they think I have it? What's on it, do you know?"

"I know you took it, Quinn. All you have to do is turn it over to them, and we can walk away from this."

"Are you really that stupid that you think they'll just open the door and let us walk out of here as they tell us to have a nice day?"

"We can bargain with them. Give them the thumb drive and promise to keep our mouths shut. I know I will. These are powerful people, and they'll watch us to make sure we forget they exist, so I damn well know I'll wipe them from my memory."

He really was stupid if he thought he'd ever see the light of day again. "What powerful people?"

"You're better off not knowing." He gave her a sly look. "Unless you already know because you saw what's on the thumb drive. Why were you in Hope Corner, Quinn?"

"How many times do I have to tell you and these *powerful people* that I. Do. Not. Have. It? If I did, believe me, at this point, I'd gladly give it to them."

"You don't have to yell. I'm right here."

"If I want to yell, I will," she yelled. "I'm tired, I'm hungry, I'm very thirsty, and I'm in handcuffs. I think that gives me plenty of good reason to scream my bloody head off." She glanced around. "Do they feed you or give you anything to drink at this resort?"

As if on cue, the door opened and Deputy Dog walked in, a bottle of water in his hand. "You want this?" He dangled it in front of her face. "Tell us where the thumb drive is, and it's all yours."

A low growl sounded behind her, and she yelped when Jasper barreled past her, his head lowered and aiming straight for Deputy Dog's stomach. The deputy dropped the bottle and brought his knee up, right into Jasper's groin. Jasper made a horrible sound of pain and fell to the floor in a fetal position. Deputy Dog landed on him, his fists pounding Jasper's face.

"You're going to kill him," she shrieked.

With her hands cuffed behind her back, she couldn't try to pull the deputy off Jasper, so she kicked his leg. "Stop it."

The deputy grabbed her ankle and pulled her foot out from under her. She hit the floor with a hard thud and pain ricocheted up her arm, bringing tears to her eyes. "I think you broke my hand."

"Roll over. I'm going to take the cuffs off you, so be a good girl or I'll put them back on."

After he removed them, he pushed her onto her back again, then fell on top of her. He aligned his body so that they were chest to chest and groin to groin.

Lust darkened his eyes as he stared down at her. "You want to play, little girl?"

Chapter 35

Liam frowned when Quinn's phone was on the move again. She—or at least her phone—had been stationary for twenty-nine minutes. "Quinn's phone's traveling."

"Coming at us?" Grayson asked.

"No. The opposite direction. Do we stop at the senator's house or follow the phone? She could still be there and someone else has her phone."

Before Grayson or Cooper could respond, the car's Bluetooth announced an incoming call, and their FBI friend Sean Danvers's name appeared on the screen.

"Grayson here. I'm in the car with Liam and Cooper."

"Correct me if I'm wrong, but I have a feeling you'd rather I not ask where you're going. Am I right?"

"Why you're a good Fed," Liam said.

Sean chuckled. "Just try to stay out of trouble. I have some news for you boys. Turns out Jasper Garrison is not dead."

"Then who was the body in the cabin?" Liam didn't like this at all.

"Garrison's cousin, Joey Garrison. Coop, I'm sending you pics of both men. They could almost be twins. It was assumed it was Jasper because his wallet with his ID in it was found at the cabin. Fingerprints didn't match up, though."

"Where is Jasper if he's not dead?" Liam asked. He had a very bad feeling about this.

"In the wind. I wanted to give you a heads-up. If I hear anything more, I'll be in touch."

"Thanks for that," Grayson said.

"Anything you boys want to tell me?"

Liam shook his head as he shared a look with Grayson.

"Not at this time," Grayson said.

"I was afraid you'd say that. Listen, you're walking a fine line here. Don't cross so far over that I can't get you out of trouble."

"We'll do our best," Liam said, but he wasn't making any promises. He'd cross all the lines it took to keep Quinn safe, trouble or not.

Sean knew Garrison had kidnapped Quinn. They'd had to tell him that much to get him to keep an eye on the investigation into the murder. They hadn't shared with him that it appeared a powerful senator was involved or just what he was involved in. If he knew, the Feds would step in, and that would have put Quinn in even more danger.

"That doesn't reassure me, but I didn't expect a different answer. Stay safe." He disconnected.

"He's not going to be happy when he finds out what's going on," Grayson said.

"Don't care. You agreed that if we brought in the FBI before we were sure Quinn was safe that we wouldn't be able to protect her." She would've been their star witness and considering the people they were dealing with, that would have put a target on her back. An even bigger target.

"I did, and I still believe we did the right thing. Just saying, though."

"We'll just have to ask for forgiveness when it all goes down. Hell, we'll be handing the FBI the case on a silver platter."

"Look at these pictures," Cooper said, holding out his iPad. "The cousins really do look like twins."

Liam studied the side-by-side photos of the two men. "I'm not sure I'd be able to tell them apart in person."

"The house is a half mile ahead," Grayson said, stopping on the edge of the road. "What's the plan?"

On an operation, Liam had a reputation in his Raider team for being able to sense things, especially danger. His teammates called it his Irish woo-woo. "Drive by the house slowly."

The house was a two-story, one of the biggest in the area. As they passed, he opened his mind, trying to feel Quinn. He got nothing. Didn't mean she wasn't there, but he was going to trust that he'd know if she was.

He tapped the screen of his phone, his eyes on the dot no longer moving. That was where she was. *You better be right, O'Rourke.* "Keep going. I'll tell you when to turn."

When they reached her phone's location, it was to find a boarded-up restaurant with no cars in the parking lot. "Let's check out the back," Grayson said as he drove around the building. "There's a car back here."

"That's the car the deputy drove away from our place." *She was here!* "I can feel her." His brothers didn't roll their eyes or question his sanity, and for that, he loved them.

Without a discussion between them, Grayson drove away. He found an empty house for sale and parked the Range Rover in the open carport. They slipped out of the SUV, moving swiftly and silently toward the restaurant. There was a dumpster at the back of the building, and they stopped behind it.

"It's your party," Grayson said. "How you want to do this?"

"We go in hot and heavy, we risk Quinn getting hurt, so we go in stealth mode." He leaned around the dumpster and scanned the door and windows. Although the windows were boarded up, the plywood didn't reach the top, leaving about a six-inch gap for light to enter. He glanced at Cooper, who was scanning the building with an infrared camera, which would pick up body heat. "What you got?"

"I'm seeing three bodies, all close together in the back left corner."

"Think the missing Jasper Garrison's one of them?" Grayson said.

Liam nodded. "Wouldn't surprise me."

"Weird," Cooper said. "All three are horizontal and low to the floor. One isn't moving, but two are..." Cooper hesitated, then lifted troubled eyes to Liam. "One of the larger bodies is on top of a smaller one, and it looks like they're fighting."

"Quinn's the smaller one," Liam said, knowing he was right. "We're going in hot and heavy." To hell with stealth. Quinn was in trouble. He took off running across the back parking lot, his brothers on his heels.

The back door was unlocked, and the first thing that hit him on entering was the moldy smell. The door opened into the kitchen, and a rat ran across his foot as he raced through the room. Fury burned through him that the deputy had brought Quinn to a place stinking of mold and home to rats.

Cooper had said she was in the back left corner of the building, so he raced to the left, running past bathrooms and down a hallway.

"Get off me!"

That was Quinn's voice, filled with raw panic. He reached

the closed door at the end of the hall and kicked it so hard that the handle flew off and the wood splintered. The sight that greeted him turned his blood to ice, and a red haze colored his vision. Rage like he'd never known exploded. Unleashed, the beast inside him had only one thought.

Kill him.

Chapter 36

Quinn's heart hammered against her chest. Each breath a struggle. Her terror that she was going to be raped sent panic racing through her. She tried to scream but fear paralyzed her voice. The deputy wrapped one hand around her throat, squeezing his fingers, choking her. He reached down with his other hand, unbuttoned his jeans, and pulled his zipper down.

He rocked against her, and she could feel his erection pushing into her. No! She wasn't going to let him do this to her. When he put his fingers on the button of her jeans to snap it open, she spit in his face.

"You little bitch." He let go of her throat and put his hand over her mouth.

She bit his finger.

"You want it rough, bitch, I'll give you rough." He pushed her T-shirt up. "What the hell is this?" He grabbed her phone, pulling it out of her bra.

Oh, God. He'd found it. She couldn't let him destroy it. Not only would she lose the recording, but Liam wouldn't be able to find her. She fought him like a wild animal, beating her fists on every part of him she could reach. When she dug her nails into his cheek and scraped down, shredding his skin, he roared in anger and hit her on the side of her head. The pain in her ear was excruciating, and white stars danced behind her eyelids. Tears burned her eyes.

Taking him by surprise, she was able to snatch her phone out of his hand and toss it across the floor. It was safe for now, but unless she could somehow overpower him, he'd still destroy it. After he finished with her.

He laughed. "The more you fight me, the more I'm going to enjoy fucking you. So, go ahead. Do your best, bitch." He wrapped his hand around her throat again. "Every time you move, I'm going to squeeze harder." He reached between them and pushed his jeans and underwear down, exposing himself. Then he pulled the zipper of her jeans down.

"Get off me!" she screamed.

He laughed again. Then he crashed his mouth down on hers and forced his tongue into her mouth.

She tried to bite it off, tasted his blood. Felt victorious when he yanked his mouth away from hers. The fury in his eyes terrified her more than anything he'd done to her by now. He was going to seriously hurt her. He raised his fist, and she squeezed her eyes shut, anticipating the blow.

It never came.

His weight left her, and another voice roared out in rage. "I'm going to kill you."

Liam? Afraid she was hallucinating that he was here, she kept her eyes closed. She couldn't bear not seeing him if she opened them. Then the sound of fists hitting flesh and the deputy grunting in pain filled the room. She wasn't imagining Liam was here.

She opened her eyes, and for a woman who abhorred violence, she felt nothing but relief and gratitude at the sight of Liam battering the deputy with blow after blow, his fists connecting with the man's face with sickening thuds.

"Hey. You're going to be okay."

She tore her gaze from Liam at hearing the soft voice. Cooper was squatting down next to her, and when he gently pulled her T-shirt back down, covering her exposed breast, she was unable to stop the tears.

"Where are you hurt?"

"I—I'm o-okay." She tried to sit up.

"Just stay where you are for a minute. Let's make sure you really are okay."

"That's enough," a different voice said.

She turned her head back to Liam. Grayson was pulling him off the deputy, who was out cold. She looked at Cooper again. "You're all here."

He smiled. "Of course we are. You matter to Liam, so you matter to us. Did he…hmm—" His gaze slid down to her unbuttoned jeans.

"No, y'all got here in time."

"Really glad to hear that."

"He hit me on the side of my head, and my ear is ringing. My hand hurts a little where I fell on it. Other than that, I really am okay. He stuck his tongue in my mouth, and I tried to bite it off."

Cooper laughed. "You go, girl."

"He hit you?"

She turned her head to the other side to see the most beautiful face in the world. Her Liam. "Yes, but I think you paid him back for that. Hello."

"Hey. I was afraid we'd be too late."

"I knew you'd find me." The truth of those words hit her, and she lifted her hand to his face. "I'm sorry for the things I said. I know you're not like Aiden."

He put his hand over hers. "We have some talking to do, but right now, we have to take care of things here."

"My phone." She pointed to where it had landed against

the wall. "There's some good stuff recorded on it. Help me sit up." He slipped his arm under her back, supporting her as she rose.

Grayson was putting the cuffs the deputy had taken off her on him. Once the man was secured, Grayson put his foot on the deputy's back. "Don't move."

"Is Jasper okay?" At Liam's narrowed eyes, she said, "I don't like him, but I don't want to see him dead."

Grayson leaned over Jasper. "He's fine, just out cold. What happened to him?"

"Deputy Dog happened."

Liam grinned. "Deputy Dog?"

"Fits him, don't you think?"

She looked at Liam, and they both laughed, which was amazing, really, after what had almost happened to her. "Thank you for coming for me," she whispered.

"I'll always come for you, Quinn."

Cooper handed her phone to her. "Guys, you have to listen to this." She opened her phone and played the recording. "Is that who I think it is?" she asked when it finished.

"Where did you get that?" Liam asked.

She told them about being taken to a house and about the man wearing a mask. "I just had the feeling it was Senator Hanson even though I couldn't see his face."

"It was his house you were at, so it was likely him," Liam said while Grayson called someone on his phone.

"You need to get down here ASAP, Sean. Bring a team with you…" Grayson eyed the two men on the floor. "And a few handcuffs." He gave whoever Sean was their location. "Trust me, you'll want to personally handle this one. We'll wait for you here."

Grayson slipped his phone back into his pocket. "He'll

be here in two hours, so we have to hunker down until then."

"Who's Sean?" she asked him.

"The assistant director in charge of the FBI."

"Wow, go big or go home."

"I'm going to go get the car," Liam said. "Quinn will be more comfortable waiting in it than in here. It's filthy in here and it stinks."

She wanted to grab his hand and beg him not to leave her.

Cooper stood. "I'll get it. You stay with her." He glanced at her and winked.

While they waited, and although she'd told him she was okay, Liam had insisted she get checked out. Two EMTs had shown up and, after examining her, determined that she didn't have a concussion and her hand wasn't broken. The verdict was just to keep an eye on her, and if anything changed to take her to the hospital.

By that evening, she was exhausted and just wanted a shower to get the dirt off, and then she wanted to crawl into bed with Liam and have him curl around her and keep her safe while she slept. She'd been questioned by Sean—who she'd liked a lot—for two hours before he was satisfied that he had all he needed from her. He'd shown her a photo of Senator Hanson. She'd recognized his eyes and had positively identified him as the man who'd questioned her. She gave Sean proof that she was in his house by describing his office.

She was so tired that she only half listened as Sean outlined the plan to arrest Senator Hanson and the men who had destroyed her father's house. Jasper and Deputy Dog had already been taken away by two of his special agents. Honestly, she didn't really care anymore what happened from here on out. She'd done her job of bringing attention to the illegal dumping of chemicals into a lake children played in. The senator was going down, and that was all that mattered.

"Time to go home," Liam said, waking her up.

Sean had sat in the car to question her, and after he'd finished and left, she'd fallen asleep. "Yes, home please. Your home."

"Our home someday, I'm hoping."

She sleepily smiled. "Maybe."

He was still in the back seat with her when she heard the engine start. She noted that Cooper was driving. "Where's Grayson?"

"Staying behind with Sean," Liam said. "You've had a long day. Go to sleep."

"Okay." She toppled over onto Liam's lap and went to sleep.

The next morning, she awoke in Liam's bed with him curled around her just like she'd wished for. She didn't remember arriving home and barely remembered his taking her into the shower with him and gently washing her. She peeked under the covers to see that she had one of his T-shirts and her panties on. She smiled. Liam O'Rourke was a good man.

"Make me a promise," Liam's sleep-laced voice said from behind her.

"If I can."

"Don't go and get kidnapped again, okay? My heart can't take another one."

She rolled over to face him. "I'll do my best, but maybe I'm too much trouble."

He grinned. "You do have a way of making life interesting." His eyes turned serious. "Is it too soon to tell you that I love you, Quinn Sullivan?"

Well then. Her heart did a happy bounce, but she wasn't ready to say it back. Not yet. "Maybe a little too soon." She traced her thumb over his bottom lip. "Keep those words handy, though. I think I'll need to hear them before too long."

"They'll be on the tip of my tongue, ready to say them as soon as you're ready to hear them. Just say when."

"Speaking of tongues. Mine is missing yours."

"Is it now? Let's remedy that." He leaned in and captured her mouth in a soft, lingering kiss. Then his tongue found hers, and she sighed from the pure pleasure of being with Liam. And when he made love to her, softly and beautifully, she floated away on the feel of him, the taste of him, the scent of him.

Maybe she was in love.

Chapter 37

Two weeks had passed since the arrest of Senator Charles Hanson, and the attention to his arrest and the illegal dumping was finally dying down. It hadn't taken long for reporters to ferret out that Quinn was a major part of the story, and Liam had spent every minute of that time by her side, protecting her from the vultures who wanted an exclusive from her. They waited for her outside his condo, outside The Phoenix Three offices, followed her to the grocery store, and anywhere else she went, yelling their questions to her.

The one good thing to come out of all this, she'd postponed her trip to Ukraine, and it had been her idea, which was a relief. He hadn't had to be the bad guy and convince her she wasn't ready for that kind of trip.

She'd finally agreed to an interview with Felice Robertson, a reporter with a local Myrtle Beach television station. The big guys from the networks were mystified as to why she wouldn't talk to one of them over a reporter no one outside of Myrtle Beach had heard of.

That's my girl, he thought with considerable amusement when she announced her decision. Never doing what one expected of her. He stood out of sight of the cameras in the studio, listening to her answer Robertson's questions. They'd been at it for twenty-five minutes now, and the interview was winding down. He could tell Quinn was exhausted, and he was close to walking onto the set, picking her up, and carrying her out of there.

She hadn't slept well since he'd brought her home, and he didn't like the dark circles under her eyes that had been covered with makeup for this interview. The first week, she'd had a nightmare every night, would wake up crying and struggling against the covers that were holding her prisoner. Sometimes it was Jasper in her nightmare, sometimes the deputy, and once it was Senator Hanson. The second week had been a little better. She'd only had two nightmares. She was talking to a therapist, and that was helping.

His girl was strong, and he knew she'd fight her way back to herself and do it surprisingly fast. She had not only him, but her father, along with Grayson and Cooper and Harlow in her corner, all of them there for her. His friends had welcomed her into their little family. She was laughing again, and that was great progress.

"A question many are asking," Robertson said, "is why would you risk your own life for people you don't know?"

Liam smiled, knowing what her answer would be.

"How could I not?" Quinn said. "Children were getting sick. What kind of person would I be if I turned my back on that? Whether I personally knew those children or not didn't matter. The EPA has identified the children in Hope Corner who are sick, and they are receiving treatment. That's what matters."

"You brought down a powerful senator, a possible future vice president," Robertson said. "That had to be—"

"He brought himself down. End of story."

Liam wished that was the end of the story. Hanson had a team of the best lawyers in the country working to get the charges dropped. Sean had told them there was no way that was going to happen, even with all of Hanson's expensive attorneys. Quinn's recording from when she was in his home was some of the Feds' best evidence that Hanson was not only aware of the illegal dumping but of the kidnappings and the murder of Garrison's cousin.

Quinn shook hands with the reporter, then headed his way, her eyes locked on his. He got the message. It was *get me out of here*. So he did.

"You were great," Liam said after they finished watching Quinn's interview, which the station had aired as a special report.

"I'm just glad it's over."

He didn't tell her what they already knew. It wasn't over yet. There would be a trial, and she would be the star witness, but that was likely years down the road, so for now, she was right. It was over.

"I think we should turn off the TV, put on some love music, dim the lights, and let me show you how special you are." They sat in his recliner, her in front of him. He loved sitting like this, her back to his chest, his legs on the outside of hers. "Sound good?"

"Sounds like a perfect ending to this day."

"Great. Why don't you start with a bubble bath while I get everything ready, and then I'll join you. I'll bring you a glass of wine when I come."

She turned and straddled. "Or we could just get it on right here." She kissed him. "Right now."

"Tempting, but no. I'm going to romance you tonight." He patted her butt. "Go. I'll be there in a few minutes."

"Hurry." She was only a few steps from him when the doorbell rang. She stopped. "Are we expecting company?"

"Not that I know of. Probably a neighbor wanting to borrow something."

"Okay, I'll be waiting for you. Don't be long, or I might start without you." Knowing his eyes were on her backside, she slipped her shirt off and swung her hips as she walked away.

"You better not." He almost followed her, but the doorbell rang again. Whoever was on the other side was only going to get about ten seconds of his time, long enough for him to tell them to get lost.

"I'm busy right..." *Now.* "Mom?"

"Of course, I'm your mom. Who else would look like me?"

"I... I wasn't expecting you. What are you doing here? Does Dad know you're here?" She had a few gray hairs now, but she was as pretty as she was the last time he saw her, ten years ago.

"Are you going to invite me in or just stand there?"

He snapped out of the shock at seeing her at his door and pulled his mom into his arms. "You're really here." He couldn't wrap his mind around that. She'd wanted to meet secretly over the years, but he'd always been too afraid his father would find out and it wouldn't go well for her.

"I really am, and so is your father."

"What?" He leaned back and looked down at her. "Here now?" At her nod, Liam scanned the hallway but didn't see him.

"Yes, he's downstairs in the lobby. Your doorman is holding him hostage."

"Hostage?" Maybe he was dreaming his mother was here and his father was a hostage because that was the only thing that made sense.

"Your doorman, Wilson, wanted to call up and tell you

that you had guests, but I was afraid you would refuse to see us if you knew your father was here, too. So, I convinced him to let me come up if Patrick stayed with him until you gave permission for him to come up, too. Are you going to invite me in?"

"Of course. Sorry. This is just a surprise... A good one." He smiled at her. "Really good." He kept his arm around his mother as they walked inside.

"Do you need some money to buy furniture, son?" she said as she took in his living room and empty dining room.

He grinned. "I guess it looks like I might, but no. Quinn and I intend to go furniture shopping, but it's been a little hectic lately." They hadn't been in a big hurry because Quinn had been quite happy sharing the recliner with him.

"Where is she? I want to meet in person this woman who saved those poor children."

Right, Quinn was naked, waiting for him. "Let me tell her you're here, then I'll go down and rescue Dad." He needed to get to her before she came looking for him, wearing nothing but a towel...or not even that.

"There you are," she said when he came into the bathroom. "I thought you got lost."

"I kind of did. My parents are here."

Her eyes widened. "What?"

"You're no more surprised than I am. Mom's in the living room. I have to go downstairs and get my father."

"They're *here* here?" At his nod, she shot up and grabbed a towel. "I have to get dressed."

"Like you better naked, but that's probably a good idea."

She grabbed his arm. "Are you okay, Liam?"

"I don't know. I feel like I'm in a weird dream. I better go downstairs. Come out when you're dressed."

When he returned to the living room, his mother had

his balcony door open and was looking out at the ocean. She turned and smiled when she heard him. "Who needs furniture when you have this view?"

"Yeah, it's pretty awesome. Be right back."

As he rode the elevator down, a hundred butterflies took flight in his stomach. The last words between him and his father had been bitter, and he'd walked away angry and heartbroken. He tried to think of what to say to his father for the first time in ten years, but nothing came to him. Not one word.

He reached the lobby and found his father leaning against Wilson's desk as they talked. Liam stopped and studied the man who'd said his son was dead to him. Patrick O'Rourke hadn't been an easy man to feel close to. He was opinionated, demanding, intimidating, and never wrong. But the man was his father, and in spite of the hurtful words hurled at him that day, Liam had missed him, had especially missed his mother, had missed being a part of a family. He'd always felt he was owed an apology, but did that even matter anymore?

No, it didn't, so he banished his hurt and approached the man who had the power to undead him. Would he? "Dad." Damn that quiver in his voice.

Patrick O'Rourke stilled, then turned. "Son."

Son. He hadn't been a son since he was eighteen years old. His father's gaze roamed over him, and Liam forced himself not to show that his nerves were a crackling live wire. He still didn't know what to say, so he didn't say anything more.

Patrick darted a glance at Wilson, then he lifted his chin toward the lobby seating. "Let's go over there and talk for a minute."

A minute? It was going to take longer than that to repair the damage that had been done, but again, he stayed mute as he followed his father to the chairs. They sat facing each other, and Liam waited. What would his father say? Express more of his disappointment in his son? Make excuses for the years of silence?

"I...ah, I've been following the news about Quinn Sullivan's involvement in the arrest of Senator Hanson." His father frowned. "Knew there was something untrustworthy about that man."

"That's what you want to talk about? The senator?" He couldn't help the bitterness in his voice. He was expecting too much to think his father might apologize for the things he'd said.

"No." His gaze softened slightly, a flicker of regret passing through his eyes. "I wasn't an easy father, Liam. I know that. I pushed you because I believed in you, because I wanted you to be the best possible version of yourself. I had thought you would step into my shoes one day. Then when you said you were joining the military, well, I thought you were ruining your life. I was angry."

Not an easy father? That was an understatement. "The kidnapping changed me. I tried to talk to you about it, but you told me to just get over it. To man up."

"I did. But you were still a boy who'd gone through a terrible experience, and I was wrong. I've known that for some years now."

"Yet you didn't think to pick up the phone and call me? To ask to see me? I called your office once, told your assistant I was your son. I thought if I was the one to reach out, that it might be a step toward a reconciliation. You told her you didn't have a son. That was the day I gave up." Tears stung his eyes, and he glanced down at his feet to hide them from his father. His bare feet. He hadn't put shoes on.

"Pride got in my way, son. Would you look at me?"

Liam lifted his eyes to his father's. Let him see the tears swimming in his eyes. Let him see the hurt he'd lived with for ten years.

"I came here to say I'm sorry. I was wrong. Terribly wrong. I don't expect you to instantly forgive me, but I'm hoping that this is a chance to start over. That you'll give me a chance I know I don't deserve."

There were tears swimming in his father's eyes, too, and that was jarring. He'd never once seen Patrick O'Rourke humbled and even close to crying. A part of Liam wanted to refuse the chance his father was asking for. To get up and walk away. Let him see how it felt to be abandoned. But the bigger part of him had longed to have his father back in his life, to rebuild what had been broken.

"I'm a firm believer in second chances," he said, feeling the weight of years of hurt and resentment lift after saying those words.

"Thank you, son. You've grown into a man any father would be proud of."

He never thought he'd hear his father say those words, and to finally hear them, well, he was close to losing it, which would embarrass both of them. Before that happened, he stood. "Let's go upstairs so I can introduce you to Quinn."

"I want to meet the girl who took down a powerful senator. Your mother told me that the two of you are together now."

"So, you found out I secretly talk to her?"

His father chuckled. "I've always known, *Lisa*."

Well, damn. "And she thought she was so clever having a book club friend named Lisa."

He and his father looked at each other and shared the first laugh of what Liam hoped would be many more.

Later, as he and Quinn sat out on the deck with his parents, Liam leaned back in his chair and smiled at how Quinn had his father on the edge of his seat as she told him everything that had happened.

"Son, you've got an amazing woman here," his father said when she finished.

He had his family back, including one special addition, and he smiled at her. "Believe me, Dad, I know it."

Epilogue

One Year Later...

For the tenth time—probably even more—Liam eyed the board announcing arrivals. It hadn't changed since he'd checked it two minutes ago. Quinn's flight was still showing as late. Didn't the airline know she was on the plane and how much he needed to see her, to feel her in his arms again?

They'd talked almost every night that she was in Puerto Rico following a devastating hurricane, FaceTimed whenever possible, engaged in phone sex many of those times, which was hot but wasn't the same as being able to touch her. In—he glanced at the board again—twenty-one minutes her plane would land, and he would be hard-pressed not to go open the aircraft's exit door himself and dare anyone to move before he got to her.

He'd even bought a cheap ticket to fly from Myrtle Beach to Charlotte that he wouldn't use just so he could get past security and wait for her at the gate. He was a goner. He knew it and didn't care. When his brothers had teased him for doing that, he'd shrugged and said, "Bite me."

Keeping his mouth shut about her going on this particular trip, knowing she was pregnant, was the hardest thing he'd ever done, but he'd made a promise to himself that he'd never be *that guy*. The one who tried to control her or thought her job wasn't important. If he wished she would lie low until after the baby was born—and maybe a year or two after that—he was a smart man and would be keeping that thought to himself.

It felt like hours, but finally the board showed that her plane had landed. He laughed as he put his hand over his pounding heart. The woman would always send his heart racing, and he was grateful every day that he'd found her.

And there she was. Her eyes widened at seeing him at the gate, and then a big, beautiful smile greeted him. He wrapped his arms around her. "Welcome home."

"You bought a ticket, didn't you?"

"Guilty. Couldn't handle waiting in baggage for you to get down there. Couldn't wait that long to see you." He took her camera bag from her and slipped it over his shoulder, then he kissed her with all the longing of missing her the past two weeks.

"I love you, Liam."

"Love you more, Quinn."

"Nuh-uh."

"Uh-huh." It was a little game that they played every time she returned home. From the first time she'd finally said it to him, hearing those words from her mouth was a blessing he'd never take for granted.

"Let's go home where I can give you a proper welcome." Needing to touch her, he took her hand as they walked. When they reached baggage and were waiting for her suitcase, he put his hand on her stomach, and his breath caught. "You have a baby bump."

"Popped out overnight. Little bean's growing like a weed."

He pulled on her hand. "Let's go."

"What? I don't have my bag yet."

"Don't care. I'll come back for it. Right now, I need to see you naked. See this baby bump for myself." For the first time, it felt real, that his baby really was in there. There wasn't a happier man on this planet than him. He was sure of it.

The bell rang that luggage was coming out, and he sighed. His escape plan foiled, he impatiently waited for her suitcase. As soon as he saw it drop down, he went to get it. "Now can we go?"

She laughed. "Yes, Daddy, we can go."

Daddy! Hot damn, he loved the sound of that.

Liam sat on the edge of their bed, his gaze on Quinn's stomach as she undressed. They hadn't planned for a baby so soon, but because of her travel schedule and constant time zone changes, she'd chosen an IUD over birth control pills. It rarely happened, but hers had dislodged and she hadn't realized it for a few days. Next thing they knew, they were having a baby.

"We need to look for a house," he said as he held his palm over the most beautiful thing he'd ever seen. Who knew a baby bump could bring tears to his eyes?

"We do?"

"Yeah, a condo's no place to bring up our little girl."

"How do you know it's not a little boy?"

"Because I want a little girl with red hair and green eyes who'll wrap me around her little finger."

"Maybe I want a little boy with blue eyes."

"Next time." He caressed that precious baby bump. Honestly, he didn't care whether it was a boy or girl, but he loved that she got salty every time he insisted their baby was a girl. "Why don't you go take a bath, get the travel grime off. By the time you get out, I'll have dinner ready. We're eating on the balcony."

"You really know how to treat a lady."

"Only this lady." He tapped her stomach. "Go."

While she bathed, he got everything ready. He'd had to use the discipline he'd learned as a Raider to not toss her on the bed—yes, she still loved for him to do that—and make love to her as soon as they walked in the door. It had been a close call, though, when she'd stood naked before him having been gone for two weeks and with her new baby bump. But tonight was the night, and when he made love to her, he wanted it to be with his ring on her finger.

He was nervous as hell. He surveyed his efforts. Her favorite pregnancy food and drink were a steak and peanut butter milkshake. Weird on the milkshake, but his lady had a craving for it, so that's what she'd get. Then the icing on the cake was…literally cake icing. He chuckled as he opened a can of the coconut pecan frosting she craved, stuck the *special* spoon in it, and carried it out to the balcony. He wondered how long it would take her to notice.

The grill was hot and ready for the steaks, and the asparagus were seasoned and wrapped in foil, ready to go on the grill. He paused to appreciate his efforts. He'd spread candles out on the balcony, scattered rose petals over the table—so far, the wind hadn't blown them away—and had soft music playing on the outside speakers he'd installed while she was gone.

"Perfect." Those romance novels he'd read on deployment had taught him much. Now he just needed the woman all this was intended for.

And there she was. He quickly stepped inside, stopping her in the kitchen. "Stay here a minute and close your eyes."

"Why?"

He laughed. "Always with the questions. That's an order, Little Marine, and good soldiers don't question their orders."

She saluted him. "Sir, yes, sir!"

Once her eyes were closed, he got her peanut butter milkshake from the refrigerator, and after taking it out to the balcony, he returned for her. He took a moment to just look at her. Her hair was down and wild, the way she knew he liked it. She'd put on one of his white dress shirts with the sleeves rolled up that she'd stolen from him and loved wearing. There was something about seeing her in his shirt that did it for him.

"I can feel you staring at me."

He loved that she was that attuned to him. "Can't help it. You take my breath away, baby." *Wait for it...*

"I'm not a baby."

"No, you're all woman." *My woman.* He didn't dare say that either.

"Can I open my eyes now?"

"Not yet." He took her hand. "We're walking out to the balcony. I'll tell you when you can open them." When he had her facing the table, he let go and stepped to her side so he could watch her face. "You can open them."

Her gaze took in the candles, the rose petals, and the table set with her mother's delicate china. "Liam," she whispered.

That was all he needed, to hear the wonderment in her voice and to see the pure pleasure in her eyes.

She stepped to the table and picked up the can of frosting. "What's this?"

Well, that didn't take long.

She pulled the spoon from the icing. "Is this..."

"A baby spoon."

"It's pink."

"Yep, for our little girl." *Wait for it...*

"Our little boy's not going to like eating out of a pink spoon."

Her attention returned to the spoon and what was tied on the end of it. "What's in this lace? Oh, it's... Liam?"

When she turned to him again, he was on a knee. "Quinn Sullivan, you are my heart, the reason for the smiles on my face. With all that I am, I love you and our baby girl..." He grinned. "Or boy. I promise to respect you, support you in all that matters to you, and to always protect you and the family we're creating. I—"

"Yes!" She fell to her knees in front of him. "Yes, yes, yes." She peppered kisses all over his smiling face. "I thought you'd never ask."

He laughed. "Well, technically, I haven't yet."

"Then for God's sake, get on with it. I want to put that ring on."

"Impatient little thing. I have a long speech I've been practicing, but I guess I'll just skip to the end. Quinn, will you marry me and make me the happiest man who ever lived?"

"If you missed it the first time, my answer is yes. A hundred times yes." She pulled the lace from the spoon and untied the ribbon holding it closed.

He took the ring. "With this ring, I promise to do everything in my power to make sure you're never sorry you love me." He slipped it on her finger. "If you don't like it, we can exchange it for one you do."

"Hush, you." She held her hand up. "It's beautiful."

"You're beautiful." He'd taken Harlow ring shopping with him, and when they'd seen the white gold two-carat emerald cut diamond engagement ring, they both said it was perfect for Quinn. Beautiful in its simplicity.

"I love you, Liam."

"Love you more."

"Nuh-uh."

"Uh-huh."

He stood, bringing her up with him. "How hungry are you?"

"Very… For you."

"Good answer." When she reached to set the frosting on the table, he shook his head. "I have some ideas for that. Bring it with us."

Her eyes lit up with delight. "You wicked boy."

"You have no idea." He carried his soon-to-be wife to their bedroom, where he showed her just how wicked he could be.

Later, after they'd gone back to the balcony and had their dinner, then a little more wickedness under the stars, he'd carried her back to bed. As she slept with him wrapped around her, he rested his hand on her baby bump.

"Hey, little girl," he quietly said. "Your daddy can't wait to meet you."

"Boy," Quinn mumbled.

He buried his smile against her neck. Liam had his family and knew he was a lucky man.

* * * * *

Harlequin® Reader Service

Enjoyed your book?

Try the perfect subscription for Romance readers and get more great books like this delivered right to your door.

See why over 10+ million readers have tried Harlequin Reader Service.

Start with a Free Welcome Collection with free books and a gift—valued over $20.

Choose any series in print or ebook.
See website for details and order today:

TryReaderService.com/subscriptions